ETHEREAL EMBER

Twilight Tales

Marisa Loretta

Know that I am built up of death from head to foot and that it is a corpse that loves you and adores you and will never, never leave you!

—Gaston Leroux, *The Phantom of the Opera*

A MAP OF
Ethereal
Ember

Ethereal Ember
Emeraldine
Lunavale
Amoria
Grimstone
Stardalia
N
W
E
S
Evermore Woods
Bailengra
Anamchara
The Desire Lantern
Fauna's Cabin
Flora's Cottage
Pakena's Log Cabin
Elderberry Forest
Mistmeadow Kingdom
Pearlpoint Kingdom
Lazy River of Love
Aphrodite's Manor
Temptation Empire
Cinderine 'capital'
Estate of Desire
Belinda's Atelier
Praline Patisserie
Edwin's Antique Emporium
Luminaria
Miserymoon Castle
Psychic Parlor
Lupine Dynasty
Scarlette Rainforest
Man-Eating Mansion
Nemerosa Kingdom
Malumice Court
Thorne's Lodge
Labyrinth Kingdom
Lifeblood Isles
Dewvalley Domain
Eclipse Academy
Witchweaver Resort
Unrequited Cemetery
Bellbrook
Winona's Townhouse
Thornhill Chateau
Twilight Falls
Saltwater Sea
Aqualine
Swanlake Lagoon
Roseveil
Apple Orchard
Heartbreak Café
Hellbore District
Honeycomb Haven
Hazelnut Inn
Brambleheart Castle
Wisteria Ballroom
Renva Province
Mirabelle's Healing Hollow

Fantasy
Grimoire
Witchcraft

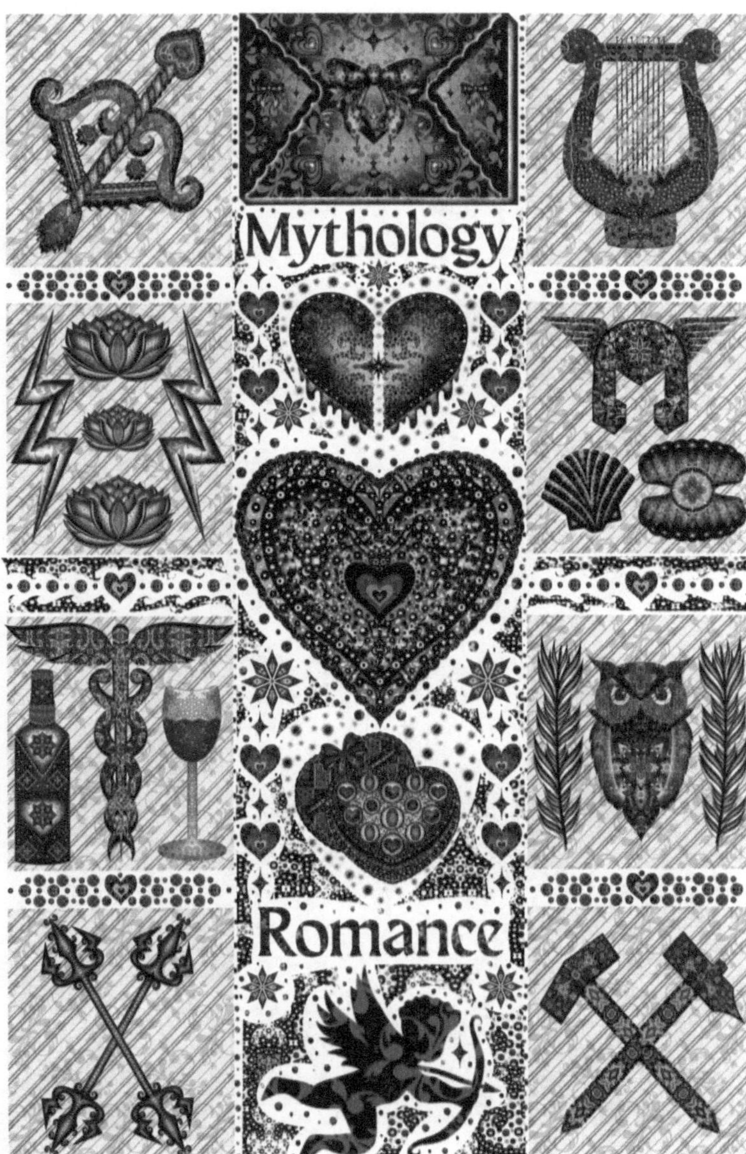

Mythology
Romance

Nightshade Masquerade

Promises of debauched mayhem pranced within the Wisteria Ballroom
Of the lavish Brambleheart Castle, a ten-towered acropolis of affluence
For 'twas the eve of the Nightshade Masquerade, a *murder mystery* bash
Where élite partakers modeled bespoke cufflinks, slingbacks, or circlets
Before situating decorated papier-mâché masks over unhuman features
Just as sentient double doors unlatched and rabid hedonism unleashed

Psychedelic liquor in her intestines and wayward zeal in her diaphragm
Gwyneth, she-devil descendant of the Garden of Eden banished, Lilith
Glorious in a décolletage-divulging gown of nine thousand sequin frills
Meandered her way through the tempestuous masses of assorted beings
Socializing with gorgons, flirting with half-fae, gossiping with Valkyries
That is, up until a tell-tale scream rippled across the disorder in the hall
For the faux homicide, insincere demise by deadly poison, had befallen
And as the designated fatality of this festivity, a thespian wyvern-shifter
Performed a convincing play of passing, lying prone with eerie stillness
The invitees, *she-devil included*, were saddled with troubles of their own
For every facial façade hardened, binding to cheekbones with longevity
Adhered by the enchantment of the event, like impishly adamant paste
Indentured to persevere—never to falter until the night's crime cracked
Some guests toiled in groups, like covens brainstorming sound theories
While others, such as introverted vampires and independent spiderfolk
Endeavored upon their lonesome, rifling for clues like practiced sleuths
But in the end, it was our Gwyneth who detected a glint in the distance
Born by the revelry's starlike lighting refracting off of a *minuscule* object
Almost indiscernibly peeking out of a manticore's corduroy side pocket
But as she focused her scarlet corneas—seeing with perfect satanic sight
Gwyneth noticed the item was none other than a vessel of mock toxins
Which, shown by an artificial autopsy, could have slain our staged prey
After describing her hypothesis to the charismatic master of ceremonies
One nod validated our she-devil's suspicions, thusly shattering the spell
Urging ornate masks, beaded, feathered, or bejeweled, to *detach at once*
And yes, the incantation did irk, and the castle's energy did overwhelm
But at this time the very next year, all will revisit the Wisteria Ballroom
For no matter the theme or title of the perennially awaited masquerade
It was not a solicitation any hybrid or hellion would *ever dare to decline*

Cliffside Captor

Swaying atop a rocky overhang in the periphery of a dour, coastal town
Plummeting travesties await, for gravity yields to not even the innocent

While the atrophying effects of aging weathered the seagull-strewn ether
A warlock of subpar status with an irrepressible appetite for invincibility
Dedicated his discontented existence to satisfying *any and all evil whims*
Before adopting the pertinent alias of the Cliffside Captor, terrifying all
As a fanatical abductor just like the Odysseus-obsessed nymph, Calypso
With secrecy, our culprit skulked into the market square to seize females
Beatific goddesses, shoreline selkies, endowing genies, seaside sorceresses
Any who withheld critical sparks of potential, wholly ripe for the taking
Our veteran kidnapper injected vulnerable arms with power suppressors
Before aligning abrasive burlap sacks over insulted, *hysterical* expressions
Only to be thrown, one by one, over his shoulders like packs of produce
And hauled up the mountainous hike all the way to his inclined address
At the extreme precipice, our criminal heaved the hostages onto the dirt
Ready, *at long, ravenous last,* for his prudently planned scheme to launch
Although his derisory brew-boiling and charm-crafting gifts incited pity
This warlock's caliber of thieving witchery from targets was *anything* but
Like a malign magnet, our captor siphoned envious heaps of supremacy
Sapping with speed until their figures weakened and ligaments withered
Left to lament the confiscation of formerly embedded, steadfast abilities
Not knowing that soon, it was their succinct lives they would mourn as well
For their souls, lackluster when bereft of magic, negated their usefulness
And so, our hijacker flung each female over the bluff, like flightless fowl
Leaving them to the fates of hydras and rusalkas circling the misty tides
Cradling past victims, broken-limbed and stock-still, at the *very* bottom
And while their bruised and bloody forms never felt bodily strains again
Miserably, their spirits experienced dire suffering, even on the other side
For death so idolizes imitating the horrors and hardships of a taxing life

As for the Cliffside Captor, *never once* has he regretted his wrongdoings
For the exhilaration of metaphysical prospects surging inside his vessels
Proved more than enough of a distraction to impede any tears of shame
Even now, addicted he remains to debilitating his present-day prisoners
For just like leeches of any type, our warlock's cravings shall never cease

Grimstone Warfare

Within the picturesque galaxy, a paranormally hypnotic realm persisted
Known by saints and satyrs from neighboring worlds as Ethereal Ember
Where the spiteful continent of Grimstone accrued barrels of animosity
Until negotiations were needed no longer, and war was rightfully waged
Commanding enemy regions to train for absolute butchery and bedlam
Before diving off combat's brink, powers primed for *perhaps the last time*

By decree of the triad of rival monarchs, the following territories shall enlist:
With the horizontal scenery of lowlands, the Labyrinth Kingdom dazes
Named by the Minotaur as a triggering homage to his worst nightmare
For long ago, plowed were the patterns of a puzzling geographical maze
Extended across the length of these acres, fortified with fatal safeguards
Like blockades fitted with acid-tipped machetes to spear pliant tendons
And hornet nests stashed in every intersection meant to mortally attack
But bleakest of all is the factor that the maze assumes a mind of its own
Forever rearranging winding roads and repositioning bewildering paths
Vowing none hellbent upon storming this web of dead-ends will ever escape
Next in line are the Lifeblood Islands, flaunting a viscous patina of gore
Atop a cluster of swampland isles just off the continent's southern coast
With hemoglobin-fixated tenants poised to manipulate opposing blood
As capillary-varying virtuosos, rousing influenza-inducing temperatures
Though most notably, or most advantageously amid this era of turmoil
All inhabitants may reawaken the familiar spilled treacle from axed foes
Goading the gelatinous cells to strike just like an unforgivable plasma flood
Closing the enrollment is the Lupine Dynasty, a grassland of vegetation
Established by Lupa, the maternal yet merciless beast from Roman lore
Motivated by their moon-exalting icon, the wolves revert to baser goals
Raring to rise up and impound spines, vertebra after impaired vertebra
While masticating upon the cartilage between torn out Bronchial tubes
Before howling to their founding idol as their foaming mouths hunger, still

As follows, Labyrinth aches to level Lifeblood into a six-foot-deep grave
The Islands insolently strategize to trounce each canine across the ocean
And the Lupine population plots to *abolish them both* with an iron claw
But when the battle horn blows, it will be up to the fickle fabric of luck
And the overriding deciders of *destiny* to elect who will reign in the end

FEBRUARY
SUNDAY MONDAY TUESDAY WEDNESDAY THURSDAY FRIDAY SATURDAY
1
2 3 4 5 6 7 8
9 10 11 12 13 14 15
16 17 18 19 20 21 22
23 24 25 26 27 28

Elysia's Devotee

When the calendar of the cosmos leaped into *the rosy month of romance*
Something endearing occurred within the luxuriant shire of Luminaria
Elysia, crystalline elf revealing a sparkling aura and sunglow-hued irises
Acquired an unidentified admirer of the mythological-and-marble kind
A genuine gentleman and anonymous advocate for *traditional* courting
Well, as traditional as one could get without disclosing himself, just yet
And so, Elysia's fan deposits an envelope upon her front steps every day
Oblong cardstock offerings sealed with wax stamps of symbolic maroon
Housing pink-shaded papyrus exposing shockingly elegant penmanship
The swirling ink of which shines shall his crush deign to read past dusk
Each scalloped letter, in polite fashion, details this enthusiast's thoughts
Signed, *with a soul unflinchingly desiring only you, your monstrous devotee*
Our gleaming elf never gathers the courage or grasps the words to reply
Though she awaits, with giddiness, every punctual delivery, all the same
From the introductory first to the thirteenth, Elysia locates one missive
Yet when daylight breaks amid the *flushed* early hours of the fourteenth
Rather than the peaceful fluttering to the floor our elf typically harkens
An *impassioned thump* reaches Elysia's ears as a stack of valentines arrive
To commemorate this supremely starry-eyed holiday with proper praise
And even after the Cupid-central celebration ends, *halt, her notes do not*

After accepting inscribed parcels of affection for twenty-eight mornings
Dejected, our Elysia becomes as February finally diminishes into March
Before peeking toward her porch amid the inception of this third phase
But rather than a new message, our damsel finds her devotee *in the flesh*
Much to Elysia's undisguised delight and her admirer's bashful suspense
Acquainted with his visage at last, a colossal gargoyle of grey stares back
Utterly off-putting or unapproachable to the standard, hypercritical eye
Exactly why Elysia met her correspondent by means of lovely longhand
Before coming clean, longing to start their enamored epic with honesty
Giving Elysia the grace of determining if her sentiments match his own
With the knowledge of his imperfections—so unlike her blatant beauty
But upon musing, our elf feels connected to her calcified writer, already
And without any revolt in reaction to his form, just the *opposite*, in fact
Elysia eagerly unchains her ajar entry, ushering her unveiled love inside
Now amenable toward the genesis of *this next chapter and so much more*

Razor-Sharp Coffin

Sharper than a broadsword's edge, a quartet of fangs plunged into flesh
For a barrier so delicate never stood a chance against a creature so cruel
And as spotted owls crept across the skies upon a lethally imbued wind
A nocturnal predator of darkness raided the internal wine of his quarry
One with a name entirely irrelevant whose vocation was evidently clear
A fervent novice of the infamous cult of sanctimonious *vampire hunters*
Inducted into this stalking society to eradicate species deemed macabre
Allied alongside those panicked by the certainty of death's looming call
Or those lost to envy's seduction, bitter over skills beyond mortal reach
Either way, this pursuer, the shameful rogue in every vampire's memoir
Steadily failed the fight to breathe—released from reality *and* his league
With wrists grieving musical pulses and visions of only blackened voids
All vigor left the human, stolen by annihilation cloaked as an icy squall
And in one decisive puff, the reaper cackled, *and the huntsman was gone*

Imagine the see-saw of imbalance wavering between the discordant pair
Like goldenrod brightness dying so the lofty silver spotlight may prevail
Recall that as the vampire gulped his greedy fill with a gore-fueled haste
And his middle inflated with swallowed life, the hunter only grew *gaunt*
Starkly sunken, as his ending transpired in the most permanent of ways
For the two shall seldom survive on this earthly plane in amicable unity
As the threads of their adverse spirits are tied—coerced to make contact
Yet fated to *stereotypically* clash, unwilling to uncoil the yarn and coexist
Though, in this case, our creature of fantasy fretted not of this disparity
For the vampire Anatole, egotistical as any with his smoldering exterior
Left every ambush victorious—never facing the vicious bite of downfall

As merry as a reckless god—willfully ignorant of the definition of guilt
Anatole's slashing teeth withdrew from the deceased's disfigured jugular
Leaving his sopping mouth hollow, requiring spare rations far too soon
But past the burgundy thirst consuming his mind, the vampire sobered
Before unfurling the hunter's rapier of titanium from digits already stiff
For loss is a *selfish and swift* lover, implementing rigor mortis in its wake
Dagger in ashen palm, Anatole prowled the frost-slicked streets of 1901
Unafraid of the *unnamed* creeping among nightfall's cocoon of shadows
For nothing would prove deadlier than his own soul of opaque *obsidian*

Slotted just below sodden earth where vanilla suggestions of verve lessen
An ancient lair endured, surrounded by the potpourri of decomposition
For all entities found next to reeking elements renounce their livelihood
Even centipedes and stag beetles loiter on the periphery of Hade's portal
But within Anatole's underground abode, any gangrenous whiffs waned
Extinguished by the breathtakingly *ghoulish grandeur* projecting indoors
Such inviting warmth filled the opulent space, rife with vintage touches
Relics from planetary vacations as dated reminders of his immortal state
From eighteenth-century candelabras traded in the amatory city of Paris
Ochre goblets thievishly looted from Dublin cathedrals in medieval eras
And Italian Renaissance settees upholstered with handspun spans of silk
Tinted cobalt and merlot, the vital color of veins and what dwells inside
To *meticulously* embellished mirrors mounted strictly for ornamentation
For the glass itching to behold a reflection remained sorely disappointed
Still, this bloodsucker's hideout circulated an air of melodramatic charm
With an *incomparable* asset exhibited in the epicenter like a gothic pearl
Elevated atop a sturdy pedestal laid a vampire's one requisite possession:
An unfinished coffin of victory, backlit by the constant glare of a hearth
Amalgamated from patchworks of *homicidal* materials and harsh metals
Assuming the shapes and structures of surgical scalpels or stiletto blades
Gripped by zealots amid futile assassination attempts all against Anatole
Yet, ever a recycler, our vampire repurposed his razor-sharp compilation
Utilizing their *ineffective* tools of torture to assemble his venue of repose
Not one to distress over stockpiling more and more, not for one second
For as long as the sands of time will spill, hunters will undoubtedly lurk
And daggers will be transferred into Anatole's clutch, but never his chest

Impelled by barbaric hormones, Anatole affixed his most topical trophy
A dagger shaped from Damascus steel—as impressive as it was incurable
Attached across from *warped* Viking knives sporting leather-bound hilts
And Norse battle axes with chiseled engravings, once familial heirlooms
Reclaimed to serve an altered aim, like tinny angels obeying a novel god
This prize was no different, concluding the vampire's coffin with finality
And one stolid heartbeat later, Anatole tumbled into a *relieving* slumber
Dreaming beside weaponry as neon rays of solar heat rose and retreated
Until the vampire's fatigue vanished, *and he awakened, parched yet again*

A TALE
ORCHESTRATED
BY TITANS

A Tale Orchestrated by Titans

Titans, our original playwrights, molding souls for their own recreation
Such ingenuity, both terrible and tender, within their everlasting minds
The Bard of Avon will indeed *tremble* from the threatening competition
Should their dramatized works drift from the clouds to the stages below

Complementary rapport runs between the narrow gaps of *contradiction*
True for these forces of nature, undeniably palpitating with dominance
Yet their elemental capabilities materialize in manners clearly divergent
One entity *torpedoing* through the oxygenated ether in which he resides
While the other deplorably blisters tenuous stretches of land way down
All beginning with a Titan of meteorology, impatient for entertainment
Who, upon a lark in 1599, formulated a Zeus-inspired god of lightning
Bustling with *frenetic* essences of electricity beneath a pallid appearance
Using galvanized gifts to generate blinding flares of charged conductors
Unfolding across the sky at climbing intervals amid *strict thunderstorms*
But long before his labor, the paternal icon of all climates had colluded
Plotting beside the conflagrant fire Titan—a female of turbulent talents
Who bore the idea that while one character may be thrilling to observe
A double-feature débuting unwitting co-stars would surely multiply the fun
And so, as a self-serving mother, this red-hot Titan built a lava goddess
With a body dyed by coals, underscored by fluorescent vermillion veins
For this goddess's decimating endowments encompassed molten messes
Ejecting rivers of liquified volcanic rock, declaring to destroy *everything*
But then, the Titans agreed, the only thing greater than two inventions
Would be if their isolated lives merged into one of outright infatuation
For romance will always surmount as the sovran choice for amusement
Like engaged audiences, our Titans rowdily applauded as their kin met
Locking *invigorated* gazes while transfixed feelings arose out of the blue
Hatching alien emotions augmented by the arrant potencies of passion
Until the trappings of unrivaled respect strengthened their relationship
Evolving into an exemplary pair, *even if they* were *penned to be just that*

And although the lovers know they were sculpted for nothing but sport
Neither find themselves bothered, for they may be marionetted around
So long as their raucous love saga, manically matched, never terminates
And their smitten appendages remain entangled, eternally and onwards

Candid Confessions

Those without candor lined atop their lips quake from imminent *doom*
When cowering in the perceptive company of Trixie, sorceress of verity
For *truth-saying* flairs pierced our witch's soul from her very conception
Blessed with a deceit detector, oh-so-helpful in a world laden with liars
And presently, one dishonest individual in particular must be punished
Emboldening our turquoise-haired Trixie to concoct a salve of integrity
To coax a confession from the throat of a cheat into the ears of a *skeptic*
Setting in motion her procedures, Trixie simmers spring-sourced waters
Before introducing lingonberry wax and rosehip oils to the tepid broth
Marrying the mixture only to transfer her handiwork into a shallow tin
Hurriedly, so as the steam still mounts, our mage may vocalize her spell
Inoculating the solidifying salve with sincerity-retrieving enchantments

Let libelous perjuries be ransacked; replace fraudulence with flowers of fact
Articulate with authenticity so exact, lest my penalizing powers rapidly react

Balm cooled and clotted, Trixie turns to the *two-faced* male in question
Fused to a beam with sailor's knots—forced to watch while she worked
Choked by unbelievably cumbersome cables of worry as time ticked by
Only exacerbating as Trixie spreads her salve upon his heaving sternum
Soaking into skin *so susceptible*, for the ointment's magic is transdermal
Excavating through dermis and tissue until accurate affirmations reveal
For Trixie's jailbird has been suspected of directing ritualistic slaughters
Murdering with the corroded scythes of Satan *all to oblige a bestial liege*
And this slaying admission, spiraling to the surface without his consent
Confirms that blameless he was never, for Trixie senses his lack of lying
As forthright murmurs breed far diverse refrains than those of duplicity
Inside our witch's auditory sphere, sour untruths mimic deafening cries
And legitimate lyrics imitate calming countryside cowbells upon a loop
So, with the newfound noises of *truthful* concertos echoing in her head
Trixie cheerfully summarizes this underling's hard-earned chastisement
Which she inflicts upon the immoral male herself by way of witchcraft
Rewiring his brain to block all future ordinances from his infernal king
Then cutting his eliminating fingers and crocheting his oral cavity shut
Guaranteeing that this devil shall *never* again brandish a killing weapon
Nor delude any other, *leading Trixie's heart to exult in* yet another *success*

Midsummer Mead

Excerpt from "Bewitching Cocktails and Mocktails"; page 87

Pure edible ecstasy portrays Midsummer Mead, the finest of fairy wines
First prototyped from inside the Tulipterra Court of botanical breweries
Now distilling the *rich libation* for yearly festivities and feasts of faekind
From the Gossamer Gala and Sunburst Carnival to the Freesia Equinox
Saved only for these lively events as the drunken effects are unsteadying
Markedly *delectable* yet also eleven times headier than human beverages
For mortal-made cognac, scotch, or cider shall provoke dizzy sensations
But this midsummer luxury melts inhibitions with *inebriating outcomes*
Midsummer Mead *best* pairs with soft cheese and garlic crostini starters
Lamb and mushroom stew entrées and deep-fried apple donut endings
A three-course meal befitting highborn members of winged monarchies
Yet all humans and halflings alike are prodded on to sample a taste, too

Our incandescent brew's ingredients are to be followed exactly as listed:
Heaped pours of honey from whimsical bees, eleven diced dragon fruits
Macerated maraschino cherries from dryad orchards, dashes of nutmeg
Pints of peach liqueur, citrus-steeped ocean water, Seelie-sprouted yeast
Twelve scant gooseberry syrup dollops and eight spoonfuls of ambrosia
Together, every component complements one another ever-so-dreamily
For after all, this recipe was tested by *many fairies over many generations*
Far before Midsummer Mead was initiated into these instructive sheets
Succeeding four fruitful months of fermentation, a ritual of converting
Craft cocktails by upending the *outstanding* potion in an airtight shaker
Then decant, like aromatic rain, into a coconut-rimmed, chilled goblet
Before garnishing with fizzing seraph teardrops and a crisp orange twist
Until all that remains is to whisper wanton words for a truly *hazy* night

Sugars and berries and saps galore, greet my bloodstream 'till I call for more
Expel any modesty, this I plead, so the eve turns wild, all thanks to my mead

In the very dead of dusk, experience the liquid entering your esophagus
Reap the more-than-tipsy results until tomorrow shines through, at last

Not liable for any skull-throbbing or stomach-turning post-consumption!

Sorcha's Kiss

What unforeseen boons a fleeting kiss may bestow in the face of fatality
Like an angel of resuscitation, Sorcha's looks sidetracked historians *little*
Instead, archivists recount the vitality in her cherry lips, admired by all
As an unmatched female with a *salvaging prerogative* powering her steps
Sorcha visits tumultuous frontlines, trudging through the mass hysteria
Scanning for cold chainmail-clad soldiers, javelins still furtively clasped
Just as often as she surveys infirmaries swarming with nurses so harried
Concerned over irredeemable patients submitting to grievous abrasions
Our Sorcha pinpoints these *unresponsive* individuals, deceased as of late
Their ousted spirits still clinging onto this bountiful realm of breathing
Yet struggle they shall not, for the recently departed may be *rejuvenated*
Through Sorcha's kiss, not sexual or romantic or drawn-out in any way
Just an imperative press of her merciful mouth upon their airless orifice
Exhaling the slightest semblance of survival inside motionless skeletons
Miraculously gasping, each saved soul does not awaken exactly the same
For their brains remain baffled, confined within death's disorienting net
Consciousness not completely stripped, yet not quite as whole as before
But still, far better to accept a pseudo-life than to undergo *only oblivion*

For those who passed in days gone by—just past the point of no return
Sorcha may snatch their waning souls from limbo and bring them back
As revenants: undead beings possessing their *very own* postmortem skin
And for those with dismembered bodies, innards haphazardly extracted
Sorcha may not sew split limbs and restore organs to make a man anew
Dissimilar to Frankenstein's scientific kin, *a point she prides herself upon*
Although Sorcha's urgent kiss may resurrect—piece by disjointed piece
Should she graze a splintered cranium, newfangled thoughts shall form
Should she peck a haywire heart, it shall rhythmically restart, and so on
And while these *estranged* units lack the faculties to live an inclusive life
Thankful they still find themselves, alert yet fragmented as they may be
Consider a committed husband's uprooted eye able to regard his spouse
Or a military commander-in-chief's guillotined head able to roar edicts
And understand that our Sorcha's unconventional yet opportune magic
A persuasive caress of power and the demi-reality it fortuitously awards
May mean *everything* when confronted by an existence of *nothing at all*

Witch Hunt of Evermore Woods

Tendrils of profound exhaustion paired with stanzas of prophetic truths
Beleaguer the battering heart of Ravenna, *harmless* witch of white magic
Sprinting through the Evermore Woods, discarded thorns prick her feet
Yet the scrapes, crimson and sore, burn less than what will surely follow

Forged decency as justification, male mortals roleplay as righteous gods
Though their forms never course with gilded ichor, metallic and mighty
No, their musculatures house nothing but erosion, so sordidly polluted
Padded with fetid chasms for termites to *fester inside, lodging incessantly*
It is these foul males who hunt, yet bison or elk or deer they never seek
Banded together as braggart mercenaries, waylaid Wiccans become prey
Mistakenly judging sisters of the coven to be mistresses of hellish deities
Indoctrinated by the overpowering witchcraft within Lucifer's teachings
Amid their pursuits, the villains invent false egos inside their frail minds
Arrogant, assured that their quest shall never culminate in a neutral trial
But a finale of *demoralizing* outros that only female targets may prewarn
And as Ravenna, their latest recipient for reasons untrue and unmerited
Rushes past wilted greenery, she fathoms that detest her they likely may
But so too, with vulgar stares and lecherous asides, do they covet *her as well*
Abhorring her enough to cause chase—hurtling over ivy-coated terrains
Yet not enough to curb their urges from treating themselves to her body
And when all is through, it will not be Ravenna's sorcery that damns her
But her palpable splendor, luring in ways she never dreamed nor desired

High-handed oppressors closing in, our mage fears her fate when taken
And yet, with a mage's insight, she equally dreads her *destiny after death*
Unconscious, many an assaulting sin will befall beneath the Milky Way
But unalive, the sickening and sacrilegious likelihoods are, alas, endless
Favoring one deed of self-destruction over limitless turns of desecration
Ravenna ultimately resolves to retreat upon a cross of her own creation
Electing to perish by her *humane* hands than under their *violating* ones
Breathless from weaving through the woods, Ravenna recites her chant
One every witch memorizes from early girlhood for events just like this
And so, from shaking lips slips a spell of shelter to protect as she passes

Sought by huntsmen with aims unjust; leave this flawed earth, now, I must
Save my body from certain defilement to come; erase my bones as I succumb
Crowd my fallen flesh with cypress leaves; banish my form from lewd thieves
So their roving palms may never act, and I may move on auspiciously intact

Ambitions voiced to the *loyally* listening attention of her High Priestess
Ravenna plucks a slim sachet of wolfsbane from her poison-lined cloak
Always presuming and planning for the worst, as is the life of all mages
Swallowing the plum blossoms of defeat, Ravenna decelerates her stride
Distantly wishing to secure a strangling noose, scratching and scabrous
Sure to leave behind displeasing bruises dotted along her snapped neck
If only to depict herself as defective or disagreeable in some crucial way
Rendering the final remarks spat at her *bereft of any unwanted lust at all*
And yet, poison is her last resort, and it is functioning at a frenzied rate
When the banshees wail, Ravenna, guiltless all the way to her grave, expires
Exiled from our problematic mortal coil with a sigh of bittersweet relief
Escalating their pace, the huntsmen reach Ravenna's vacant death place
Yet her corporeal casing has dissolved, soul already absconded elsewhere
Presenting the fuming crusaders, spewing indignant saliva, with *nothing*
No casket to invade, no corpse to besmirch, and no carcass to consume
For that was their intent, and in this, all witches and women shall agree
Only once their devious senses discern no one to assail do they disband
For unseen, she is out of mind, overlooked, and undesirable at long last

With an empathetic welcome, Ravenna settles into the other side easily
Solaced by those who were once well-acquainted with her predicament
Consoled by none other than the scorned witches deriving from Salem
Chiding scars and censuring burns haunting defaced, intangible figures
Yet their mutilations will never dissuade their stories from being shared
Several express they were publicly beheaded or immolated upon a stake
While others, desperate like our Ravenna, did the executing themselves
But here, their grievances are cathartically voiced, all plights in the past
For this unburdened afterlife encourages the aged custom of witchcraft
Never to be reprimanded—as it was never a *true* misdeed to begin with

Aphrodite's Soirée

Nothing material nor magical shall ever outdo unfiltered odes of love
Ageless mantra of Aphrodite, nude goddess of attraction and adoration
Archetype of all physical fantasies and everything languidly pleasurable
Yet, above all, our not-so-shallow idol honors the grandness of *devotion*
To rejoice affection both affable and ablaze, Aphrodite arranges a soirée
Scheduled biannually, when all who are wedded and all who wish to be
Obtain beautified invitations handwritten by the Greek goddess herself
Unable to pass up such a summons, guests enter her sumptuous manor
An abode of *romantic* architecture rivaling the Palace of Versailles itself
Within, a perpetual ambiance of desire ascends from cerise mosaic tiles
Before gliding over fresco-painted walls, trimmings of cordiform décor
And *prim* tablescapes with canapés and cocktails and confections for all
Like any proficient planner, Aphrodite fixes blood bags for vampiric ilk
And tops off thermoses of youthful nectar for goddess and god cohorts
For those with a more *mortal* palette, flutes of passionfruit punch await
Next to Aphrodite's banana fudge brownies, a recipe of dairy *decadence*
Much later, amid farewells so wistful, ardent party mementos lie ahead
But the guest's exits shall not ensue until the eve's activities are through

Further into Aphrodite's bash, where the perfume of admiration surges
Festive pastimes, both olden and unheard-of, are ready to be competed
Seven, *or more*, heady minutes spent in heaven as bottles of wine swivel
And pairs divide to engage in scavenger hunts with *brain-teasing riddles*
Finding rose-scented clues the subtle shade of a ballerina's pointe shoes
Leading the parted couples up sleek stairways and into moaning rooms
Before guiding them back to the lover they had arrived with an age ago
No more to-and-fro, the partners revel in the affair, together once more
So too, may any unmarried and unmated individuals *teasingly* converse
Indulging in their own game of winning earnest, enthused connections
Able to do so without error—due to the precision of Aphrodite's magic
For those leaving this recurrent gathering forever set forth worshipping
With affiliations labeled inseparable or informal, their hearts are *hooked*
Amid the get-together, our hostess holds happiness for all in attendance
Though, quietly, only within the soundproof privacy of her pretty mind
Aphrodite hopes that at this soirée, she may fall head over heels, herself
For heartfelt love may transcend all, but *only if attained in the first place*

Veiled Nightingale

Unexaggerated rumors of quintessential appeal sweep across the nation
Muttering of an enigmatic damsel famed for her prepossessing exterior
Or, at least, every report blathers of her beauty from the neckline down
Displaying a curved, *comely* figure and windblown locks of light yellow
While everything else remains covered behind a silk chiffon veil of ecru
Like a virginal maiden of virtue, too sacred to be seen by *degenerate eyes*
Envisioning her with mesmeric irises suitable for a museum installation
But only when a *boastful* contender enquires, one with gullible defenses
Does she cajole them to edge closer and closer, only to shed her shroud
Although a statuesque countenance, complexly fetching, never is bared
For when her cryptic veil rises, the form of this seductress shifts *entirely*
As the waiflike mantle acts as a tether to her shape of synthetic pretense
But undraped, this exquisite being rediscovers her biological silhouette
Sliding into the brown and beige skin of a little nightingale, effortlessly
Tabling impartial enticement in exchange for a purely errant avian aura

To quell her prey's preliminary tension, twitching in an anxious uproar
Our nightingale, with stout lungs, emits a whistling sonata of rhapsody
Like an operatic aria evoking lulling visualizations of copacetic serenity
Serenading until their shouts quit, though slackened jaws remain agape
Granting our plumed shifter trouble-free circumstances for admittance
With a condensed body, our distinct bird breaches lips parted in denial
Descending through empty pharynges and dipping past interior viscera
Until her anatomical jaunt brings our nightingale to her victims' spleen
Where she harms the filtering organ with her dutifully *penetrating* beak
Vaccinating helpless lymphatic pulp with her personal brand of venom
For our formerly camouflaged female is outfitted with *powers of reversal*
Which diffuse from lanced spleens in feasible efforts to activate anarchy
Forcing compromised bodily higher-ups to stick to subversive briefings
Until bones liquefy, intestines pollute, livers deregulate, and hearts crumble
And when the vile impact initiates with the timely efficiency of sorcery
Our nightingale navigates her way out of terminally doctored skeletons
Sailing over sedated tongues, *lingual tarmacs*, before sipping allaying air
And with one curt blink, the lithe charade of her damsel veneer returns
Abating prey expiring in the backdrop as she lowers her veil once more
Likely to shift soon, for impressionable males are never in short supply

The Beauty of Bloombriar Grove

Earth, the organic soil binding our connection to all *prolific* ecospheres
Remains entirely ample within this arboreous continent of Emeraldine
But march deeper still and detect Mistmeadow, a west-facing kingdom
Housing the insulated coppice of Bloombriar Grove, a riot of greenery
Where cacao dirt bears the touch of those with *foliage* filling their veins
For this verdant and vined grove inhabits a synergetic faction of dryads
With oak-related origins, every forest nymph survives as a nature spirit
And although they represent evergreen pines, laurels, and edible apples
Fae-like females are the lissome, lovesome physiques the dryads assume
With chlorophyll-infused skin and twig-based circlets of ferns or floras
Appearing as *perennially lovely* as living bunches of yarrow and daylilies
But the fairest of them all was the pleasing, praiseworthy dryad, Sylvie

Clothed in petaled brassieres and sarongs of moss and mocha gradients
Sylvie's splendor, as environmentally sightly as a mirage, hypnotized all
Though her true illustriousness was historically tied to her regal lineage
For our mythical creature was a descendant of the *original* dryad queen
And as a modest royal maiden, Sylvie's days indicated woodland luxury
Nestled within the flowering hold of Bloombriar Grove, forever restful
Having dwelled in a hardwood home of exfoliating bark and elm leaves
From there, Sylvie viewed storks dropping off new saplings and shrubs
While mooning over blossoming huckleberries, clovers, and toadstools
And if any humans stumbled upon her sacred grove, *as they so often did*
Sylvie could influence their emotions, more than able to impart trauma
Though she did not, aching for all to worship the forest as much as she
And so, she evoked fanatical favoritism, ensuring that when they exited
It was Sylvie and her dryad sisters they would pray to from then on out
Adopting a nymph-leaning divinity as their timbered religion, *evermore*

Sun-dappled Sylvie valued her days, as she knew with glum resignation
That while her beloved tree was once robust, it could not exist eternally
And alerts of aging, *acorns leaping, branches lurching*, had already arisen
Finally, when the fatal eve arrived for her abode to go forth into demise
So too, did Sylvie likewise perish, cast into the endless riptide of expiry
For the *soulless butcher* sensed the bond between the dryad and her tree
And thought it a mercy, one he hardly grants, to end them *both* at once

Alchemy Sorceress

Within a baroque bedchamber Marie Antionette would have begged for
And atop a European-style champagne credenza rests a true *tour de force*
In the shape of an oxblood-varnished jewelry box with hinges of copper
Housing trinkets prompting jealousy, more often than one would think
Every formation dispensing abilities far beyond simply seeming voguish
Soldered by the *creative* Alchemy Sorceress—a mix of mage and goddess
With witchery of altering alloys and conjuring revolutionary gemstones
Modifying commonplace materials into iridescent brooches and bangles
Our sorceress welds, invokes, and workshops wearable regalia for others
But the objects from her own receptacle of riches remain *only for herself*

Rigid padlock removed, the satin-lined box bares an orderly initial level
A mood ring standing perpendicular amazes, yet it is no *sham* of a stone
For the ensorcelled rock, ellipse-shaped, wedged among prongs of silver
Toggles between tints based upon changing temperaments—*so unerring*
Across the tier, a dainty charm bracelet of yellow gold grants invisibility
While a chain appointed with a stellar crystal mirroring a waxing moon
Operates as a notable amulet, ordained with powers of lunar protection
Finishing the primary tray, a divine twosome of pavé drop earrings *stun*
For all the quartz inlaid around the hoops propels shapeshifting services
All irreplaceable, yet her inventory carries on as an ancillary layer awaits
Incorporating inserts to store surplus odds and ends of all classifications
Take, for example, a birthstone band of peridot full of remedial energies
Lying adjacent to an adjustable filament carrying a reflective ruby locket
An oracular saving grace, for past the exterior prophesying skills prosper
So too, did our Alchemy Sorceress develop an anklet adorning tanzanite
Harmoniously infiltrated with the euphonious propensities of a lyrebird
Reclining parallel to her *cutting-edge creations*: stud earring sets of amber
Equipped with the talents to teleport from one known realm to the next

At times, the accomplishments of our mage doze inside her jewelry box
Lounging, a listless vacation of sorts, in close immediacy to their maker
But amid other instances, our witch-goddess meld *dons every decoration*
Festooning her skin to the limit—just like an heirloom-amassing queen
While letting the witchcraft in her precious accessories engulf her spirit
Relishing in the proof that power often lies within the *prettiest* of pieces

Strawberry Moon Skies

Just as the gruesome dust from a strenuous campaign of tyranny settles
A worldwide conflict waged eternities ago, only now coming to a truce
Our sympathetic goddesses of the galaxy reward the newly serene realm
By stringing up an orbiting strawberry moon, a *pure* poppy-red satellite
Whenever this stemless circle rises, seldom so, the whole world changes
Renovated into an untainted domain of loveliness for one extended eve
The very next bleary daybreak—before the exhibition abates altogether
Fade in upon Clementine, nymph with frizzy locks and freckled cheeks
And umber-tinted Theodore, most docile werewolf one shall ever meet
Intoxicated off the emotional endorphins from their honeymoon phase
Our newlyweds set up a solstice picnic outdoors, like a quaint breakfast
Underneath the *rubicund* hues of the leisurely leaving strawberry moon
Within a regional and rustic vineyard enclosed by white nectarine trees
Clementine and her husband-to-be, Theo, unload beige wicker baskets
Bursting at the seams with small, sheer pots of Concord grape preserves
Batches of warm buttermilk pancakes with homemade whipped cream
Antiquated earthenware jugs of sickly-sweet glaze born from maple sap
Meyer lemon miniature madeleines baked with grapefruit zest surprises
Lattice-crusted pies of huckleberry and spiral rolls of mulled cinnamon
Chocolate bundt cakes slathered with silky ganache and jovial sprinkles
Breathable cartons of fruit *so* ripe, not to gorge oneself is a true misstep
Atop tartan blankets, Theo and his free-spirited Clem feed one another
Reminiscing over their love story, chatting faintly, unraveling *completely*
While the strawberry moon, speckled not with seeds but spores of light
Shines its unsurpassed radiance upon them, seeming to poetically sing:
Huzzah, war is over, so shower your tongues with the flavors of midsummer
And take in this time spent beside your darling, as nothing shall last forever

After, our nymph hoists her head from the crook of her werewolf's arm
And as they lick *pampered* lips to divest astray crumbs while packing up
Readying to return to the charming villa Clementine and Theo co-own
So too, does this seasonal strawberry moon vacate from view—for now
Just as the consequential bells of battle inundate the recently relaxed air
Making soft moments like these lovers just shared scarce, from now on
Trading mellow sounds of percussive wind chimes and warbling tweets
For the uniform marching of combatants, as another war has *just begun*

Beauty Room
Bedroom
Kitchen
Library

Ginevra the Genie

All mortals seek to convene with the *coveted* sister species of sorceresses
Genies, who disobey the bylaws of nature diligently coined so long ago
Made of malleable molecules, bending and shifting whenever beckoned
With cranial nerves and coronary arteries as *wish-fulfilling* headquarters
And while these sexpot creatures are categorized as to-die-for celebrities
None shall outshine our groundbreaking genie, well-known as Ginevra
Who drenches the atmosphere in a cascading outpouring of confidence
Spun from interior spindles of undisputable magnetism and persuasion
Like a supernatural supermodel, Ginevra garners fans just by breathing
For her upturned espresso eyes and severe brows stimulate such interest
Just as her braids of sapphire waterfalling to hipbones instantly *intrigue*

Yet, when frost-bitten folk songs begin, and heat stroke yields delirium
When none retreat from their rooms to face erratic episodes of weather
Ginevra gleefully remains both unnoticed and unbothered—for a time
Left to unwind inside her lush estate, just as *priceless and popular* as she
A bottle of attention-grabbing eminence dreamt by prodigies of design
Erected from only stained glass and shavings of burnt gold and sterling
An *extravagant triumph* of witchcraft different from any other residence
Matchless in style and stature—seeming slender and swollen all at once
Upgraded with heart-halting, head-hurrying *finishing touches of stardust*
Ending up as a phenomenon of engineering, pushing all to peer within

Ginevra's bottle not-so-meekly brags of its aesthetic setting of amenities
With a yawning floor plan awash with navy accents and teal appliances
Offset by furnishings of charcoal and fixtures of titanium—so very chic
Center stage lies a crescent-shaped bed, as cozy as a cashmere raincloud
With soothing textiles sewn upon mountains of cushions and coverlets
Arranged atop Egyptian sheets of cerulean, ensuring a *heavenly* slumber
Equally enviable, an expansive wardrobe stands within a domed corner
As Ginevra's magical aptitude is bested *only* by her knowhow of fashion
With a figure suiting any fabric, this genie favors gauzy attires of risqué
Methodically sifting through midriff-baring, topaz-laden two-piece sets
Moving along, Ginevra's tour next leads into her contemporary kitchen
Before concluding in her vaulted library shelving worn novels of erotica
For Ginevra's bottle is truly a *tantalizing* habitat for a *trendsetting* being

Amid blackbird-chirping mornings and propitiously clichéd midnights
Ginevra, with her inactive timepiece of immortality never ticking away
Flicks through tactless popstar tabloids and hems ultra-short miniskirts
Soaking in every transient second of solitude she so frantically clings to
Certain that when the climate steadies, temperatures turning amenable
Entitled mortals will resume their avid errands to ascertain her location
Only to lure Ginevra out into their secular world based on *selfish* wants
Disturbing her seclusion by speaking an *age-old* invocation of yearning:

Beloved genie, grant me the grace of one wish before I slope into the abyss
And let my existence be kissed by the resulting precipitation of radical bliss

As their words swim skyward, Ginevra levitates from a wraithlike spiral
For her limbs had no choice but to contort, *forced* into a vexing exodus
Leaving this genie sulking before her summoner, superpowers laid bare
Bringing to light her capacity to cerebrally manifest pleas and petitions
From bodice-ripping romances to replete coffers, she wills it *all to be so*
Knitting the agile twine of fate as easily as Penelope wove her tapestries
Until appeals are approved and attentions briskly reorient *anywhere else*
Ginevra then acknowledges the universe for its indispensable assistance
Before *blitzing her body back into vapor* and slinking into her sanctuary
Contemplating, for the hundredth time, investing in a *trustworthy* lock

Lazing once more upon her high mattress like a depiction of deluxe life
Ginevra, more cunning than any ever assumes, *seethes* from indignation
Stewing with ire for her autonomy is cavalierly infringed upon so often
Until each raging resentment within the fibers of her being bubble over
As her ornery spirit *bellows for retribution* over this chronic exploitation
And so, whenever forcibly subpoenaed, Ginevra distorts their demands
Twisting negligent phrasing, until perilous storm omens tarry overhead
For the behests they necessitated never do slant in their expectant favor
Courtships disunite, coins disappear, contentment remains *out of reach*
Leaving the spell-caster in need of one more wish, now more than ever
A vain likelihood as Ginevra is inaccessible in her irreproachable bottle
Temporarily living in tranquility, pacified by the residue of her revenge
Until that galling spell is sung yet again, as a genie's work is rarely done

Draconic Epiphany

Across the Saltwater Sea, Fabergé egg glimmers point to a coastline cave
For beyond stalactites and salamanders lies a trove of *monumental* jewels
As the dragon Elijah, a goliath of graphite, dappled with veins of pewter
Bears a single-minded brain, dreaming only of his exorbitant discoveries
And while *fossilizing* particles flood his trachea, switching soil into stone
Elijah instead slavers over the forte of swapping calcium for multi-carats
But alas, our dragon must travel the map to find his overpriced artifacts
Exhuming aristocratic tiaras, talismans of agate, and alexandrite scepters
Before hoarding every harvested palatial beauty within his humid grotto
And resting right on top of his treasures, shielding the relics *even in sleep*

One vibrant sunup, Elijah overhears wings skimming the water's surface
As a female wyvern soars into view, *utterly* opalescent like a frosted pearl
A proper assessment, as our silver Evie originally hatched from an oyster
Labored into life with a respiratory system stored with *holographic smoke*
And although Elijah's eyes have homed in upon heaps of first-class assets
None have ever, not once, seemed as extraordinary as this exotic wyvern
Elijah would sacrifice much more than a diamond, *no, a million of them*
If only to tuck her glistening form, tail and all, into his side forevermore
Luckily for Elijah, Evie feels similarly, panting from burgeoning feelings
And before dusk arrives, early signs of love settle within two scaled souls

Just like disciples of the monastery pledging themselves to their religion
Elijah's draconic priorities amend while his territorial infatuation swells
And despite the welt-leaving lacerations he stomached to grow his stash
In an epiphany, Elijah cedes each gem to corroborate his *change of heart*
Doing so by setting aflame his stockpile—fashioning puddles so useless
For tangible belongings convey zero meaning in comparison to *his* Evie
And while our wyvern surveys the grand gesture with definite gratitude
Evie rushes to notify Elijah that he may keep his rubies and her respect
In the nick of time, she averts her dragon before his total inventory razes
And to replace all that burned, Evie nudges her own collection forward
Emotional as ever, Elijah reels from the weight of his wyvern's kindness
Beholding the remains of his fortune mixed with his loves, Elijah *weeps*
For a life interlinked with hers, *he admits,* is all our dragon ever needed

A Deadly Apple a Day

So implausibly similar to a scene from the pages of Grimm's Fairy Tales
A pastoral, *pick-your-own* apple orchard planted in the county, Roseveil
Entices the nurturing, marigold-eye of Greta, award-winning hatmaker
Ambling with her sketchbook in hand, searching for alfresco incentives
But in this place posited in her wildest reveries, Greta strolls no further
As this arboreous land, faultlessly farmable, parodies a pretend paradise
Until, like in every *twisted* parable, something menacing abruptly arises
Everything abundantly airy and angelic now seems alarmingly ominous
As if revamped by perdition's paintbrush—submersed in rancid acrylics
Even the tree's waxen treats, so tempting, tolerate *putrid transformations*
All, except one—as viridescent as the grassy meadows Greta often visits
Mysteriously twinkling with the tropical allure of an unblemished lime
Dazedly passing hedgehogs and hollyhocks, our hatmaker strides closer
But to Greta, it is as if she is twirled forward upon wings of fascination
And although she abstractly thinks that something awful *must* be amiss
Carry on, our spellbound maiden shall, just inches away from salvation
For the self-discipline to deny the crème de la crème of irresistible fares
Remains an option no longer, not with the apple somehow in her palm
And as Greta ruptures the smooth skin, giving in just like Eve once did
Unbidden moans float from her open mouth, dribbling with tart juices
Treating the ether to tunes so mellifluous, bees flock to the erotic noise
But such serendipitous palatability produces misgivings *speedily* verified
When she squints downward and the fruit, bereft of a bite-sized chunk
Outlandishly assumes the unconcealed exterior of deteriorating horrors
For the toxins within tarnish, bestowing more than Greta *ever* expected

As time edges forward, as it is always keen to do, and a decade drags by
Septic atoms from the cursed apple still vandalize our hatmaker's blood
Asphyxiating her aorta, dismantling her ventricles, cremating her joints
For the nectar under the flesh of the fruit *held cataclysmic poison aplenty*
And just one ingested morsel still ravages her reality all these years later
Greta, or what is left of her, haunts a liminal space betwixt life and loss
And as emaciated as she is, far too *feeble* to flee from the orchard's acres
Here Greta hurts, never to craft again, stuck crying below oak branches
Powerless to warn naïve females lest they make the same mistake as she
For in the midst of such decay, none can resist the pull of *sheer splendor*

Undying Desperadoes

Painstakingly stationed in its predetermined slot, the moon hangs high
While scalding conditions below singe as the end-of-spring rays defrost
Strain unblinking eyes toward that globe of luster, a unanimous marvel
And witness a webbed cauldron of hair-raising bats take flight together
Illumed by the albino afterglow of space accentuating their winged forms
But as these silhouettes cruise closer into view—*lurching* toward terrain
Mammalian fur warps into flesh as hovering extremities grow flightless
For when the onyx colony alight in the bounds of this mountain range
With graveled spans of bluebonnets, kicked-up dust, and tumbleweeds
Our night-flying entities then emerge as slayers of a *much* different sort

A clan of *vampiric* gunslingers dismount—bandits down to their bones
Nicknamed the Undying Desperadoes, western parasites in every sense
Archaic myths correctly chronicle that each of their *utterly whetted bites*
Inoculate specific impressions into the emptying bodies of their victims
One array of sharpened incisors gifts an anesthetizing variant of venom
And while tingling fear will remain, the sensations of torn skin will *not*
Another supernatural set of lips bequeath hints of aphrodisiacal arousal
Though their virile appearances often induce attraction, mauled or not
Next, this mouth plants rose-colored delusions within petrified psyches
Goading prey to imagine their necks are accepting pecks in lieu of ruin
Lastly, as punishing as Perseus, this undead brute renders mortals mute
Honed teeth infuse muzzling compulsions, halting lungs from hollering
Allowing the parched cowboys to summarily swallow in electric silence
Well, save for the *swigging sounds* of their throats working until glutted
The Undying Desperadoes travel as a crew, changing from bat to bloke
Transfiguring *every single eve*, pandering to patently nocturnal wildness
Setting the stage for other homicide-inclined degenerates to follow suit
After striding onto soil, these vampires mount their breakneck stallions
Adroit equestrians, just as all fanged outlaws are coached to be out west
Before charging through the nebulous nightfall, tracking down humans
Aftershaves of driftwood and death oozing from their pores as they ride
Spurred on by a carmine thirst water or whisky will never quite quench
Permitting the proximate fragrance of mortal gore to act as their guides
As they trail intravenous gluts of plasma with platelet-hungry anticipations

Amid the majority of moments, the Undying Desperadoes quickly trap
For this foursome of masculine cowboys seem to elicit unmitigated *eros*
Soon-to-be victims become put under by their devil-may-care attitudes
While lost inside extra-bawdy daydreams, *much too crass to be described*
Clad in durable attires of canvas and pelt—fashioned for frontier living
Each avaricious vampire dons wide-brimmed suede hats, rawhide boots
And belt buckles of brass—which lads and ladies alike pray to unfasten
Enlivened by lust, the blood banks for the desperadoes give in willingly
Lured toward the dim backstreets the *piercing* renegades cage them into
Jerking paisley bandanas around collars that shall never sustain wounds
The Undying Desperadoes drink, consuming deeply, almost deliriously
Before lifting their scarves—hiding away smirking mouths once slaked
Disguising discolored ruby-stained chins, *the sign of a well-savored meal*
But sometimes, no-nonsense mortals shoulder level-headed practicality
Wise enough to pour energy into evading, conscious of their fate if not
Yet, the callous-handed cowboys catch them slickly—like snaring cattle
Hogtieing their fright-filled limbs, no strangers to managing hefty rope
For reasons both ranch and bedchamber related, all too sinful to define
Prey restrained, grinding their jaws, the tall desperadoes crouch to glug
Favorable additives of *overt dismay* spiking otherwise *toothsome libations*
Bitter as java, piquant as cayenne—tangs the sponging beasts so cherish
Just as much as they value the titillated essences of not-so-chaste targets
No matter the profile, blood is blood, akin to ambrosia for all vampires
And they will celebrate whatever they may get—or, more precisely, *take*

Any unfortunate souls who happen to perceive their inflight alterations
Shall never live to perplexedly communicate the *fanciful* yet factual tale
But one being's misfortune so regularly results in a godsend for another
And in this case, these Undying Desperadoes never even need to search
For their next supper will be *directly, deliciously* in sight when they land
And while this unpredicted incident shall generate a stroke of true luck
Any prosperity in these disaster-prone mortals will be altogether absent
Standing where they never should have been, at the *worst* possible hour
These apologetic individuals will pay for their blunder with their blood
And then with their final gasps, for the greatest compensation is *demise*

Lilypad Enchantress

In the depths of Dewvalley Domain, an everglade ecosystem of nirvana
Fantastical foliage lives atop fertile topography found only in this region
Here dwells the charitable Seelie Court of all spritely, scintillating souls
Wandering over oscillating treetops and ostentatious fountains of fancy
Pocket-sized fae born within this marsh bear sorcery of *benevolent* sorts
Consider Fleur, aerial female crowned as the petite Lilypad Enchantress
With garden-fresh wildflowers plaited into her strawberry-blonde locks
Suntanned wisps framing her heart-shaped face, *fitting with her persona*
And moth-like wings in multiple shades of juniper bracketing her back
Namesake denoting her homeland, Fleur rules from a calming reservoir
Always lying upon a lily leaf or suspended above the midpoint of a lotus
And since our enchantress's cousins are sirens and mermaids and selkies
Fleur embraces aquatic witchcraft from her floral, genetic configuration
Replenishing the rippling contents of rivulets and millponds and creeks
Feeding the lifespans of both shoreline and submarine botanical beings
Maintaining the camaraderie between bettas and minnows and guppies
All while keeping up resounding security below each Seelie Court wave
Safe, should Scylla, *starved for a male menu*, ever swim to lesser streams
And deliberately deprived of any prohibited Unseelie Court trespassers
Maliciously craving, *as those dissolute cads often do*, to defile Fleur's tides
Spoiling Dewvalley Domain's customarily positive, placid environment
Which our loveable Lilypad Enchantress toils so thoroughly to preserve

While intoning promises of immortality on behalf of her piscine wards
And keeping dual raspberry retinas glued upon her habitat's well-being
Unfailingly, Fleur is graced by the nearness of her chatty partner, Piper
A prolific fae of artistic renown, with ceramic powers and paprika curls
Fellow Seelie Court subject—overjoyed to obey her commendable ruler
While walking upon air to have tumbled into love with our protagonist
Familiarized amid an afternoon social, shy curiosity bred strong crushes
And by sundown, enriched longings ended up as something everlasting
A five-star-rated romance repetitively envied by fae and fish everywhere
For Piper does all she can to embellish her girlfriend's *enraptured* mood
As loyal as our Lilypad Enchantress is in defending her affiliated waters
Undertakings these overachieving females *succeed in for now and forever*

Athena's Wisdom

By the crackling fireplace, settle into your relaxing armchair of chenille
Then lend readied ears toward the speculated lore of a sought-after witch
And the unbearable consequences of the incantation she ruefully recited

Amid the very didactic Age of Enlightenment, in a Tudor-style cottage
Lodged a generational mage, Natalia, specializing in force-field sorcery
Yet, as a priestess so abiding, her leading focus centered around Athena
All were mindful of our witch's association with the goddess of wisdom
Desiring but a tiny sliver, *a drop in the infinite well*, of Athena's acumen
Thusly so, Natalia served the supplicatory askers just what they wanted
A cinched pouch full of feathers from robins to slide below one's pillow
A corked tube sloshing with olive oil to sip the minute before moonrise
A curled scroll scrawled with a concise spell to voice beside the shadows
Head positioned just above the parcel; stomach lubricated as instructed
And drowsy lips having spoken the assigned script, they sank into sleep
Fathoming, partially so, that everything would change after awakening

My mistress, madame, mentor: when mortals visit my terrace to implore
Grant them a speck of the sage you bore until their begs forge on no more

Natalia's patrons stirred to the refreshing morning light, altered indeed
Gaining tactical thinking, encyclopedic knowledge, and ace perception
But real intellect, *meant only for Olympus occupants*, carried a grave cost
For the restricted expertise they reaped embezzled something esteemed
Some involuntarily sold dear memories—missing snapshots of the past
Intuiting everything about everyone yet recalling *nothing* of themselves
Others inadvertently relinquished their legacies, memorialized by none
Clever enough to highly appreciate tributes, but bankrupt of their own
No matter what was waived, *each mortal ended up with distended brains*
Entirely too shrewd, claustrophobic minds were so completely besieged
For a restful hush idles in the unknown—peace they *never* sensed again
Natalia and Athena foretold this inevitable fee from the very beginning
But a mortal upon a mission remains willful, firm in their earthly ways
Therefore, our *dreadfully* contrite sorceress capitulated to any entreaties
Leaving Natalia's astute clientele in an irreparable quagmire of remorse
As such wisdom still left them unsure *of how to return to the blissful before*

Edwin's Antique Emporium

Hark the secondhand melodies streaming from just down this pathway
For along a *bizarre lane* starring pubs, cosmetic salons, and perfumeries
An acclaimed business nestled in between Hugo's Wandcrafting Studio
And Mystic Ink Tattoo Parlor, opposite a delicatessen and donut outlet
Releases an aura of oddity, more than any rival retailers in the kingdom
For Edwin's Antique Emporium has always been anything but *ordinary*
Externally, copper composites and stone resources encase the storefront
Offset by flower boxes of violas and veined leaves of evergreen climbers
Past the studded entrance of stained rosewood, scattered wonders await
Made of unending, zigzagging hallways and five, *no*, six stories of wares
Refuting the humble image the shop's outer guise leads one to visualize
Embroidered wall hangings, murals, and candelabras—*lit by dragon fire*
Decorate spacious sections of saturated emerald, sapphire, and eggplant
Like a panorama of salvaged prizes, all curated by our kind connoisseur

Edwin Darlington, halfling with elven ancestries from his paternal side
As gentle as a guardian angel, with elongated helixes and a love for loot
Claims an apprizing regard toward vintage memorabilia and heirlooms
Collecting wrinkled and worshipped pieces amid in-depth explorations
Touring fairy-managed flea markets and auctions at vampiric mansions
Until his eccentricity for moth-eaten *curiosities* flew from town to town
Bringing druids, trolls, and dwarves from afar right to his private stoop
With pitches to trade their *one-of-a-kind* objects and *bygone* belongings
Taking them off overflowing hands, or talons, and into deferential ones
So, with his customer base cultivated, Edwin bought a historic building
Setting up shop with sensible expectations for a modest revenue stream
For his spirit worried not over wealth, only aiming to display with care
But little did he know just how lucrative his gamble would prove to be
Soon, the high-traffic entry to Edwin's estate was nearly never not busy
Receiving with open arms a magical and monstrous mass of consumers
Raring to search built-in shelves, racks, boundless baskets, and endcaps
Gingerly sheltering primordial or peerless items that others readily sold
For everyone, local or tourist, knows his emporium is the ideal location
To either peddle, purchase, or both, enchanted articles of exclusive awe

On the chockfull ground level of handpicked baubles, books, *and more*
Behold one goddess-surrendered record player once owned by Calliope
Next to a harp with *spelled* strings and seraphim-composed sheet music
Step over slanted hickory floors into tapestry-tacked zones of sublimity
Rampant with lace-tied bundles of succubi diaries noting illicit liaisons
And a sentient calligraphy set complete with monogrammed stationery
Climb the looping flight of steps, bemused, to ogle at *exceptional* décor
Like an artisanal portal-sending armoire and rune-etched writing desks
Alongside an oil portrait with imprisoned subjects, once a costly dowry
And steel figurines and fixtures hewn by a blacksmith-working warlock
Only halfway through, saunter upwards yet again but *sideways this time*
And uncover elf-sewn deadstock petticoats and a time-traveling brooch
Beside black hole elixirs from astronomers and a bejeweled genie bottle
Which may or may not *include a certain woman with three wishes inside*

Edwin's Antique Emporium's layout features far too many uphill layers
With inestimable partitions, alcoves, passages, and teeming backrooms
To list what lies inside every last one, *though the contents are worthwhile*
But our halfling, neck consistently craning, reticently reasons to believe
That everyone will find an optimal occasion to come around sometime
Anytime actually, as the emporium runs upon a twenty-four-hour cycle
Handle unlocked, mid-day or night, providing all a chance to breeze in
Whether that be to analyze, merely gawking, or to decisively check out
Edwin minds not, so long as each browser or buyer employs veneration
For the nostalgic ephemera, netherworld keepsakes, and *pre-loved* relics
Our halfling has doggedly been a sentimental lover of all things antique
But trained entrepreneur and savvy genius of financial literacy, *he is not*
Our vendor's prices are more than justifiable for what customers receive
And yet, Edwin is as adept at bartering as he is at baking or beekeeping
Which is to say, *not very skilled at all*, and so he panders to every patron
Enabling mortals, golems, and imps to pay whatever sums they suggest
Be it two shillings for upscale furs or half of a stone for a sorcerer's staff
Only gratified when special merchandise move into novel, *happy* homes
Which, really, was all Edwin ever aspired for his antiques from the start

Nautical, Nebular Love

At the helm of a pillaging brigantine ship traversing crystal-clear waters
Captain Ripley, unscrupulous pirate, carries a nautical repute of devilry
Buccaneer with gem-gathering purpose and a cutlass-carrying presence
Though decked in garbs hardly covering the cords of obtrusive muscles
Consummate male is not Ripley's real identity, for when his crew dozes
Our captain's plundering aspirations readjust as soon as starlight ignites
Just as his skin switches into a leviathan, *submerged serpentine scoundrel*
But amid each nighttime overhaul, an astrological queen gazes lovingly
For Ripley surreptitiously landed a partner in crime hailing from above
Absorbed in a shared obsession with Stella, *transcendent* Astral Empress
Regulator of every ethereal entity from comets and asteroids to meteors
Turning moon-governed whitecaps into stable lulls for her pirate's trips
For Stella longs to ensure Ripley's safety, as she has since the very outset
A *kismet* introduction amid Stella's weekly sojourn to our earthly world
Brought about an interstellar *love* undeterred by their eventual distance
Both born as sons and daughters of the effervescing sea and endless sky
Though Ripley remains handsome in daylight and *horrid* come twilight
While our Astral Empress gives off raw allure—reinforced by the galaxy
Making Stella and her part-time bandit the most *suitably synergized pair*

Together, their coupling spawned seeds of Schadenfreude, ready to rise
After sundown, Stella dusts the distant cratered sphere with extra tinsel
Before glazing the planets with pearlescent gloss as a breathtaking boon
But too soon does her impossible illusion, too trancing to be true, *falter*
As her slithering leviathan strikes—charging the hapless future fatalities
Sinking fileting teeth into flimsy flesh, yet not to scarf down tacky gore
Interested only in any *powers* his targets possess, displacing their energy
Into his own paranormal piles, right before swallowing skeletons whole
Where they suffer a subaquatic death in his middle, beside *all the others*
Embarrassed to have been diverted by the Astral Empress so effortlessly
Their fading existences, fleeing from Ripley's sizable maw into the ether
Magnify Stella's already superlative extraterrestrial sorcery for the better
After their gradually festering bodies nourish the leviathan—literally so
And though expiry has ensued, lives sheared short before their very eyes
Pirate Ripley and his nebular sweetheart have, conversely, never felt so alive

Unrequited Cemetery

Here lies every dearly departed soul trapped inside an eternal stalemate
Who many moons ago underwent disenchanting *revelations of rejection*
Around the Unrequited Cemetery, the alchemy in the air remains grim
Wailful hummingbirds uncork their sorrows atop neglected headstones
Encircled by sterile wastelands and washed-out mausoleums, all austere
Inverted from the whereabouts of affection, ever-so-demonstrably lurid
To adore another is to entrust their existence with your pounding heart
Never to have those aches unattended precipitates a *discouraged mindset*
Offering up your body and brain, guarded essence of your spirit and all
Just to be subjected to sharp dismissals, which the graveyard prophesies
For highly sweetened starts often give way to overly *cloying* conclusions
Suffocating from sickly fixation never to be returned, only to be ruined
One-sided evangelical emotions wreck these rebuffed beings in the end
As if their destiny was done for as soon as immersive feelings instigated
Too soon finding their prostrate forms lying in lowered wooden caskets
Having died unaccompanied and unwed, *barred from life as well as love*
Physical frames powerless to exist while bearing such forlorn anatomies
For their reality was fated to be uneventful, never to be caressed by any
Save for all the maggots dragging across their necrotizing cavities, ceaselessly

Specified plots inside the Unrequited Cemetery hold not flatlined souls
But reverent relics to commemorate the deaths of disparaged devotions
Whenever their malaise grows intolerable, and aghast recognition arises
Mortals rest tokens relating to their crushes underneath begrimed mud
Burying handkerchiefs and square spectacles worn by their infatuations
Out of sight before marking the coordinates using a carved slab of slate
As the boneyard's witchcraft sets a spell of forgetting inside their minds
Letting the reviled parties move on, though a sense of emptiness loiters
Shortly thereafter, when these solitary humans reach their *closing* hours
Revisit, they must, the phantasmal necropolis of calamitous familiarity
But this time around, rather than routinely roaming in between crypts
Dormant bodies end up in graves of their own in the depths of the dirt
With the totality of their expunged memories rushing back, *far too late*
How terrible that all who become tenants of the Unrequited Cemetery
Never faced joint fervor, never enjoyed exultations of perfect alignment
And now, will never shirk afterlives of solo grief—all alone, *forevermore*

Tempest of Fury

Rustling whines from unsettling drafts designate acrimonious intensity
Brought about, as mythology *swears*, by the destructive, hybrid Harpies
Antagonistic wind incarnations and official intermediaries of vengeance
Seething with hankerings for reprisal as they coast across the open skies
Before shaming unrelenting miscreants on behalf of Olympic divinities
For Harpies autographed an *ironclad contract* of employment with Zeus
Laboring as his unshakable enforcers, hard-hitting in their assignments
Just as liable to sprees of heated wrath as Norse god and warlord, Odin
Though amid *outbreaks* of anger, toil upon their own, Harpies never do
For millions of sunrises ago, aid arose in the form of bloodshot females
Titled the Furies—an underworld-residing trio of goddesses, truly livid
Famous for their proclivity toward penalty—missing the trait of mercy
With enflamed hearts, Furies retaliate against males worthy of reproach
Before tormenting or terminating any who verbalized duplicitous vows
Certain that insensitive individuals disregarding all fairness and fidelity
Warrant the whole extent of their outraged umbrage *and so much worse*

United by a protracted treaty, the Harpies and Furies apprehend targets
Who purged *inculpable* humans or incensed gods with Grecian statuses
Having transgressed without any allusions of guilt pestering their souls
Before forced into personalized episodes of punishment, unendingly so
Furies motivate their prisoners into madness, as Harpies impose *torture*
But, these periods of maltreatment remain not as their final castigation
No, that does not begin until both species, drenched in extricated gore
Have attained their sated fill of doling out days, if not years, of carnage
Only then, each knuckle split from *smiting*, do they evacuate their prey
Propelled into a ghastly pocket dimension—a place of pure lawlessness
As unsavory as the circles of Hades combined, *stuck in a state of squalor*
Where an ill-famed penitentiary dwells in the dead center, so daunting
A site even the deities of death and princes of purgatory strive to avoid
Within, these captives are afflicted by methods that cannot be recorded
By means of mere ink, as the parchment would erupt into demonic ash
And so, the tribulations endured are never exhaustively elucidated upon
But ask the Harpies and Furies, stern wardens unlikely to enable parole
And all will be reassured such persecutions are most definitely deserved
But never fret, for their incurred agony will renew until the world ends

Flora and Fauna

Although much remains incompatible throughout this mystical nation
The symbiotic relationship between blossoms and beings is very certain
And none understand this little fact of life better than Flora and Fauna
Our attuned enchantress duet, exuding botanical and beastly overtones
Upon Ethereal Ember's predominantly *verdant* geography of vegetation
Characterized by bucolic florets budding in each junction of the world
Flora, green thumb witch of all overgrown organisms, comes alive here
With pear-tinted curls, irises of orchid, and a matching halter sundress
Flora, dirt saturating her stem-like veins, supervises all garden blessings
Organic magic spawns from her spirit, raising azaleas and baby's breath
Repairing malformed petals of pansies and defective seeds of calendulas
Sprouting loquats and currants with nothing more than a *mental* signal
Just as intuitively as she persuades the terrain, binding roots to her will
While moistening topsoil for growth and shuffling mulch to recirculate
Or, Flora may very well alter her appendages into bouquets of any type
For she bears the prowess of a shapeshifter—just like her wildlife equal

Animalistic with a complexion in shades of khaki and eyes *just the same*
Fauna, taming witch like her mentoring mage, the swine-turning Circe
Leads every mindful creature, be they scaled or tusked, spiked or tailed
From indigenous emus to fluid invertebrates, Fauna speaks *each* tongue
Bleating to elks, cawing to unpropitious crows, and chirping to cicadas
Documented as a dungaree-donning zoologist with peculiar credentials
Fauna, like a shepherd, beseeches owls and jaguars to trot to their ruler
Migrating no matter the miles, moving based upon sorcery's directions
Obediently trekking, for our witch urges their steps as surely as her own
So too, shall Fauna sway actions, inciting critters to feast when starving
Or drift off into joyful stillness when on the weary brink of exhaustion
But like any selfless queen, Fauna compels only to comfort and cherish

Harnessed by leashes held by all ecosystems, our witches live adjacently
Dwelling in habitats rife with character on either side of their farmland
Remote enough to offer respites when needed, though often that is not
And near enough to relish each other's presence, as they so regularly do

Just beyond the cobblestone bridge over top of a sudsy babbling brook
We find the lattice gate adorned with bluebells preceding Flora's abode
A mauve fairylike cottage, just small enough for sprites to feel at home
Overrun with damp moss, fringed by shade-granting trees of sycamore
And brimming with snapdragons to beckon buzzing pollinator helpers
Out back, past unbeatably planted patches, lies an undying greenhouse
A conducive setting for Flora's many flowers and fruits and foliage alike
Where they each will never wilt nor wither nor want for anything at all
Though *want*, they are able, as all of Flora's protégés bear consciousness
Capable of doting on and deferring to their mage, *both daily occurrences*
English roses trill Flora's favorite anthems praising our abnormal planet
Succulents and dandelions rehearse self-authored plays to induce mirth
And honeysuckles alternate narrating lines of iambic pentameter poetry
With eloquent ferns and eucalyptus leaves ending the expressive stanzas
All to regale their horticulturalist mother—who never seeks out fanfare
But Flora, watering pail in muddied hand, still closely listens *every time*

Upon the corresponding side of the koi-strewn waters below the bridge
Fauna's fur-accommodating cabin, in the earthy color scheme of safaris
Bares a paw-printed wraparound porch and bird-perched bay windows
Appropriately disorderly in the most welcoming and well-worn of ways
In the rear courtyard, environments fitting for every species are exposed
Tin roof barns for dairy cattle and arid enclosures for herbivore iguanas
Seafoam aquarium exhibits for otters and icy sanctuaries for polar bears
By virtue of Fauna's veterinary witchery, her animals adopt immortality
Never to submit to or suffer from the *drastic effects* of aging or ailments
Immensely indebted, sheep and snow leopards choreograph tap recitals
As Arabian horses and expeditious cheetahs form bracelets of *friendship*
Aspiring to convey their appreciation one handcrafted present at a time

Nature's children artlessly animate beneath Flora and Fauna's attention
Releasing their inner beauty with the poise of progeny well-attended to
And this self-effacing coven of two, with magic ever-so-complimentary
Encourages their pets' laughter and light to spring free in *idyllic infinity*

Room No. 192
Room No. 313
Room No. 825

Miserymoon Castle

Atop the snow-capped mountain's peak beset with toxic hemlock seeds
Lies a windowless fortress with echolocating bats as capsized watchmen
Fear the Miserymoon Castle cast in grey like a Romanesque tombstone
Lest snapping magpies feast upon your complexion so caked in naïveté
Should any neglect this notice, a hellscape of *unspeakable despair* awaits
Where cold-blooded fiends massacre and posthumous distress prolongs
Told by cautionary tales, every chamber holds people turned phantoms
Reliving their expiring episode, caught in Satan's cycle with no end in sight

Room No. 192: Splat goes the gore onto the disgraced mahogany floors
On account of a crystal letter opener lodged in a perforated midsection
For this spirit suffers the sting of stabbing, in and out, flinching in vain
Room No. 41: Retaining the surefire mark of a vampire's dermal dinner
A once tawny, now colorless spectral frame bears the evidence of biting
Mauled from jugular to wrist, *brutally* drained like a succubus to a soul
Exorcising enough penny-scented carnage to make Bram Stoker queasy
Room No. 825: Heavy are the cranium-hugging arms of this apparition
Stroking their severed head before regeneration resumes sinew by sinew
Only for this replacement skull to fall into waiting hands all over again
Room 78: Critically struck by a warlock with specialties of retrogression
Ordered is this casualty to obscenely rot and writhe from the inside out
Decaying like an untreated mummy for as long as this realm continues
Room 313: Habitually, this ghost sips from her chalice before *collapsing*
Poisoned by the Belladonna Butcher, only to then regain consciousness
And sate her thirst, for the sap may be sullied, but so too is it *irresistible*
Room 666: Worst is the grisly victim of the Creature of Collected Faces
Whose skin shall *not* suture after thin layers of frontal tissue are molted
Wading past ample blood, peeling back bone, left with a desolate crater
Before disembodied digits trail down—for there is still *much* to be shed

Like a *sold-out* bed and breakfast, the Miserymoon Castle must expand
Building extra lodgings for the latest invisible guests unable to sign out
Never meant to mingle with their murderers, for death often sequesters
Though the convulsing aftershocks of sadism remain inside their rooms
And while poignant sobs are muzzled beyond double-latched doorways
Make no mistake: pain reigns within as certainly as Cerberus maims below

Witch of all Wings

With a mother-of-pearl set of spider silk and velour-plumed extensions
Knitted into the crucial cells under her shoulder blades, kissed by cedar
Giselle, with all the grace of an airborne savant, glides without exertion
Upon her inaugural, ineffable set of wings, long past her initial passage
For it was forever and an eve ago, before the birth of pixies or sphinxes
That our Giselle, *neverendingly elevated*, became the Witch of all Wings
A sovereign of sorts, presiding over akin mammals, pests, and monsters
Viewed as a goddess to phoenixes, risen from the ashes of *reincarnation*
And an unadulterated patroness to fresh-faced cherubs praying upstairs
Giselle takes off into the thermosphere, overseeing with an *overhead eye*

In days of yore, this ambitious sorceress tinkered with her strange skills
To produce a built-in-parachute elixir of levitation—the *first of its kind*
Permeated with the idea of invading the aloft arena like a song sparrow
In *whichever* way the prima mages of magic agreed it shall come to pass
And soon, as a fantasy fulfilled, Giselle's wings made a grandiose arrival
Green-lighting idealistic intentions to twirl above the highlands, at last
Over time, the guidance of our Witch of all Wings *gained amplification*
Allowing Giselle to affix each sky entity with a pair of additional limbs
Sparing Harpies and glowworms, and hippogriffs and geese and herons
From a terrestrial fate, *never* fathoming what excellence lies in the ether

By way of the powers that guide, I gather my gifts with Wiccan pride
Awaken all infant angels and fae, unlock birdlike ways upon this day
In all that's weightlessly divine, grant them wings that may match thine
Raise them to a hovering height until they complete their very first flight

As the Witch of all Wings, Giselle *also* announces penal condemnations
When coasting beings clearly swindle and perjure, or plot and slaughter
Giselle *roasts* their unearned appendages until they drop, just like Icarus
Or, in a capricious frenzy, she breaks their spines like vertebral branches
For starlight wings and the migration they mete out are *premium honors*
That not every tiger moth or gargoyle or mockingbird ethically deserves
Yet Giselle herself, unpunishable, needs not to pout over these tragedies
As her steady wings shall never let her soul or her body down, quite literally

Mellivoxa's Melody

Saddled with plagued souls crushed by the burdens of deafening chores
Banshees, the predictive creatures whose cries echo throughout folklore
Remain bound to spew *shrieks of shrill proportions* from overtaxed lungs
Foretelling uncontrollable upcoming happenings of life-ending disaster
But this lesser-known species, inverse relatives of all earsplitting entities
Spun inherited traits of thunderous volumes into something far more subtle

Conjure up the corporeal avatars of flawless pitch into one's cognizance
And the mellivoxa's, females of esoteric fame, shall suddenly materialize
With layered tresses tantamount to the interior of lemon chiffon loaves
Practically translucent when in the sedative company of soft moonlight
And bloated, baby-pink lips offset by the tapered eyes of a jungle feline
Yet in lieu of likely irises, mellivoxa's possess eddying marbles of asphalt
Abounding with stimulating images of successive deaths to soon follow
But those scenes remain sealed, unlocked only by unearthly individuals
Gaze downhill to preview the depresses of concave facial characteristics
And lean frameworks barely tolerating dense features of muscle and fat
For mellivoxa's *never* necessitate a lick of nourishment in order to stand
Obediently desiring only to open wide and sing to the crow-filled skies

As if living in a transposed mirror realm to their cacophonous ancestors
Mellivoxa's, far more arresting than banshees—though just as unnerving
Prime their throats all the same, preparing not to release a *sullen* screech
For what falls out instead is a harmonized composition laced with death
Holding half-notes pulsing from tremendous sparks of treacherous hope
Emerging as a touching masterpiece of aural art, so downright evocative
Mount Helicon muses helplessly weep, raining *exalting* tears in response
Swiftly sycophantic, overawed to overhear such a superb cadence prevail
For the mellivoxa's mollifying disposition transfers into their intonation
Discreet yet *introspective* as morgue-impending lyrics set themselves free
Still, the moving melodies insinuate not vibrations of *loss* but rather, life
Acknowledging the ever-present hazards of causality waiting in the haze
While highlighting the mezzo-piano power of a well-timed premonition
For the mellivoxa's will forever be categorical *dreamers* of second chances

Heed their spelled soundtrack—like globs of agave nectar made audible
And watch the reaper's skeletal grip relent for one providential moment:

Imitating winter rivers, soon too shall oceans of lifeblood freeze their waves
For notifying clocktowers have chimed with the promises of incoming graves
And the footfalls of one caustic predator ricochet according to a divined plan
But consider our call, dear deathly man, and delay this end, as only you can

Mellivoxa's sense the kiss of killing settle upon their temples like threats
And with each uninvited caress, glimpses of pending executions *flash by*
Torsos hacked open past fixing; capillaries nicked with violent abandon
Airways clamped by stiff vises or hearts regressing into stagnant tempos
Until a discerning elegy—hatching from a proverbial egg of perception
Leapt from larynxes like vocal colonies of metrical wasps wafting about
Alerting the alarmed atmosphere to the nightmares inside their psyches
Though the resultant libretti called to life are not imprinted onto stone
For if the mellivoxa's song is deemed as riveting as Narcissus's reflection
Armed with *just enough* musical virtuosity to steal the breath of destiny
Departure's incoming twister is tentatively foiled as but a brief reprieve
For the merry-go-round of demise *always circles back around, eventually*

Near-casualties, leniently left alone, remain astounded by their rescuers
Whereas the cadaverous general of lethality is left aggravated to no end
For he is fond of so little, save for dispensing pitiless verdicts of passing
And yet, whenever the mellivoxa's tune interlopes into his discernment
Death turns defenseless, droning out each competing chirp and chatter
Tuning his otherwise unswerving focus toward only the soprano spirits
Ever-so-angelic when bedtime billows disperse to reveal their physiques
Costumed in colors indicative of the *unhinged* tale of everyday endings
Mixed with the vivid tones of peroxide pouring from the vast hereafter
And death, decidedly devoid of any lust, becomes inflamed at the sight
Imploring to rest his cheek beside their own for a closer look and listen
Intriguingly entranced in a way no other living being has *ever* managed
For as insistently as the mellivoxa's thwart his time-honored techniques
Nor can this pining deity help but brighten as their ballad begins anew

meriweather's
musings

Dearest Diary

None appreciate the act of immortalizing the *prancing* thoughts of love
More than Meriweather herself, for affection's effects flatter her *liberally*
Staining her skin, extremities and all, with the coquettish hues of blush
And coloring such tousled curls in the *permanent* peroxides of magenta
For this rare female, conceived with the dueling fragility of humankind
And the organic fluidity of mermaids stamped upon her chromosomes
Floated into the open lasso of love's vortex, but abandoned, she was *not*
Never again would she stand alone, not so long as Magnus still respires
As sure as the hunter's moon will materialize each russet-toned autumn
Meriweather's oh-so-towering orc, hewn like an oversized statue of jade
Will kneel at her precious altar—just as he always has and ardently will
And so, with their heartwarming saga singing in the divots of her brain
Meriweather, forever flushed, takes to journaling in her treasured diary
Birthed from *flowing freshwater* and bound in boysenberry-dyed leather
But just beyond the embossed designs idling across the eroded exterior
Copious sheets of cardstock contain penned proclamations of romance
Acting as *never-failing* confidants for this half-mermaid's introspections
Bristling with expectation as she raises a roseate arm, picks up her quill
Soaks the point within a waterproof potion for transcribing, and writes

Dearest Diary,

My philophile stack of parchment, there is much to express on this eve
For I know my words feed your fibers just as surely as they *sate* my soul
Lately, my mind has wandered to the balmy morning my orc and I met
Having long shared the Elderberry Forest, starring panoramic plant life
Although, just like steel waiting to clash, our paths had not yet crossed
As I prefer the peripheries of our land, surrounded by my arcadian lake
While my Magnus favors his limestone cave further in the forest's heart
But this sunrise, when our goddesses prematurely expelled the early fog
Uninterrupted light roused me until I opted to take an *uncharted* stroll
But my orc felt the same, for we soon collided, unalike frames crashing
And while the impact was indeed forceful, it led to the lightest landing
For he bracketed his body against mine and took the brunt as we tilted
Cradling my skull with his *substantial* palm, whispering that he had me
And as you know by now, my orc kept his oath and *never* did let me go

Dearest Diary,

Voiceless sister, what a tonic it is to visit you and reflect upon my mate
When goldfinches whine to the pitch of yearning, I find myself calmed
As I pine no longer, *not when my orc speaks all known dialects of devotion*
Admiring my flesh, like a study in lychees, now his most besought fruit
And revering my ringlets, brushing each rosy strand before we slumber
Yet, above all, my partner cares for both my mermaid and mortal forms
Whenever I must mutate, forgoing feet to *reenergize* beside amphibians
My Magnus guards from the shore—tracking the movement of my tail
Ensuring no harm reaches my ears or eyes, securing my complete safety
And when I emerge, seaweed hugging my hips like a slippery paramour
Blinking back into my legged silhouette, he watches with equal wonder
But I hope he knows, I hope I show him enough, that I *idolize* him too
And so, when a gale lifted the greenery hiding his home a fortnight ago
My deft hands repaired it before he awoke to spare my orc any concern
For his hermit habits are reclusive—yet he never seeks respites from me
But if ever he did, I would simply assent, for I am sure he would return
Just as I melt into his arms after every swim, *reined in by true love's rope*

Dearest Diary,

My lipless listener, unburdening upon your pages parlays such pleasure
As I increasingly imbibe adulation's brand of liqueur—leaving me dizzy
How astonishing it is that my other half and I began as contrary beings
Magnus—a prototypical orc with barbed horns and strength *so extreme*
Versus my willowy existence—a sinuous blend between fish and female
But wedded, our hearts coalesced by the indivisible adhesive of passion
And while his tusks pose a problem, if we ache for somatic reassurances
My Magnus drops his brow to mine, and I press my fingers to his chest
And at once, our radiating endearment is understood—unquestionably
How I honor that our *unpublicized* union stays inside these forest walls
Never divulging our bond to anyone—barring birch trees and begonias
Knowing nature prospers with every day we spend fearlessly committed
For whether Mercury retrogrades or meteor showers spill upon our soil
The connection between my one and only orc and I will *always conquer*

Angelic Menagerie

Amid the blood-clotting aftermath of amputating wispy *heavenly* wings
Having alienated their saintliest attributes in an outburst of malcontent
A clique of bleeding angels *toppled from above* like clipped meadowlarks
Descending a realm-defying portal landing just outside the underworld
Only to tour the abyss's atrocities, entirely as depraved as Dante alleged
Upon their fifth stop, Charon's river-residing ferry sailed them forward
Rowed, *with the haste of hell*, to the altar of the devil's nonreligious heir
Alastair, a capitalizing demon of satanism in this habitat of the damned
Respectfully harkens testimonies of the angel's blasphemous epiphanies
How they sought exoneration from the deities and doves and decorum
Petitioning to adopt the impure behaviors of Beelzebub and his legions
Having heard this same spiel so many a times, Alastair doles out advice
Notifying the defunct saints they may *never reenter* their empyreal gates
Should he ever greenlight their distraught applications for immigration
As one, the angels reply they *cannot return*, for their backs are bare now
But be it that they could, none would plan a visit for any prize or price
Pacified by their obedience to live in the fiery *underbelly* of the universe
Alastair sanctions their stay while adding on the stipulation of a rebirth
For if the emancipated angels remain, they should at least look the part
Leading Alastair to pronounce a pithy couplet of monstrous conversion

Fugitive angels, once full of belief, accept this peck of perverse relief
Holy and hellish is my ongoing plea; ensure both they shall forever be

Alastair's Molotov cocktail of realignment ceases as hellfire disintegrates
Raising the flamed curtain covering the hybrid mixes of virtue and vice
For as bluntly as the demi-angels thirst to embody the spirit of iniquity
Their pureness is *indelibly rooted*, unable to be exclusively exterminated
And so, their immovable halos now rest atop the apex of satanic antlers
Just as their sheen of dignity endures, tinged with drab gradients of sin
Most remarkably is the unthinkable appearance of once axed posteriors
Bare no more, for a unique pair of chiaroscuro wings have grown anew
Favored by Alastair, who extols his angels like dolls of debased integrity
Just as he hails all of the others who knelt before him, begging, over the ages
For this accumulating demon is a collector of crossbreeds above all else
Cherishing his amassed angelic menagerie with his whole charred heart

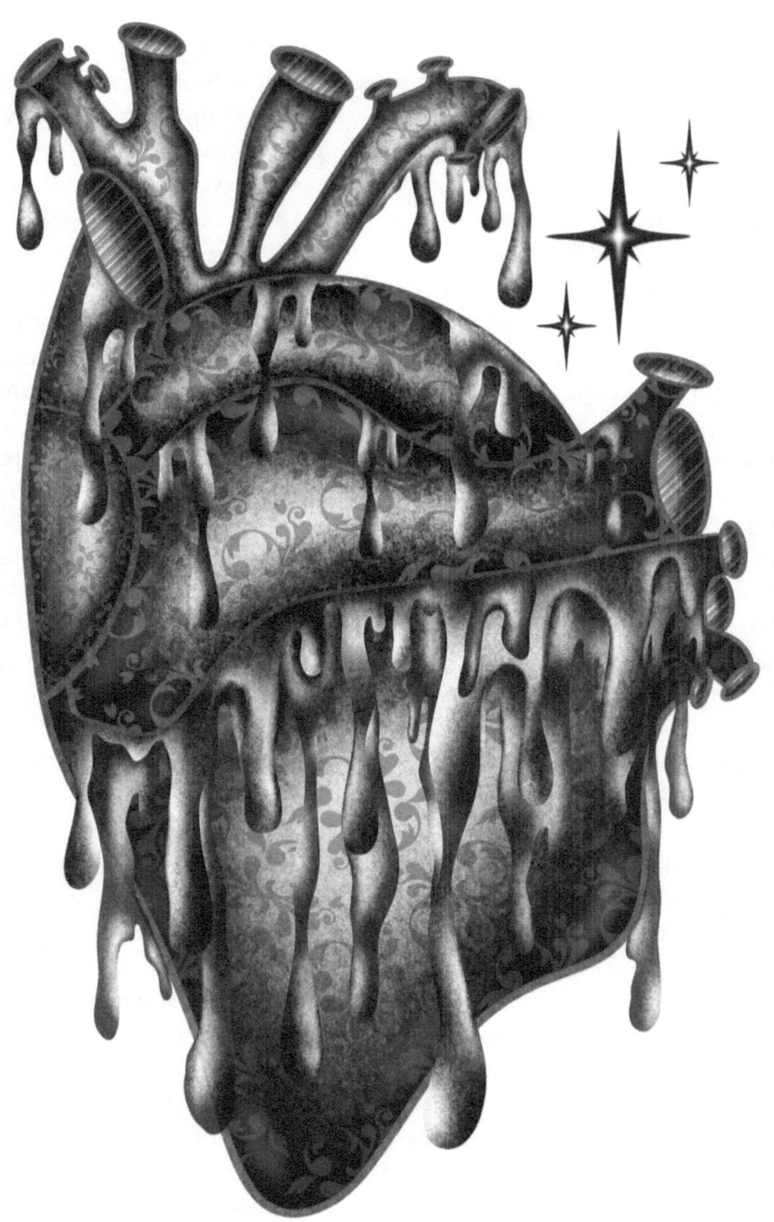

Heart-Stopper

Tangled together like entities created solely for the aim of being adored
How eased Elsbeth had felt in her lover's embrace before all the trauma
Before the bygone, yet operational, spell wormed its way into her skull
Through a prehistoric language once used by antiheroes from allegories
But Elsbeth experienced such pleasure, the arcane words mattered little
As this unfaultable individual was *surely her soulmate*, mislaid no longer
On second thought, Elsbeth strains to recall the origin of their meeting
When this new suitor entered her life, or why she ended up in his arms
Attempting to recoil, needing to perceive his face and place his features
Elsbeth, discomfited mortal, realizes her limbs are inflexibly unmoving
Struggle as she might, our misinformed maiden cannot move a muscle
For the incantation inserted numbing spores in the weeds it embedded
And the buds of stasis have sprouted, the poison in their petals *cackling*
Rendering Elsbeth's regretful body, raring to protest, to a stupefied fate
Hoodwinked, yet not as the first nor the last, by an unsparing offender
Dubbed the Heart-Stopper—a not-so-gentle gentleman of elimination
And it does not take much time at all for our human to recognize why
As the fingers once stroking pebbled flesh land atop her catatonic chest
And with one sudden motion, nails become pilfering pincers of keratin
Enabling the Heart-Stopper to uncivilly extract Elsbeth's arrested heart
Revoking her pericardium, pulmonary valve, vena cava veins, *and more*
All while discontinuing her existence within the same appalling second

The Heart-Stopper never conceals nor consumes his burglarized organs
Only ever presenting them to the obscure master he compliantly serves
For amid his *long* lifetime, there has seemed to be no finer contribution
Than a disengaged heart once before beguiled, *quick as it may have been*
Now contaminated by the rancorous grudge stemming from deception
Yet what his cutthroat lord does with all these donations, he knows not
Only proud to be a pliable follower, appeasing his tyrant so thoroughly
And as for our dead and divested Elsbeth, rib cage removed of its pearl
All she ever desired was to parcel out love only to gain it back in spades
But in the end, the Heart-Stopper seeded amorous attitudes in her soul
Feigning believable sincerity in reply—just as she had always hoped for
Yet it just so happens that after saving Elsbeth from her woes of wanting
So too, did this killer damn her to death, as no love comes without *cost*

Belinda's Atelier

Ever since Gaia spilled her *secrets* with another fertile divinity of realms
And Ethereal Ember was constructed, *so too*, has our Belinda been busy
Slight sorceress of tailoring, our needlework mage exists as a seamstress
Toiling away alone in Belinda's Atelier, her passé yet popular workshop
Specializing in shaping articles of clothing with first-rate magical merits
Drafting original sketches using bristled implements carting watercolor
Before buying cotton and crêpe bolts to be fitted upon her mannequins
Spelled to conform to the specific measurements of Belinda's customers
With bobbins and buttons strewn about, our stylist forms double hems
Donning paranormally protective thimbles all along to shield her digits
And when the work is nearly done, a charm crafts costumed perfection:

Enrich the outfits pouring from my heart; enhance every last bias and dart
Imbue my attires with sorcery's care, filled with the fame of the flairs I bear

With an emptied spool and enunciated song, her requisitions are ready
Backless ballgowns, opera gloves, balconette brassieres, woolen capelets
Contracted by everyone from duchesses to deities and farmers to fiends
For Belinda earned a repute ascending beyond immaculate embroidery
When worn, our witch's goods dish out every buyer's bona fide dreams
Should they be wealth or welfare, beauty or brilliance, prestige or peace
Belinda's apparels, houndstooth or herringbone, heartily provide for all
A usurping princess purchased a stately dress of taffeta to aid in ousting
While an assassin ordered *formfitting* catsuits to become lethally hidden
A lovelorn deity demanded see-through chemises to entice a lustful god
Just as a Valkyrie craved pieces of armor to deter her fleshly destruction
And a plebian mortal, without any rank, needed a plain skirt of muslin
To take control over those who machinated to prey upon her *innocence*
And for her, this sorceress of couture was more than agreeable to oblige

Bit by bit, amid the intermissions after influxes of commissioned orders
Belinda, banning any requisites, fashions an item for no one but herself
An Angora cardigan of cream, or a lattice bustier laced just to her liking
For if dawn to dusk is spent stitching garments for her *clamoring* clients
Ensembles that foreshadow uplifting spikes in self-assurance amplitudes
Why should Belinda, our seamstress *so* unselfish, not feel the very same?

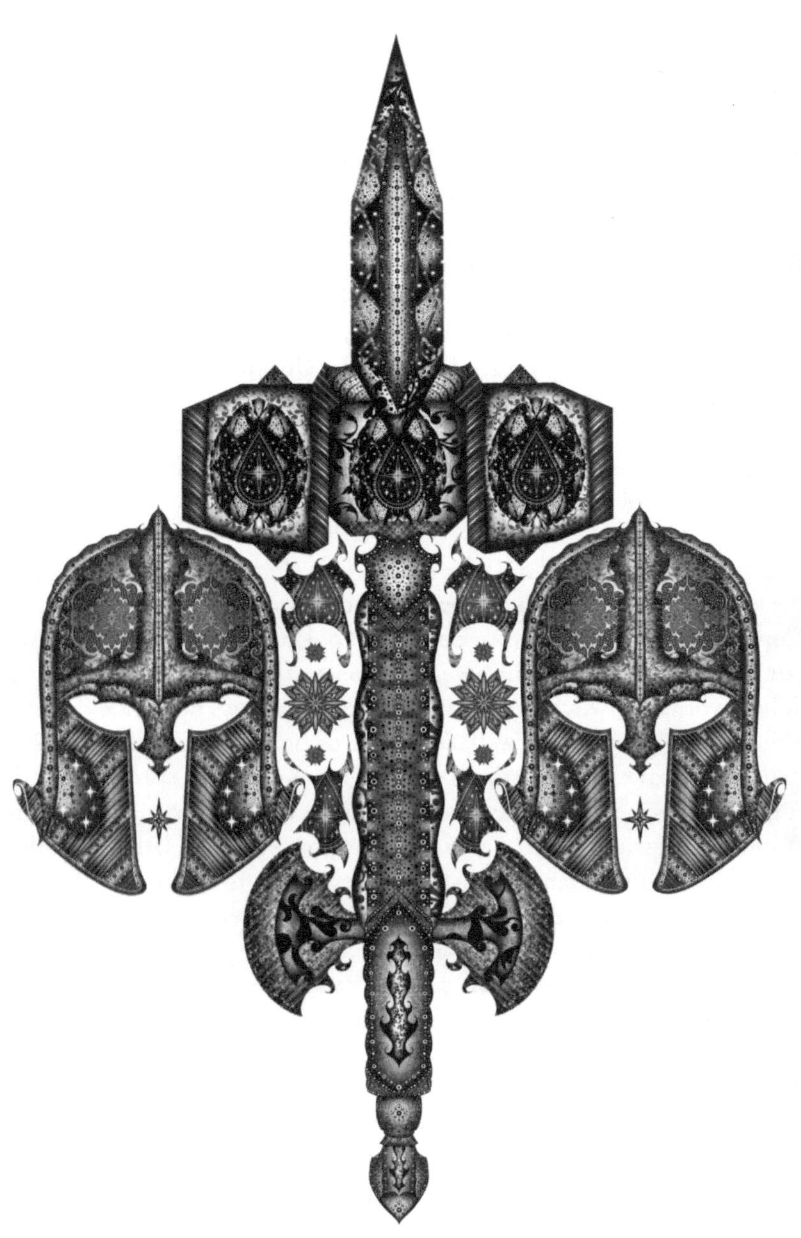

Medieval Rendezvous at Midnight

In the *nonpareil* capital city of Cinderine, within the castle's boundaries
Past bountiful citrus trees showcasing ivory clusters of orange blossoms
Beyond lantern-lit achieves of literary classics, around fragrant kitchens
Led upstairs by lavish banisters not far from an astronomic observatory
An over-the-top chamber, only the finest, houses the *pinnacle* of royalty
Where the queen dozes deeply, for a Knight of the Royal Guard patrols
Upon a bronzed balcony, overhanging enough to evaluate the premises
While warranting Her Majesty, whom he swore upon his life to protect
Shall stay unharmed amid daylight and unmarred amid firelight *forever*

Raphael, with a rugged visage—coarse to the touch from full facial hair
And a robust frame starring raised wartime scars and well-honed brawn
Assumes peak masculinity, as if hewn from unrefined leather and wood
Yet most are left tragically unaware of Raphael's provocative appearance
For our noble knight remains veiled behind impervious plates of armor
But still, quite a few ladies and lords around the stone stronghold muse
That his brutish stature, exuding *dominance*, is almost just as appealing
Nevertheless, Raphael's intents amid this eve stray not toward romance
Immersing himself only, using masterful skillsets and equipped reflexes
Within various shielding and surveying responsibilities, *never to hesitate*
Until, despite such staunch, observant vision, hour after dimming hour
A petite blade, *as slender as it is sharp*, pressing into the steel at his back
Informs Raphael that, rebelling against all reason, no longer is he alone

Idalia, svelte as ever, could not fault this strapping knight for his shock
After all, she knows he is, indeed, abnormally hypervigilant—loyally so
But the furtiveness gifted by the imperceptible wings of true witchcraft
Made this hellcat of an intruder *undetectable* until she desired not to be
Living upon a paved row of spice merchants and brownstone dwellings
Idalia remains Cinderine's premier sorceress, with invisibility specialties
And while performing private, self-serving invocations gives her a thrill
Amid this particular date—beneath the subzero darkness of wintertime
Idalia was contracted to breach every barricade and *eliminate* the queen
Using untraceable spells, an assignment she *loathed* yet could not reject
For our witch's solitary acts of sorcery stoke the flames within her spirit
But much to her vexation, *pay the dreary bills such spelled hobbies do not*

With a conscientious pace, wisely divining his invader's *anomalous* aura
Raphael twists, knowingly not reaching for his iron lance or longsword
Lest his spine becomes *skewered, disc by disc,* upon the tip of her dagger
Mutely, our knight's now dilated gaze takes in this *bewitching bombshell*
With velveteen flesh in Mediterranean olive tones, heterochromia irises
And lengthy, textured tresses of blackberry twisted into a tousled up-do
Out of the way of her ebony-dyed organza cape and scantily-clad gown
Fantasizing, Raphael pines to let down her locks with reverential hands
For our knight is no stranger to scandalous flings with chefs and maids
And, so too, was he once smitten with agile archers or lusty laundresses
Though this feeling was novel, *more potent* based on a far different scale
For upon first perceiving Idalia, it was as if all of Raphael's training fled
Washed away into the icy ether, replaced with something *much stronger*

Capitalizing on the knight's dissociating reveries, Idalia slyly turns away
Expecting to tiptoe into the targeted ruler's chambers with little fanfare
But Raphael returns to reality, seizing not the witch's wrist *but her waist*
In a movement so charged, Idalia stumbles into his metal-covered chest
But then, sooner than bickering with words or sparring with weaponry
Our knight and witch remain still for several seconds, *intensely assessing*
Speechless until Idalia whispers as to not alert any sentries within range
Brave knight, are you scheduled to release your hold upon me anytime soon?
To which Raphael's rough fingers only sink deeper into her supple skin
That depends, he drawls, *Will you do something wicked with your freedom?*
Melting into his arms, Idalia turns her mismatched eyes into silver orbs
Replying with a sickly smile, *If the tales are to be true, far worse I shall do*

Raphael should balk at that—readying to detain his beautiful trespasser
But contrarily, persuaded by the persistent Archangel of Almost Lovers
Who spirals through *prismatic illuminations* gracing twilight backdrops
Our knight, though his face remains masked, beams just a bit in return
Having long been ensorcelled by the outrageous existence of sorceresses
And the deluges of mysticism so niche they interminably supply within
Although, Raphael manages to sense that had any other witch intruded
Salient or not—none would have enthralled his mind or body this *fully*
And surely, no other would still be wrapped in his embrace so willingly

Unaccountably eager to open up to Idalia, our muscled male of nobility
Divulges *classified* information, from his title to upbringing to triumphs
Including his consecrated initiation into the knighthood, dubbed at last
A privilege, for Raphael clutches such regard for his peacemaking queen
Whom he lauds on and on until Idalia, secretly owning a sensitive heart
Admits both her mission and her aversion, *payment aside*, to complete it
In the wake of such vulnerability, neither fathom where to go from here
Idalia, bound by the terms of her task, Raphael tethered to his servitude
But perhaps, Raphael muses, such heavy decisions can delay until dawn

And so, Idalia's knight amends their stance, still interlocked in closeness
Until together, this unlikely pair overlook the stellar galaxy and stargaze
Seeking out the guiding North Star, cataloging the zodiac constellations
Basking in such faraway glory while remaining silent amid a serene stint
Content to share *wordless* space before questions arose within them both
In an impulse to comprehend everything from surface level to soul-deep
Wishing to articulate with ease, Raphael withdraws his titanium helmet
And though Idalia, a seasoned witch, has witnessed *much* in her lifetime
Never before has her skeleton, blood and bones and all, been so taken aback
Upon viewing an individual so filthily striking, with assets so staggering
Idalia grants herself one electrified minute to gape before listening *raptly*
Just as her knight shall do when she unreservedly recounts her own tales

As apricot pigments of daybreak loom and flecks of morning dew gleam
Raphael resists freeing his witch—*savoring her heat against his breastplate*
But Idalia, laden with emotion, vows to revisit when dusk blooms again
Only to converse, not to slay, stating she shall cease her contract at once
For some things, she now fathoms, are more important than trivial coin
A philosophy these two agree on, just before Idalia's knight cups her jaw
To deliver a rapacious yet reverent kiss, one this witch shall never forget
Reluctantly separating only when the castle bells chime to signal sunrise
Still reeling, Raphael ponders how his witch will exit from such a height
But before he may ask, Idalia is gone, swept away by the gusts of sorcery
Fixing *mandated* headgear back into place, Raphael resumes his position
While throbbing lips and besotted thoughts reflect upon the night's joys
Just like the meddlesome Archangel of Almost Lovers *always* anticipated

XIX
The Sun
XIII
DEATH
VI
The Lovers

Madame Valentina

Ears privy to the confidential conversations explaining what shall ensue
Eyes presented with ocular cinemas screening all that has yet to happen
Enlightened mind in express contact with the needlewomen of destiny
Who strive beside antediluvian spirits, *looping eventual events into space*
Only this oracle, Madame Valentina, possesses such omniscient insight
Expected, as her occult-oriented vernacular involves spells of *divination*
With a crystal ball charm atop her chest and scrying bones reliably near
Madame Valentina will never undergo the rankling pain of uncertainty
Though our prophet pines to assist others in grasping such acute vision
Never to be forsaken in the dark—meaninglessly teetering through life
And so, awfully early, our seer shifts as bluebirds blink away their sleep
Becoming someone who might be of use just a tad more unassumingly

Past the showroom of Psychic Parlor, Madame Valentina's arcane studio
Our soothsayer bends into the body of a vermin-sized predicting being
Changing into the Tarot Fairy—parading petal-like wings of chartreuse
In this fortunetelling form, Madame Valentina flutters across the world
Wielding shrunken Major Arcana, *or tarot*, cards from a primeval deck
Heretofore shuffled by the original oracle, a patron saint of portending
Who envisaged the conclusion of the Trojan War, *wooden horse and all*
Many eons before it ever transpired within the tangible realm of reality
Our clairvoyant fairy releases her cards over those who need them most
Teaching their out-of-focus retinas how to imagine all that awaits them
Setting *free* beclouded brains from the eclipsed ambiguities of existence
Circulating cosmological graphics of The Star, The Moon, and The Sun
Denoting healing relief, clarifying illumination, and untiring optimism
Before scattering rectangles of doom, for forecasts are not always dulcet
As Death indicates dire change, and The Hanged Man infers surrender
Yet also, our Tarot Fairy unhands several opportune Wheel of Fortunes
The Chariot of willpower, The Fool of brash spontaneity or carelessness
And The Lovers implying *limerence* when upright or *loneliness* upended
Our aerodynamic psychic does not pilot mortals in one way or another
No, our fairy simply advocates for souls in visualizing new probabilities
And picturing the trajectories their nomadic lives may *soon* travel upon
For what betters a lifecycle, Madame Valentina supposes, *more than hope*

Fatal Femininity

How utterly irresistible to exemplify aesthetics both delicate and deadly
A distant dream *not so out of reach* for the flirtatious daughter of a duke
Lady Cassiopeia—whose modelesque spitting image induces such envy
With nourished limbs and buttercream ringlets precisely laid into place
Blends in as a generously genetically auspicious member of the nobility
Bedecked with handmaiden-applied products, from powders to creams
And squeezed into *suffocating*, albeit enticing to the eye, affluent gowns
But when the aristocracy drowses, and Ethereal Ember's sunlight abates
Cassiopeia's legitimate identity emerges, subverting *clichéd* expectations
For our lady bears marrow not entirely mortal with powers of dexterity
Integral in her quest to latch onto any stimulation after humdrum days
For the damsel-like blood dwelling in Cassiopeia's showstopping frame
So too, shows signs of an unearthly edge, vying for ungracious violence

Educated by subservient duchesses to be *exceedingly* demure in all ways
Lady Cassiopeia heeds proper protocols, from punctuality to politeness
But amid alone time, she taught herself to strike, subdue, and slaughter
Until one wolf-howling twilight when deftly sparring with her shadows
Cassiopeia found herself accosted, *out of the blue*, by a schooled assassin
Recruited by a slaying guild for his undercover, camouflaging potential
Renowned in antiestablishment circles as Grimm, fully-fledged hitman
Impressed by Cassiopeia's adherence to harnessing and honing her gifts
Grimm offered, unusually charitable for a killer, to help refine her skills
While teaching her corrupt tricks only a trained murderer would know
And from that eve on—embarking upon what was societally forbidden
The makings of an extraordinarily lovely exterminator were thusly born

Gradually, Cassiopeia's spry blocking advanced, her footwork upgraded
And her inhumanity grew—greedy to greet her senses to wanton death
But furthermore, did our lady's guttural connection to Grimm flourish
Swelling with each rousing touch upon her waist, rectifying her stances
Each press of his *chiseled* torso pinning her to the ground amid fighting
And each word purred as praise as she professionally engaged her blade
After these combat and confiding spells, two hearts craved one another
Until superficial yearning reorganized into requited feelings of romance
And with this ambush of love, the time to make her *lethal début* landed

Every eventide since Cassiopeia's original offense, now years in the past
Our lady's etiquette-ignored midnight sequence has remained the same
Cassiopeia sheathes herself in lacy, lingerie-leaning bubblegum bustiers
Sheer thigh-highs with silk-appliqués, micro skirts, pink platform heels
And *Grimm-gifted* pearl earrings beneath a pair of velvet-bound pigtails
Declining to compromise her coquettish persona and pleated wardrobe
In order to imprint an air of initiative and *noxiousness* and intimidation
For her magic manufactures stealth just as her instincts are unstoppable
And so, boned corsets and cosmetics certainly shall *never slow her down*
Once unapologetically dressed as a contrastive study in fatal femininity
Cassiopeia drifts through the *gloom* of the witching hour with her beau
Stalking, hand in hand, until they discern their prey, ripe for the taking
And with one implied look, *glutted with murderous lust, our lovers attack*

Although our lady intermittently wrangles with swords, numbing darts
Or even utilizing her toned form in sweeping kicks or disorienting hits
A blend of muscle recall and magic resulting in apprehending with ease
Cassiopeia's customized, catastrophic weapon of choice is *so much cuter*
Once detained, crippling tones of trepidation bathing the stygian ether
Cassiopeia skips toward her victims, pumps clicking with *impish* intent
While retrieving a pastel ribbon of satin with a delicately ruffled border
And chrome spikes attached to both sides *as the pretty pièce de résistance*
As Grimm proudly gazes, she ties the sash around throats in tight bows
But as the pointed spears push in, ripping into rattled vessels and veins
Cassiopeia's ribbon, too taut, concurrently chokes while they bleed out
Making her killing grounds blood-splattered and beautiful—all at once

After a longwinded goodbye from Grimm, *as her assassin abhors parting*
Too fast do the stars and sun swap, bringing wisteria and waffle aromas
Signaling our slaughterer to return, under the radar, to her life of grace
Donning high-class, inconvenient regency attires, overrated and insipid
While affixing an affectation of courteous assent, veiling any *viciousness*
Amid socializing with vetted suitors or sitting through tiresome fittings
But beneath it all, buried under puffed sleeves and curtsies and politics
Cassiopeia still covets the iron scent of gore and racy touch of her lover
And so, every dawn, she decides that nightfall cannot *come soon enough*

Amethyst Supernova

After the lunar spectacle greeted the solar system, her *radiance* apparent
Nightjars and foxes alleged only smatterings of moonlight would arrive
But the determining committee of celestial activities had different ideas
Amid the gloom as silhouettes spring to life, scaring all resting humans
An interstellar entity, a blip of phosphorescence, definitively wilts away
For not even the decillion denizens of the sky are awarded immortality
And so, as this astral life enters extinction, an amethyst *supernova* arises
Mixing amaranth and azure to create truly kaleidoscopic starburst soot
Submerging this realm adjacent to Ethereal Ember, just a journey away
In flaring light like a demonstration of sorcery, for a sensational second
Cosmic carnage spitting down in *spangled, startling* downpours of rarity

But, as this deathbed individual sheds their final slabs of effulgent flesh
And the purple-pigmented awe deriving from their departure dissipates
Scorched to *sweltering* cinders befalls the fate of this transformed world
Richly sienna-hued soil and hawthorn bark bear badly blackened burns
Just as snails and button mushrooms are now nearly classified as debris
So too are the humankind citizens of this sphere left *charbroiled as well*
Yet their blisters, glowing with lilac gleams, offer more than just malice
For these gaping, worrisome wounds upon sceneries and societies alike
Grant free of charge favors relaying unprecedented, uncanny witchcraft
For their skin was earlier stroked by the tainted guts and gore of outer space
And now, beings of supernatural benefits, they themselves have become
Amaryllis bulbs and dewberries painlessly move to meadows *miles* away
And with one wink, stones and seeds alike dart across the globe rapidly
Meanwhile, quartz-tinted irises fly open amid the nightfall not yet over
Marking the launch of their novel lifestyles, left mere mortals no longer
For talents of the telekinesis sort presently live in their reworked brains
Elected objects shall hover by way of lariats made up of mauve photons
Inviting expensive and economical items closer with magic of the mind
Proving just how much has changed since the eve began, all those hours ago

Upon their *reinvented* planet, each species made anew slowly acclimates
Until another star, narrowly surviving, fizzles out into fatal nothingness
And a *sandstone* supernova with the auburn aura of death comes to pass
Assigning powers altogether dissimilar yet, abysmally, not for the better

Hourglass Overlord

Hours drain, minutes rewind, seconds slope away, milliseconds dawdle
But only if the Hourglass Overlord, time and tempos warden, allows it
Our tweed cape and chestnut waistcoat wearing antagonist of authority
Bears no branding of mortality or secular specialties within his skeleton
Surviving as a creature of chronomancy, the first and only of his species
Having exerted foreign sequential powers since his stint as a sinful babe
Guiding the largely banal global sands of time, speck by granular speck
All clocks, atomic and analog alike, bend to their dictating despot's will
Including the stainless-steel pocket watch the Hourglass Overlord owns
A noteworthy item to be sure, for when he twists the calibrating crown
Reality rotates as well, slackening or speeding to match his spherical dial
Defying set dynamics, our overlord warps present pacing incrementally
Before lagging each existence entirely, just by pausing his pocket watch
Upsetting universal circadian rhythms of humans and beasts *everywhere*
Our Hourglass Overlord *rashly revises* all of his twelve numerical etches
In order to supersede total portions of the day, deleting time arbitrarily
So too are the multiple moving hands of his device wrenched backward
To reverse already actualized eras and fall into the past—full of déjà vu
Or occasionally, our overlord prompts spells of sunshine to hurry along
Skipping right into the forthcoming future with sinister inquisitiveness
Relieved, knowing that he may recede back to *now* whenever he pleases
From adolescence to adulthood, our temporal trickster advanced in age
Just as his murderous inclinations likewise increased in terrible tandem
Until disturbing pipedreams of criminal idiosyncrasies came to fruition
For while every so often, our overlord exercises his capabilities unwarily
Squashing bouts of boredom or satisfying *unanticipated, deranged* urges
Mainly, by habit, our contrarian applies his skills to his aberrant benefit
When petulantly waiting for the stroke of midnight to start his stalking
It takes but a perfunctory phrase of acceleration until everything rushes
A little later, in the midst of slaughtering sprees sponsored by bloodlust
Out comes his watch, extending obscurity to obliterate even *more* souls
When hosting these events of torment, scored by the sounds of screams
Lengthened grows the aches of his victims, slung into a stinging circuit
And sometimes, once their forms are limp but their spirits loiter in place
Moondials retrograde so the Hourglass Overlord may have the pleasure
Of butchering over and over again—all thanks to his favorite timepiece

Poisonous Cherry Pie

Orcus, *punishing* god of shattered promises, believed in hallowed oaths
In the way devout romantics believe, head, soul, and heart, in real love
Judged as something pious, meant to be upheld with unfeigned candor
A solemn sentiment which must always withstand the volatility of time
For life's sandglass is fickle—endorsing the modifications of mentalities
But authentic affection, as rigid as a granite monolith, remains *steadfast*
Just as meaningful pledges must persist, denying all destabilizing forces
But still, Rosemary's husband broke vows, marital and moral, endlessly
With reverence contrived, principles dismissed, and fidelity nonexistent
And so, in Orcus's eyes, this devil's fate was well-earned *in the toxic end*

Fatigued was Rosemary's spirit, and indigo was her once unbruised skin
For this mistreated wife, a witchcraft-bearing woman harboring sorrow
With *lachrymose* irises of lapis and handsewn garments, *all bloodstained*
Never was properly prized with tender buccal touches or effusive words
For her disdainful stonemason partner, pulsating with injuring passions
Executed scarring tirades year after year, a testament to his evil tenacity
And while this male, undeserving of a name, abused his crestfallen wife
In acts of strangling and striking *so awful,* angels averted their holy gaze
As per her coven's code, Rosemary could not subdue using magic alone
Any lethal revenge was required to be, at least in part, by earthly means
But fortunately, though her body felt sapped, her brain remained sharp
For she was a witch of esteem, and not even censures or cuts could dull that

Our wedded pair resided atop a remote, ranunculus-laden cherry grove
Where Rosemary, day by day, fed her spouse the scarlet gems they grew
Activating his addition until he turned dependent upon the sour flavors
Until finally, after many fruit-filled months, her scheme was set to start
Beyond the barn-style sliding entry into Rosemary's farmhouse kitchen
With walls emblazoned with daffodil rays upon that June midmorning
Untidy was the wooden block she worked upon, *askew with ingredients*
Bananas for mini muffins, citrus-scented stains from mandarin extracts
Clotted cream ramekins, bergamot marmalade, and brown sugar bowls
But most importantly, were two baby blue linen-padded bushel baskets
One with whole, plump cherries and the next with piles of isolated pits
For Rosemary, baking prodigy, was inclined to make a *perfectly fatal pie*

In a checkered apron attire, our witch kneaded her elastic pastry dough
After adding smidges of salt and squeezes of lemon juice into her filling
With pulverized, *cyanide-producing* pits as final, expiring enhancements
Only then, did Rosemary transfer her mixture into a prepared pie plate
Before setting the soon-to-be *flaky* covering atop, crimping, and baking
But when daytime fled, the room taking on a far more foreboding light
And with all of Rosemary's confectionary elements merging in the oven
Steam mounting, acids hissing, pads of butter melting, crust browning
Our witch nearly inaudibly intoned a spell to sail into her bubbling pie
For though the deadly pits would administer most of the physical work
Rosemary was permitted to sprinkle in *just a tad of supplemental sorcery*
And so, to warrant her long-overdue success, with a split lip, she spoke:

Solstice delicacy with stemless cherries, flesh bursting like broken capillaries
Spiked with crushed stones once within the core, now gifting payback galore
Ingest the special treat as if by rote until the toxins flood down your throat
Intuit the poison providing a hasty death as you take your very last breath

Rosemary, attentive wife, offered her spouse a single, trifling slice of pie
Before his greed surged, *as suspected*, and he consumed piece after piece
Until the ceramic dish expectedly ended up empty—absent of leftovers
Leaving only claret puddles of cherry sap behind like a tart crime scene
In the wake of such a gluttonous feast, the chemicals within conquered
Evidenced by his seizing form, slurring out an SOS, falling to the floor
Flailing from a lack of oxygen while his heartbeat braked to a standstill
And just like that, Rosemary had slain her vile, hateful husband, at last
A feat Clytemnestra, fabled wife also wronged by her groom, would support

Wonderfully widowed with mottled contusions healing, and gore intact
Rosemary, freed from her spousal shackles, lived a solitary life of repose
Before being approached, secretively so, by other clearly battered brides
With heavy roque atop swollen scabs, they needed not to speak a word
Implicitly grasping what they sought, for their plight was once her own
Rosemary returned to her pantry with aptly mariticidal aims, *once more*
For what better way to bake than to whip up desserts not just delicious
But suffused with morbid splashes of deadly *karmic* devastation, as well

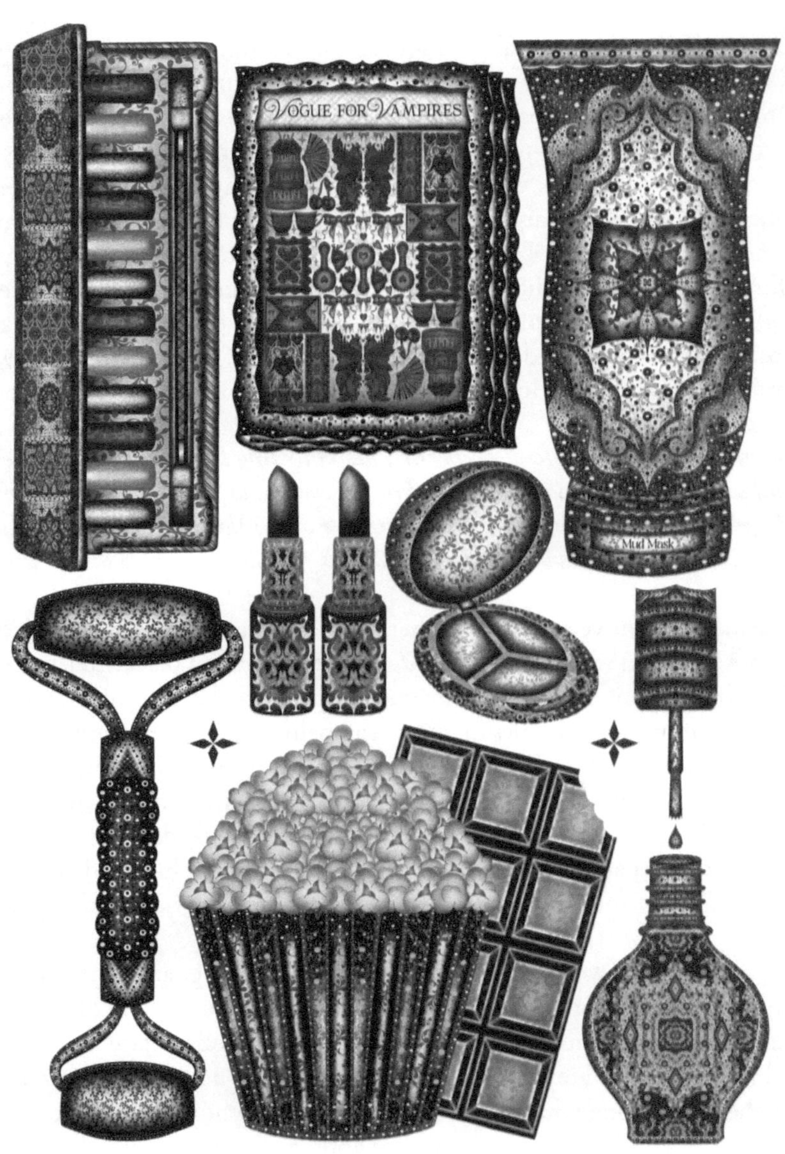
VOGUE FOR VAMPIRES
Mud Mask

Supernatural Slumber Party

Zoom in on a late-night slumber party of stereotypical supernatural delight
In the animated cosmopolis of Bellbrook, at 2928 Ruby Red Boulevard
A Gothic Revival townhouse tarries in wait, for over the onyx threshold
And up the vertical staircase rests a vogueish boudoir of vampiric décor
With walk-in closets storing designer garbs and a coffin-outshining bed
Where our event planner host, Winona, beautifully undead *bloodsucker*
Greets every guest, whether they turn up promptly or fashionable tardy
Ingrid, lily-white enveloped mummy with sun-bleached, bouncy tresses
Enters before Nora, twilight-complexioned enchantress of the dark arts
Who emerges beside Mallory, sarcastic shapeshifter of the spider variety
And Heidi, decomposing zombie depleted of any hue yet still winsome
Trailed only by Amelia, custom-made bride of a certain bolted creation
After slipping into identical silk nightgowns, *this sleepover finally begins*
Our irregular ladies perch themselves around a vintage, mirrored vanity
Testing cosmetics like lash-lengthening liquids and lip-glittering glosses
Before *double* cleansing in the midst of their sundown skincare routines
Our zombie pointlessly applies top-notch restorative grape seed serums
And Ingrid bathes her bindings in boosting mists of early morning dew
As the rest utilize hydrating avocado masks and natural mud treatments
Only to sprawl across Winona's duvet and lounge atop her nylon carpet
As Winona and our arachnid give each other *blood-lacquered* manicures
Heidi and Amelia study fantasy fashion magazines and jewelry catalogs
And Nora teaches Ingrid how to sew voodoo dolls, *satisfyingly* stabbing
Whilst trying Mallory's triple chocolate cookies, sipping mead spritzers
And gossiping and griping about males amid this most memorable eve

Meanwhile, our party-goer's respective partners restlessly grow panicked
Detesting being divided from their lovers, even for one ephemeral night
And so, a demon, legendary werewolf, and phantom, all besotted, unite
To scale the townhouse's clinging English ivy for a passing glance inside
If only to visually ensure that their prettier halves are out of harm's way
While an anemic skeleton, scientist-made monster, and insecure wyvern
Reach out nonstop, groveling to hear their wives' appeasing intonations
But Winona's ruched drapes stay drawn, and her rotary phone rings out
As these ladies pay their partners no mind, captivated only by one another
And their unbreakable connection of ultimate feminine companionship

Mirabelle's Healing Hollow

Mirabelle's Healing Hollow

Placed upon this stricken planet of ailments psychological and physical
With curative skills inside her head and helpful secrets within her heart
Our Wiccan homeopath saves individuals of every class in lowly health
Mirabelle, with opal strands laced into otherwise deeply brunette locks
And arthritic palms outright haggard from tonic-devising ministrations
Took to both herbalism and botany as tried-and-true familial traditions
Mending minds and membranes just as the wise women before her did
Based out of an archaic apothecary, *her joy*, Mirabelle's Healing Hollow
An elongated pharmacy predominately plastered with toad-tinted vines
Flowering around a firefly-lit marquee and door knob of brass and bark
Inside resides the previously insoluble answers to worrisome quandaries
Teakwood shelves house terracotta clay vessels abundant with medicine
From soporific mandrake root tinctures to remedial grains of amaranth
Timber benches stow spelled packets of feathers, seeds, floras, or spices
Beside bales of herbs, sprigs of cardamom and clove secured with twine
Marble countertops present many crystal medleys of citrine and calcite
Right next to perfume bottles of tea tree oil, atomizers of Frankincense
And small jars of hawthorn berries to the left of the transaction journal
Do not tattle but in a glamoured corner of Mirabelle's Healing Hollow
Sits somber vials of toxins from chloroform and hogweed to strychnine
Strictly to be used for the greater good, or so our sorceress buoyantly believes

Seldom referring to grimoires, for her witchcraft intellect is widespread
Our Mirabelle manifests any out-of-stock plants, minerals, and potions
Replenishing apothecary provisions without ever exiting the main floor
Unwell consumers may either purchase prescriptions to trek home with
Gathering all they desire within their baskets, thanks to Mirabelle's tips
Before paying their bill, *leaving extra coins when this mage is not looking*
Or, as a more urgent option, Mirabelle implements magic of relocation
Draining her patron's pain, separating illnesses from *poorly* plasma cells
Before distributing the afflicted atoms into her own amenable anatomy
Eventually, when hobbling back and forth advising doses or tidying up
Our mender leans upon a cane, brittle from the maladies she shoulders
Yet Mirabelle cares not as long as her customers leave better than before
Leaving our sorceress and her shop to suck in gulping lungfuls of pride
Only truly content when their assistance offers *the awaited rush of relief*

Queen of Bloodlust

Power incarnate, our usurper rules with a steel fist and salivating throat
Vampira Vox, with spider-tinged waves, full bangs, and carmine streaks
Exists as the Queen of Bloodlust, reigning over every *sharp-toothed* soul
Though, not always did she maintain such a major status of supremacy
Inundated with hemoglobin cells singing of hegemony inside her veins
And taste receptors retaining *revolting, to most,* likings upon her tongue
Harken closely, if you may be so bold, to Vampira's gory *tale of takeover*

In the midst of 1849—when the golden age of the grand opera thrived
Our future queen began as a paltry mortal, birth moniker now unused
Driven by her quest for dominion, Machiavellian through and through
Following a fastidiously summarized strategy of monarchal confiscation
Which Vampira *precociously* outlined amid the height of her childhood
A blueprint that drove our plotter to slay a stunning vampire, so servile
The pending bride of the biting king, never one to argue—as was ideal
Surprisingly to all but Vampira, to kill in cold blood brought no shame
For she utilized her injurious blade to breach the wife-to-be's skin *easily*
Stifling any sputtering pleas before severing her carotid once and for all
Beholding a direct viewing of death with the acclaim of an opportunist
For Vampira's determination, *even then,* outweighed any grating doubts
And because this late bride's face, to be unveiled upon her wedding day
Had sparsely been seen, our protagonist proactively procured her place
Posing as the upcoming newlywed, pretending to be as lovesick as ever
But so too, did Vampira need to feign a species she had not yet become
When others lazed and laughed nearby, preparing their midnight feasts
Vampira would indulge as well by *forcing down* the fluid of an innocent
Proceeding with the finesse of an actress, enacting macabre enthusiasm
Even as the ruddy libation burned like acid—pushing into her pharynx
Before sinking to her repulsed stomach like liquified onslaughts of lead
Sunset after sunset, Vampira expunged those within the king's entourage
Until, earlier than expected, with the date of matrimony a month away
Vampira underhandedly gained access into the most tucked-away tower
For every sentry was forever indisposed, unable to guard from the grave
There, in the virtually vacant turret, Vampira found the sacred sanctum
Of Renwick, unaging King of the Undead, *ruler of all who adore plasma*
And namely, the singular object of Vampira's obsession for far too long

Vampira Vox paused her pace until Renwick sensed her, *turning at once*
For she wished to witness a dumbfounded shadow fill his widened eyes
As she exploited his disbelief to her premeditated advantage as planned
In a confrontation comprised of one fatal move studied since her youth
Vampira gouged an unsanded stake into his heart, as the myths are *true*
Renwick crumpled, descending into dastardly arms anticipating his fall
Helpless but to let his executioner sway him into demise, *like clockwork*

With the prone King of the Undead evicted from life's game of survival
Toppled body but a slack ragdoll, spirit jettisoned into an impious land
And all of his cohorts and heirs and counsel settling into spectral forms
As the kings intended, the sisters of fate granted Vampira a duet of gifts
The first, thankfully so, was the transformation from mortal to vampire
Pricking fangs tore through altered gums as her pigmentation grew wan
And though the hardening treasure within Vampira's chest immobilized
Never before had such an undying adjustment made her feel more alive
But destiny's boons were two-fold, *out of character* for such stern beings
And so, a covert compartment opened with a click in Renwick's bureau
Uncovering his distinguished crown, an official symbol of omnipotence
With a base of black jade and serrated arches adorned with bloodstones
An artifact of absolute authority that Vampira wasted no time in wearing
Crowning herself with no dissenting citizens milling about to challenge
And no high-ranking council of elders congregating around to instruct
For Vampira never desired the worthless approval of anyone but herself
So, only the shooting stars passing by were present for her inauguration
Before our queen began her *blackmailing* and *blood-slurping* sovereignty
Currently, with a credible committee of courtiers Vampira hand-picked
And occupants who originally obeyed only out of misplaced patriotism
But now idolize our ruler's régime, like Dionysus does full-bodied wine
Vampira loves the reality she carefully appropriated and annihilated for
And this time, when the pangs of thirst hound her throat with wanting
Beseeching Vampira to shred into pulse points and uncouthly consume
Only mouthwatering tangs teem as she savors the gore like it is limited
Yet there is no need because, evidently, our queen may take all she craves
Whenever she so regally requires from nearly whomever she so requests
And as the *iconic* Queen of Bloodlust, Vampira Vox *never* needs to stop

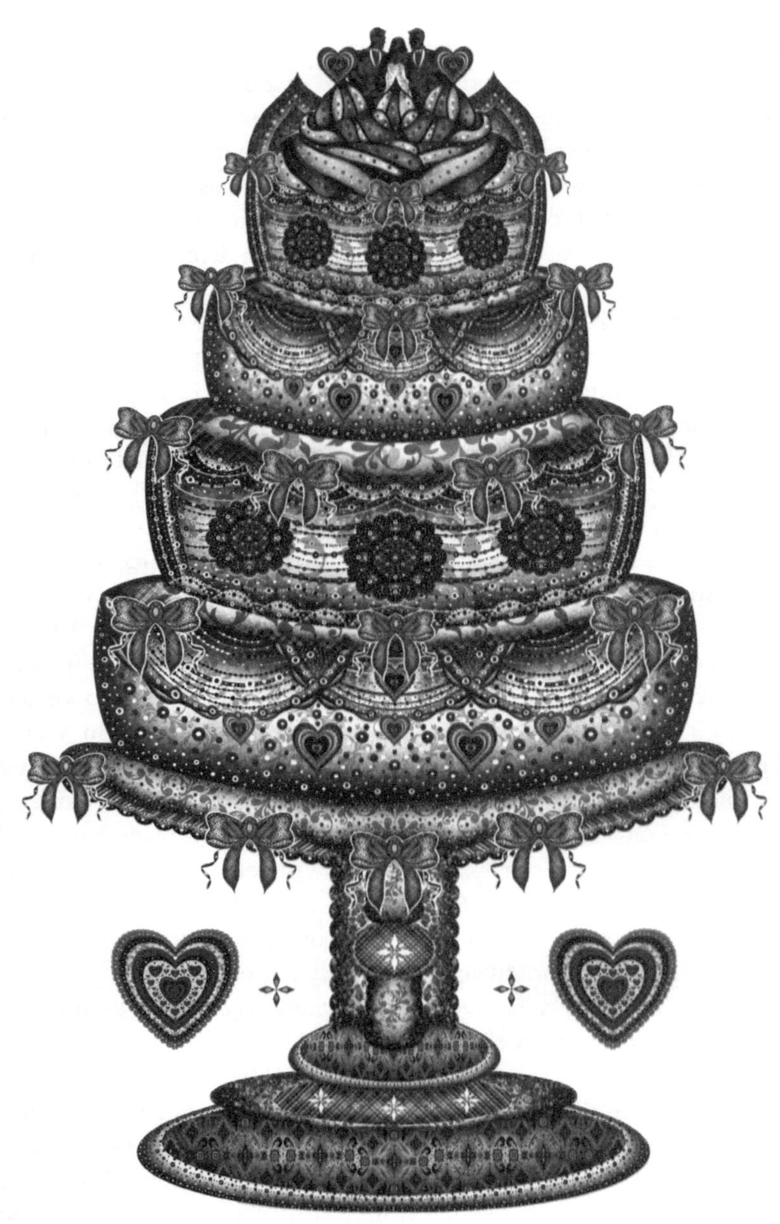

Polyamorous Promises

Through Aphrodite's portal and into the hauntingly romantic cathedral
Hushed viola melodies heighten our altar's mood of *enchanted intimacy*
For this gothic eve remains euphoric, absent of any crowds or criticism
Only attended by three ardent souls, each more enamored than the last
Enthused to eternalize their polyamorous love—in more ways than one
We begin with gentle Bellamy, beautifully ultra-pale elven earth wielder
Sewn into a corseted, champagne dress grazed by dark chocolate tresses
Fiancée of Harland, blazing half-dragon with stacked muscles and scars
Beneath a flawlessly-tailored tuxedo, baring slight flashes of ebony flesh
Lover of golden Mordecai—sporting suit sleeves that stay lewdly rolled
Plied with water-based powers from Poseidon's lineage within his veins
While this trio manipulates most of the elements, *immortal they are not*
And so, amid this ritual, united shall be their spirits over proffered gore
Just as a spell spoken as successive oaths pledges that should one perish
So too, shall the others, *deferentially fettered even in the clutches of death*
With the telepathic synchronicity of soulmates, sliced is now their skin
Blood blending as they interlock palms and vocalize their marital vows

I, Harland, plead to pronounce: *My Mordecai,* my brown-eyed beloved
Tonight, I shall speak straight from the depths of my rhapsodizing core
An extensive ode inhabits my brain of all I wish to express, my lovebug
But alas, I shall start with this and gift you the rest each tomorrow after
My candied caramel apple, it is as if your anatomy flows with ambrosia
For underneath a radiant, roguish façade, only serious *sincerity* remains
Should your torso tear, we shall realize your heart was hewn from roses
For *swoon-inducing* passion encapsulates your existence, always adoring
My toasted marshmallow treasure, even as wraiths, I will want you still
Just as apparitional circumstances shall never pry me from my Bellamy
Whose clover-irises, stippled with starlight, gleam like pastures of gems
True labor, I have learned, it takes to control my fixation, *dawn to dusk*
For you, my lovely little tulip, summon such wild sentiments inside me
Striving to shout clumsy sonnets and serenade off-key like never before
But still, I limit myself, acting with tasteful yet compassionate conduct
However could I not when your sympathy and sensuality engulfs us all
So, surely, my flower, you *must* understand my fiery need, never to fade
Through plagues and perils and poisons, I promise you both my endless love

I, Mordecai, ache to affirm: *Bellamy*, my calming dove, my carnal vixen
As Gaia's favorite daughter, nurturing to all, swallow my words as truth
Dearest, my dreams are but midnight movies of your birthmarked body
Which I long to replay upon a revering round, even after slumber ends
My humble minx, I would go to *any* lengths, illicit or immoral, for you
Our perpetual worshipping plans will endure, my peppermint princess
For I shall hold your hand until we lay beside earthworms, and beyond
But wait—my Harland, my saccharine warrior, my draconic princeling
Oh, how *highly* I deem the display of your pearlescent engagement ring
A stark contrast against flesh caressed by the tones of nightfall's horizon
But mostly, my kind knight, our gestures of reciprocal respect *steady me*
For you are patently possessive, and I so cherish being possessed by you
From your flames, I so burn, *never doused*, even when ashes we become
Should ever we divorce, my kidneys would riot, my lungs would revolt
For our bond, my gumdrop gentleman, is physical, purely unignorable
But, luckily for all my organs, never shall I leave, not now, or evermore
Through curses and chaos and change, I promise you both my undying love

I, Bellamy, desire to declare: *My Harland*, my most honorable protector
Please, permit me to gather myself, for your oceanic gaze often distracts
My brooding fire-breather, your lasting loyalty warms my bones and all
Lighting inner votives to extol, torrid wax dripping into my diaphragm
Without delay, dislodged would become my bronchi, my pancreas, too
If I trusted such tokens to correctly convey my emotions, same as yours
For my garnet organ bears the shape of your own—as if made to match
As I am yours, my noble nectarine, you are mine *in this life and the next*
But have overlooked you, my Mordecai, my blonde beau, I could never
My rakish fiend, so devilish, yet you remain the most maudlin of us all
An earth-bound reincarnation of Eros, speared with affectionate arrows
Begging, I find myself, for my blood to fill every sea as copper offerings
For only such an *extreme present* could prove to all, from gods to ghosts
That knowing you, my blushing lemon bar, has been my life's highlight
And nothing will relegate the volcanic regard I shall forever feel for you
Through toxins and tragedy and terrors, I promise you both my eternal love

Three lives are linked with a languid kiss, thus beginning their wedded bliss

Mystical Transportation

A witch's wand acts as an external extension of *numinous* energy within
A witch's grimoire archives essential spells and instructions to carry out
A witch's internal abilities emulate unceasing waterfalls of enchantment
But the *genuine* crux of Wiccan whimsy lies inside a witch's broomstick
So, Cordelia—countryside sorceress of the coven, Demeter's Daughters
With flora and fauna faculties *humming* within her shawl-wearing form
Engineers her very own broomstick, starting with the straddling handle
As a paganistic devotee of Mother Nature and lover of forest landscapes
Cordelia refashions reclaimed wood cleaved from a fallen mulberry tree
Exhilarated to incorporate the environment in such an evident manner
Then, our sorceress *uniformly* carves shallow divots into the rod of bark
Built for gemstones to be slotted into; selected for efficacy and elegance
Cordelia uses earth-green malachite for chakra alignment and creativity
And translucent smoky quartz to alleviate pressure and bestow stability
The binary rocks alternating like aggrandized rows of awing luminosity
Gratified, our mage etches fortifying sigils and symbols into the timber
Including a safe travel sign promising *protected* transit when passing by
And an illumining icon to retain unimpeded vision when in the clouds
Designs all drawn, Cordelia moves on to the bottom of her broomstick
Gathering groups of river birch twigs to create a posy of uneven bristles
Before fastening the rigid bundle upon the base with a strip of sage lace
Upon the cusp of completion—Cordelia's craft insinuating flawlessness
All there is left to do is recite a parcel of phrases to ensure its *exclusivity*
Sanctioning only Cordelia with the say-so to soar, whenever she wishes

Prodigious powers that be from within the pervasive dirt and seeds and dew
Join my wildlife witchcraft with yours, a boon you bestow upon so very few
Built broomstick of mine, encourage the hovering potential of hoisted flight
To swear my suspended flesh shall never fall straight through the moonlight

Invocation finished, lyrics saturating the stones and wood and sketches
Cordelia, emanating childlike excitement, bestrides her ethereal vehicle
Feeling breathlessly weightless when her footing atop the soil is severed
And the garden petals and wandering caribous below vanish from sight
Ascending higher and higher still amid her maiden broomstick journey
Sailing, like a partridge, *above and away into the naturally mystical night*

A Betrayal of Regal Blood

Most members of royal courts retain propriety for all palace proceedings
Some are blessed with breathtaking exteriors, some with political knacks
But our amalgam angel, Svetlana, illustrious princess of Elysian essences
Embraces it all, from decorum and brainpower to diplomacy and beauty
One-third seraph, two-thirds mortal, Svetlana stems from saintly origins
With the polished flesh of pure porcelain and unknotted, doll-like locks
Spending chaperoned days horseback riding and painting in the gardens
But all the while, our princess readies to happen upon the king's advisor
Klaus, brilliant sorcerer far beyond his age—a male of maturity and grit
Despite a strait-laced disposition, Svetlana seems to thaw his aloof guise
For progressively, Klaus and his princess established an intimate rapport
Like an amorous captive, Svetlana helplessly descended into infatuation
With a burning magnitude—though she has yet to voice such emotions
Supposing they hold all the time in the world for forthright declarations
But for now, be it glances of faux *indifference* amid ceremonial banquets
Or unescorted engagements once sunlight subsides and darkness dances
Svetlana awaits every encounter, much to Klaus's negating glee and grief

Our advisor, unexpectedly unimmune to love, idolizes his winged angel
Deeply so, for his besotted spirit belongs to her, as it has for many years
But truth be told, the engine of Klaus's soul is stoked by the fires of *duty*
For his bloodline is riddled with rebels—raring to stage a seditious coup
And reign themselves, yet as improved or inferior rulers, none could say
As part of his relatives' gambit, in the works since before his conception
Klaus applied for an advising position to infiltrate the king's inner circle
Bound from birth to be a pawn, *lest he poison his family tree with morals*

However could a disloyal Klaus choose between his beloved and his task
Such musings begot insomnia, tearfully *retching* from nightly vacillation
But when the designated date lands, Klaus feels he holds no choice at all
For perhaps his princess, *faithfully forgiving* as always, might understand
But his kinfolk, mutinous and arrogant and mulish, certainly would not
In an effort to placate his weeping mind, drowning in preemptive regret
Our sorcerer, gasping for *any* relief, attempts to romanticize his decision
Envisioning that his Svetlana will admire this perilous deed of allegiance
Even if sensibly, she could never, for it is not *her* loyalty he is promoting

With ransacking witchcraft and strapped rapiers *raring to be unsheathed*
Klaus, double-crossing affiliation exposed, annihilates the alarmed king
Through a lower abdominal slash and banned spell of profuse bleeding
Rendering the traumatized queen a dowager for one sickening moment
Before slaying her as well, eradicating the monarchy with a pivotal *slice*
All the while, Klaus's relatives invade the castle to abolish any stragglers
But amid the anarchic raid, the dissenters suffer unsightly loss after loss
Until none remain standing upon either side of this war, save for Klaus
Who grasps, amid bereft revelations, that everything this plan cost him
The stress, betrayal, and shame, was all for *absolutely nothing in the end*
Though the throne is his for the taking, Klaus remains averse to leading
The antithesis of his ancestors, never has he dreamt of donning a crown
If he truly thinks about it, all Klaus ever *sincerely* wanted was his seraph
But now, stranded in pools of decanted parental plasma, an evil eyesore
Svetlana, orphaned by her lover's own hand, views from the mezzanine
With a shaken expression, blanching as he haltingly, *hopelessly* advances
Each flinch as damaging as the daggers he drove through her close ones

Left nauseated yet unscathed, Klaus strains to stand behind his choices
Though a lucid shard seeping into his brain whispers of the bitter truth
Faltering our horrorstruck sorcerer's faith in his actions nearly instantly
Incapable of coming to terms with all he has done, all he has destroyed
Klaus suffers a breakdown of contrite psychosis, *seeing, at last, his errors*
Yet too much regal blood has been spilled to restore the lives he ruined
Therefore diminishing any likelihood of making amends with his angel
For the presence of gore stains *much more than just flesh and floorboards*

When all is said and done, it is not the fall of his noncompliant family
Or the wearisome obligation he wasted the lion's share of his life upon
Which haunts him, no, it is the fact that Svetlana, his angelic soulmate
His dear, haloed darling, the only one who *never* asked *anything* of him
Shall bind his deceit to memory with her once whole, *now halved* heart
Never to worship her intelligent sorcerer with such unconstrained trust
Or remain by his side amid trying times in the way his princess used to
In fact, never shall she revere Klaus in any way for the rest of their days
And out of every egregious blow, *that* is the most harrowing of them all

Despair of a Shapeshifter

Just as Nyctimene shifted into an owl, so too can this character change
Callum—classified as a skin-walker within the pages of Navajo folklore
Weathers the skeletal-breaking burdens of unrecognizable shapeshifting
Feminine or masculine, it matters not, for this being replicates them all
Shedding the sum of his physique or merely altering marginal qualities
Predominately unchanged, save for the affixed additions of fangs or fur
Like a chameleon with a multiplicity of repeatedly rotating frameworks
Callum may imitate other parties as infallibly portrayed doppelgangers
Or mutate into organisms of fabled fantasy like a *well-oiled* mechanism
From massive storm giants, metalworking dwarves, and hostile orclings
To forest-inhabiting Slavic leshies and half-human, half-horse centaurs
Every now and again, Callum mimics midair Pegasus or pitiless Medusa
Before metamorphizing into *mortal* beasts of earth and ocean and ether
Impersonating all animals, from coyotes, wombats, and woodland does
To mythical cryptids such as the Mothman, *emphatically real in his eyes*
Periodically so, Callum can twist his form into the contours of hybrids
Lynx-looking creatures with forelegs of felines and convex bills of birds
Displaying sunken eye sockets, pronounced shoulders, and aerial wings
Or hexapedal composites of mammals, reptilians, and marine monsters
With split tongues, spiked tails, segmented torsos, and crustacean diets
Whenever survival demands it, caught in a sticky situation of difficulty
Or whenever the immortals who introduced this talent call in an order
Callum, like a serpent, slips out of obsolete skins to expertly start again
But though the renovation may be rapid, it is indeed never free of pain
Within, Callum's always exchanging bones crack and convert and crop
As dislocating joints pop out of place and organs adapt to new settings
Flesh peels, features replace, fright proceeds, and Callum appears anew

After assuming a hodgepodge of textures and builds and temperaments
Callum, sadly confused, cannot find his way back into his initial figure
Memory failing, impossible it becomes to recall his birth-given classification
No longer can Callum evoke the slope of his nose, the shade of his lips
Or how many extremities he originally strolled or swam or sailed upon
After all these joyless years, our shapeshifter is but a body to be fissured
Veering from standard human structures to surreal fictional formations
Stuck in a fracturing identity crisis—one he will *never* be able to escape

Helena's Luminescence Spell

Excerpt from Helena's Grimoire, Volume I, page 724, circa 1692:

Wee witchlings, prepare to practice this propitious Luminescence Spell
Used to summon tangible silhouettes of light within your *electric* palms
As each apprentice mage possesses the powers to call forth illumination
Never needing to discern what hides within the ambiguities of oblivion

Begin my ritual as the eleven o'clock wolves shadow their muskrat prey
While incense of white sage purifies the chamber and calms the psyche
Arrange a bath for one—operating as an immersive, oversized cauldron
Mine remains matte black with *starlight motifs*, though any tub will do
Deluge with lukewarm water, tepid enough to dissipate any stray flares
Before decanting your ingredients one after the other as the liquid rises
Eight quarts of coconut milk to massage weary bones and bodily knots
One droplet of almond oil for clarity; five ginseng leaves for endurance
Seven yarrow seeds for detoxification; two plumeria petals for resilience
And four botanic lemon balm teabags to beseech the sun's *blinding* gift
Evenly stir with a long, mesquite ladle reserved solely for invoking rites
Until each element has assembled, and the room *skyrockets* with sorcery
Stepping over the lip, sink into the stream playing the part of a conduit
Unbridle your brain until inundated, pruning skin becomes galvanized
Visualize the *clear-cut* shape and size of light you intend to now beckon
Before reciting this proceeding request until darkness prevails no longer

Maiden, coven, mother, crone, I call upon the mages atop magic's throne
Shrouded by the stupefying dark, honor my hands with a clarifying spark
For an enchantress, I claim to be, but a clearer environment is what I plea
Grant the blurred void a garnish of light so I may abolish my unlit plight

After-spell advice: when the formation forgoes flickering—holding true
One might try casting new molds, from cubes to diamonds to crescents
And when satisfaction ensues, conclude your charm by acutely blinking
Disbanding the manufactured glow as if there was never any glare at all

Many blessings, my picture-perfect witchcraft pets,
May you all shine as splendidly as this spell surely will

Paranormal Beloveds

A myriad of eras ago, a *scathing* twister led by the reaper touched down
Amid the ruin, a duet of mortals were caught within the slaying vortex
One perishing by way of heartless massacre, the other by terminal virus
Booked upon a flight coasting from living to lifeless, earthly to ethereal
Not becoming haunting or harming ghouls, but instead, benign ghosts
For their spirits were thrust into the lackluster in-between, or *purgatory*
Where existences continue to carry on—even on the heels of execution
A stilted reality it proved, up until these expired souls first encountered
Our first ghost, a defunct university tutor, Cleo, with pin-straight locks
Sulked through the corridors of limbo, surrounded by fogs of nostalgia
Wishing to savor stacked Linzer cookies, wanting to sense July sunlight
Fixating upon mournful musings, Cleo did not grasp she had company
Until her intangible form slipped *right through* the physique of another
Instigating a clumsy introduction to our artistic, detail-oriented Astrid
Prior astrophotographer with corkscrew curls outlining a diamond face
It was as if their meeting was written in the manifesting diary of deities
Positively predestined, as our phantom females felt called to each other
Idling in the same spot *for ages*, speaking about everything and nothing
Growing blithe for what was certainly the first time since their funerals
And blushing yet not visibly so, for, *of course*, their blood no longer ran
Purgatory abnormally glowed the glorious day Cleo and Astrid bonded
Neither ghost willing to part ways, and so separate they truly never did

From then on, romance prospered, protected by the longevity of death
Conversations of casual topics led to *tectonic* discussions of significance
Nervous, momentary brushes of waiflike fingers upon paranormal skin
Evolved into hypersensitive embraces or three a.m. bodily explorations
Mutually, the pull these ghosts felt only grew with each passing month
Until their afterlives felt *eternally* attached—never to become estranged
Cleo and Astrid's adoration was largely confined to purgatory's borders
Where other lone specters found solace in the *vaporous* arms of another
But amid the witching hour, when the veil between life and loss dilutes
Astrid and her forever-erudite Cleo flew to the territory of humankind
Remaining unregarded while feeling alive, for but a temporary reprieve
Though even after returning to their indefinitely leased abode of limbo
Cleo and Astrid's love awakened attitudes of true verve every single day

Swanlake Lagoon

Amid an erstwhile age engulfed by the *never-malnourished* jaws of time
A coruscating huddle of interstellar luminaries, comfortable until now
Faced the impulse to float down to the sparkling continent of Lunavale
And ferry themselves all the way to Aqualine, famed seaport settlement
Lodging the Swanlake Lagoon, halcyon venue of *transcendent vibrations*
Where Katarina, whom these fascinated stars saw from afar, lived alone
As if a planetary daughter, her flesh and fins took after Neptune's tones
While voluminous mink tresses were conditioned by the brackish tides
Katarina was designed as a starlight mermaid, a serene spirit upon land
Body in tune with the tide-turning moon; blood spawned from far-off skies
And it was her existence that emboldened the stars to journey downhill
Demanding to be much closer to their *celestial* sister of the solar system
But after landing, connecting right away, they could not bear to depart
Hence why these blinding orbs transformed into several-limbed starfish
Eligible to linger near the lagoon's shore, next to their mermaid, always
For the more they knew of Katarina's personality—peculiarities and all
The more they comprehended how special, like an artifact, she really is

Nowadays—alongside the clams and anemones and cuttlefish and algae
Katarina quietly roves below her bottomless lagoon of bioluminescence
Swimming with fundamental simplicity, as sinuous as a coral reef snake
Incentivized onward using her hypersonic rapidity and ultrasonic range
And only when the insects belonging to twilight flit by does she ascend
Obediently heeding her sidereal stars, both close by and looming above
As a synchronized chorus, they serenade Katarina, *spilling cosmic secrets*
Renewing her rapport with otherworldly presences and oceanic powers
Amid these gloaming hours, our mermaid allies with astronomic forces
Engineering frothy whirlpool waves—exploding *high* like cyan fireballs
Instructing the whitecap surfs to hurriedly disperse, particle by particle
Only to bring the droplets back together when carving sheer sculptures
Like intergalactic, hydrogen shrines of nebulae or Mars, to name a few
Later on, Katarina urges the water to return home, airborne, no longer
And when daylight sidles in, nocturnal critters yawning in the distance
So too, does the starlight mermaid herself reenter the Swanlake Lagoon
Refamiliarizing her blue-tailed figure with this briny habitat—*yet again*

HELLO
YES
NO
GOODBYE

Thorne's Necromancing Talents

Within a forgotten boneyard where heartbreaking omens of conclusion
Mingle with murderous consequences, dwells a warped lodge of walnut
Whose stained-glass windows remain ajar, welcoming any *spectral guests*
For the abode's landowner is an occultist of the most paranormal brand
Meet Thorne, deliberately decorated to imitate a breathing Ouija board
Tattooed with transmitting letters and ciphers to relay uncanny memos
For this coal-and-chrome-haired witch came into life with eldritch gifts
Before progressing to inclusive necromancer status at the age of twenty
Generating a séance-packed line-up, as Thorne converses with the dead
Chattering around cemetery headstones, listening over chaotic clamors
For the spirits burn to convey their memories and beliefs and mysteries
And Thorne harkens each remark with round-the-clock ears every time

With an *odd resumé*, our multifaceted medium moonlights as an oracle
For Thorne may use her communications to forecast pending incidents
As the departed acquire details only those on the other side are privy to
Yet this necromancer shall never ask more than they are willing to offer
For demise grants enough unease; no need to suffer interrogations, too
Should the phantoms voluntarily comply, Thorne assuredly communes
Through the aid of a prehistoric beckoning and translation incantation
Authorizing all ghostly murmurs access into the open field of her mind
Understanding each utterance, for Thorne remains omnisciently fluent
Equipped to perceive and parse even the languages of *mythical creatures*
Like the lingo of cockatrice skeletons or the vernacular of gremlin souls
By expressing this practiced sequence of spelled poetry four times over:

A necromancer I shall always be, bring forth these verbose spirits to me
Make clear my entryway is unchained and my empathy is ingrained
Eradicate barriers of dialect and employ my brain with speech unchecked
Promising we may correspond, from the hush of night until the dawn

Thorne's supernatural and soothsaying existence contains no foul cargo
For while her life revolves around fatal reminders, *joie de vivre* finds her
Privileged to be in touch with those who never seek to begrudge or beg
Wanting only to speak with the living, cementing eternal remembrance
Just as Thorne hopes a *future* witch will do for her when she passes, too

Unholy Trinity

Somewhere betwixt the monotonous, anodyne sequences of harem life
Three interconnected wives felt their calling—their *paranormal purpose*
Did not lie, stock-still or silent, within the walls they once called home
And so, with imposing capacities bidding time beneath lithe physiques
Daphne, Margot, and Clover, all containing mystical complexities, left
And the death-defying Unholy Trinity was founded, stalking each land
For the Seven Deadly Sins, posturing as earthly males to handily tempt
Yet our newly divorced trio did not take up hunting in a bid for justice
No, they *related to*, rather than detested, the iniquities they represented
And since the sins were truly dissolute, their tastes would be unequaled
For the Unholy Trinity were not mortals, but fiends with hacking teeth
Yearning, as beasts do, to swallow their prey's brimstone-flavored blood
Wiping their tinted lips only when the seven are depleted, *souls and all*

Splitting from the rest, our first member of this feminine legion set off
Daphne, with bewitching black locks and enriched pheromone powers
Tailed Gluttony and Greed as planned, finding each in a gambling den
Spending exorbitantly, Gluttony gorged himself on the act of wagering
While Greed, *megalomaniac*, followed suit, betting more by the minute
Daphne lured both faux-men forward with her neroli-and-nectar scent
Exploiting their manifest insatiability, she subdued with bribes of *more*
But when behind bolted doors, Daphne drained Gluttony's jugular dry
Before throttling Greed into obedience and drinking him down as well
Sulfuric tangs saturating her tongue as their lives fumed in her stomach
For two were out of commission forever, with only five more to *murder*

All the while, Margot, with self-duplication skills and a ginger ponytail
Made quick work of Envy and Pride, ugly flaws their fall from disgrace
For Envy was so smoothly ensnared, thanks to jealously-inciting taunts
All alone, Margot pinned the sin in place by way of indestructible cuffs
As her decoying replica drew Pride into her clutches with compliments
Side by side, twin Margot's wounded via warfare of the emotional kind
Only to merge into one, snap Pride's neck, and imbibe his arrogant sap
Before impaling Envy, bitter to be slain *second*, and consuming him too
With both sins broken, Margot's veins inflated with spiteful superiority
Gifting the privilege of ending the next pair to our final, baleful female

Lastly, after looking left and right, our high-voltage, high-fashion killer
Clover, body plunged in earthen pigments with tawny tresses to match
Located the always passionate Lust, at last, sopping with explicit appeal
Doted on by the most brazen males and maidens inside a *lair of arousal*
Taking her time, Clover seduced by straddling, stroking, and simpering
Before prurient touches became electrocuting shocks—instantly killing
Perhaps the only time Lust despised experiencing such a physical thrill
And then, after tearing into the fruitful areas her mouth once indulged
Chic, electric Clover soon detected Sloth, as infuriatingly idle as a slug
Slumbering so soundly, a horde of locusts could not disturb his dreams
Our critically-charged fiend never even elected to wake this drowsy sin
Before ingesting every last drop of his *torpid* plasma, refreshingly acidic
Mission *masterfully* fulfilled, Clover moved on to find her loyal cohorts

After the Unholy Trinity reunited, huddled within an eclipsed alleyway
Each ex-wife snuck into a boxing arena and set their sights upon Wrath
Together, they saw his powerhouse form fight without a scrap of mercy
Wrath expressly evaded these three—for their plot had reached his ears
Which only meant his gore grew more appetizing from *imminent doom*
Feigning inelegance, Daphne loudly lost her footing, halting the round
Assured Wrath would haul her to a secluded site to prove his namesake
From there, Margot's copies tied him up while Clover's currents tasered
Before Daphne clung to his throat, Clover his triceps, Margot his thigh
And as one unit, the triad sunk their slicing fangs into this inimical sin
Until Wrath's ferocity flatlined, a first, just as *his heart did the very same*

With once-starved Greed and Gluttony lying desiccated, grimly empty
Pride and Envy and their hubris-addled frames reduced to *voided* husks
And Sloth, Lust, and Wrath bested, now bearing deactivated existences
Clover, Margot, and Daphne preened, beyond impressive versus before
For they replaced their prey as a wicked triumvirate prowling the realm
Awarded with newfound abilities reaped from those formerly devoured
From thereafter, frightful whispers of the Seven Deadly Sins stalled out
Substituted only by hearsays, all true, of the stone-cold, Unholy Trinity
Fated, as they knew all along, for something much more than marriage
But none could have prophesied just how fatal that *something* would be

A Quartet of Seasons

Solstices and equinoxes alternate abidingly—set upon a starry schedule
Dictated by a troupe of goddesses born from Greco-Roman mythology
Horae, the all-female progeny of Zeus, fostering calendar-related fortes
Cooperated with geometric constellations, thusly fashioning *the seasons*

Springtime was sown in a rural landscape rich with perennial hyacinths
Germinated from drizzles of honeycomb and drafts of powdered florals
Until a *breezy* era blossomed among a prairie of foxgloves and petrichor
Typified by stirring bear cubs and birdcalls and cherry blossom jubilees
A hay fever phase when sprites bake rhubarb and kumquat cheesecakes
And gardening brownies tend to tulip patches, pruning shears in palms
Until spring boils over into summer—begetting hell-rivaling heatwaves
Spooned from a scalding kettle of grapefruits, saltwater, and geraniums
Coining sweat-slicked spells ideal for lazy days and late-night escapades
Jam-packed with beachside junkets, melting rocky road ice cream cones
Chilled carafes of mint limeade with cucumber infusions, kiwi granitas
And perspiring merfolk suntanning sessions underneath ultraviolet rays
A sunlit period of aloe vera applications and alfresco adventures *aplenty*
But then, the air shivers, catching an alien chill, for autumn has arrived
Mulled with spiced harvest hints of nutmeg and cardamon and allspice
Dishing up overcast settings of smoky bonfires and amber tupelo leaves
A chance for plaid-vested mortals to pencil in apple-picking excursions
And friendly ghosts to glide between the straw bales of pumpkin farms
Autumn is *great* for chainsaw horror films, medieval folktales of fantasy
Maple-glazed donut mornings, and midnights of wild berry hard ciders
That is, until the final season disembarks in a wind-swept storm of hail
Wintertime straddles the line of arctic frustration and jolly celebrations
Formed from evergreen balsam fir needles and chestnut-scented stimuli
Herded inside by northern blizzards, society places bows upon presents
While frosting peppermint sugar cookies and sipping molten chocolate
For winter is a nutcracker-filled chapter of garland-decked *enchantment*

History's Horae hoped humanity could experience every season at once
But as it is, each interval lasts for the appropriate amount of heartbeats
Like cyclical clockwork, due to the *mostly* punctual goddesses up above

Paloma's Beast

Within a densely brambled jungle rife with carnivorous ivy and insects
Where sleek panthers ingest carrion and lancing scorpions slay crickets
A *purely primal* being forages, named by nightmarish reports as a rapax
With human contours and hellish needs—as untamed as Neanderthals
While bearing preternatural teeth and perforating talons of a wolverine
Rapax's regularly only ever take, *but this creature retains a bit of restraint*
Nonviolently scavenging around the leafy acreage of a remote log cabin
Until the residence's sole proprietor, a perfectly romantic poet, Paloma
With blotches of ink staining babydoll teddies over spans of sepia flesh
Slips out onto her secure veranda to offer this specific rapax sustenance
The nurturer within her spirit as strong and stubborn as his raw hunger
Paloma extends her youthful hands, presenting slices of beef and bread
Which this atypically tame rapax seizes slowly, *a struggle*, and gratefully
Before scoffing the medium-rare meat and brioche rolls with feral bites
And while his appreciation never dithers, such courteous patience does
Coral-flecked sunset after sunset, our rapax revisits for Paloma's rations
Donated profusely, even though she held little to begin with for herself
For she knows that, like a landslide, *nothing will shelve his rabid famine*
Not inclement weather, apocalyptic interruptions, or incoming warfare
Right as always, Paloma's beast returns nightly, more ravenous each eve
Howling as persistently as the bleating of sheep until his poet responds
Paloma parts ways with her last scraps until *all that remains is her blood*
And so, without delay, she reveals her neck and suggests a crimson feast

After experiencing the *bliss* of breaching her skin and downing her gore
Paloma's visitor, with her sap upon his jaw, feels more starved than ever
With obvious misery, the rapax chokes out that she made him this way
For while he loathes that his poet grows pale and poorly, *nor can he stop*
Not when such syrupy flavors linger when his split tongue licks his lips
And her pinched *yet orgasmic* expression when he drank from her collar
Fills his vision whenever his eyes flutter shut like an image of sensuality
But when parted, their roles reverse, for the rapax's mind muses lucidly
Staving off any vampiric pleas until his appetite acts up again, too soon
But when Paloma finds herself forsaken, our poet aches for his presence
After all, she would never have fed her voracious rapax in the first place
If her masochistic heart did not desire him to keep coming back, every time

Nine Hellions

Atop sloped acres of jagged floral finery remains the Thornhill Château
A neoclassical maroon manor, as if bathed by aged bottles of Bordeaux
Piqued the attention of an élite ensemble of *reprehensible* ne'er do wells
Forbidding fiends of various sorts and statuses, all panting for barbarity
As a petrifying merger of evils, they vetted this estate with hexing stares
Before autographing an indissoluble lease of the most inauspicious sort

Midnight rollcall for the wholeheartedly hazardous league of Nine Hellions:
One—Hound of Hades like his underworld-guarding cousin, Cerberus
Xavier snarls at the maw, inclined to dislodge teeth and demolish tissue
Two—Matthias, prior mortal, present poltergeist, seeks earned payback
Launching physical rackets to emotionally oppress, for his ire is infinite
Three—Slovenly Vladamir, *torturesome* Prince of Demons on sabbatical
Showing humans the iniquitous modus operandi of his brothers below
Four—Incubus of supernaturally-motivated seduction, Jasper fantasizes
Tallying the seconds until sleep succeeds, rousing him to illicitly invade
Five—Disingenuous offspring of the gilded, not-so-fabled King Midas
Donovan, metallically contagious, inherited his patriarch's bright touch
Dedicating his life to fashioning gaudy statues out of ill-fated skeletons
Six—Monochrome gargoyle of concrete, Otto's bones roil with revenge
Once assigned to act as a grotesque lookout, *mind-numbingly surveying*
Now, Otto forces his employers to do the same—as he skins them alive
Seven—Cassius, *unpardonable* vampire turned after the Elizabethan era
Thirsts only to open pulsating wrists and taste his favorite bloody brew
Eight—Considered a warlock of malady, Tobias authors jinxes of illness
Inflicting uphill pitfalls from malaria-induced chills to meningitis aches
Upon otherwise healthy souls who venture outside at the *worst* of times
Nine—And finally, Rhain, venomous shapeshifter of the scorpion order
Surges with the need to put his virulent stingers to terminally good use

Our underhanded band of Nine Hellions cohabitate in villainous unity
Brainstorming satanic tactics to satisfy their dark and degenerate itches
While the waxing moon rises, the group mutilates, curses, and murders
Only to return to the Thornhill Château before dawn—keen to debrief
And laze about in the shoplifted gore they find themselves encrusted in
Before the wrongdoers exhale, stand up straight, *and scheme to sin anew*

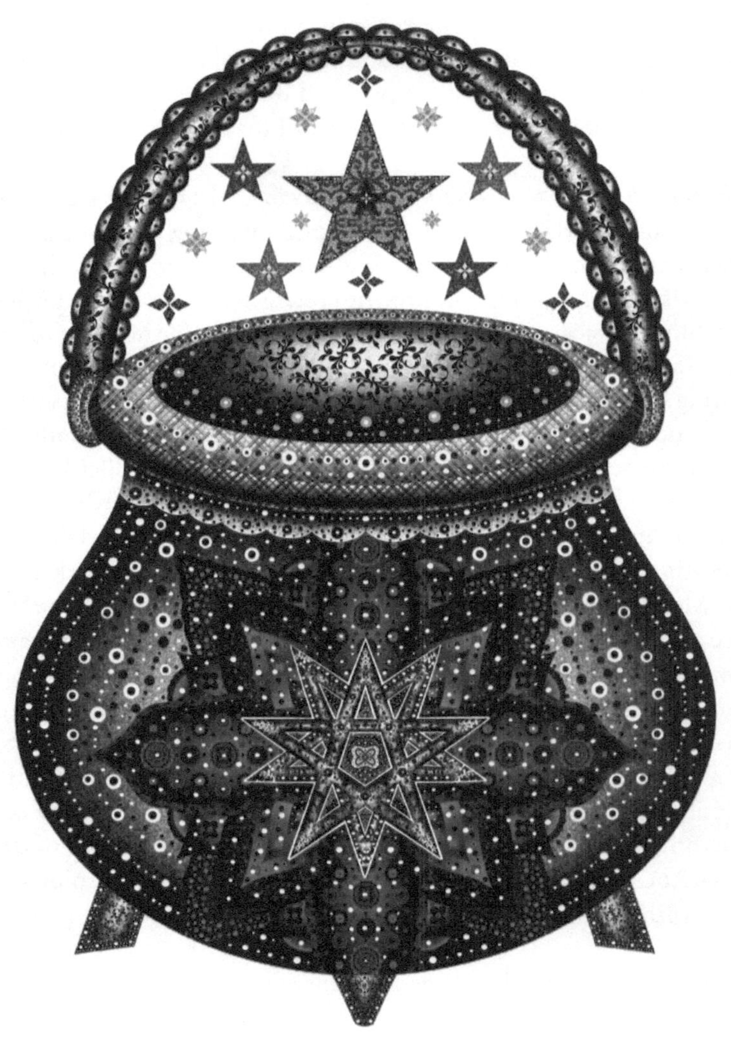

Revelry at the Witchweaver Resort

Every twenty years, when time's shadow has toured the realm and back
And an everthorn twilight trails in, shaded skies *prickling* with purpose
Modern generations of sorceresses spawned from influential bloodlines
Organize a mysterious gathering to be held from twelve until four a.m.
A quietly renowned revelry when Nyx, nocturnal night goddess, rouses
Hosted within *cloak-and-dagger* hotel rooms at the Witchweaver Resort
Where cast iron cauldrons simmer foaming tonics before being bottled
Into slim beakers carrying beautification brews and disguising draughts
All while covens of cabalistic wonderment are originated with precision
Compiling groups based on *instant* affinities or innately parallel powers
Before revealing ancestral charms, from elemental incantations of earth
To mind-moving telekinesis enchantments and teleportation summons
All to be noted inside up-to-date grimoires being telekinetically crafted
Tomes of romance, clad in soft cerise, feature fairy-painted front covers
And *heated* spells of wanting engraved utilizing Aphrodite's ardent gore
Digests of defense, Kevlar-bound to act as armor shielding the contents
Record chants to gather strength—protecting your peace and physique
Volumes of healing, rustic in hue, sure to be referenced eons from now
Penned in liquid raspberry leaf, baring medicinal solutions of mending
Books of devilry, with hell-hewn dust jackets and Hades-touched pages
Exhibit *banned* transcriptions of necromancy lessons and voodoo hexes
All to guarantee the mages will be equipped——no matter the situation
As the festivity rages on, the invigoration at every bend is incontestable
Settling any *straying* misgivings knocking around in the witches' minds
For even dispossessed of grimoires—absent of any scripted invocations
Drop-dead energy, immovable in their flesh, abounds most jarringly so
After all the toiling work is over and done, sessions of *unwinding* ensue
Sociable sorceresses relaxingly savor the Witching Hour Scarlet Sangria
A well-tested recipe of mouthwatering, tart sensations, certain to please
While others devour snickerdoodles, all born with the sweetest of teeth
Convivial invitees share needlework instructions for whimsigoth gowns
Tiered tar-black frocks of spectacular eyelet lace and vintage, onyx tulle
And gush over everyone's pointed hats—a staple of enchantress fashion
Through it all, a sense of *community* is paved into the sentimental ether
For mortals may form bonds—be they short-lived and often superficial
But *nothing* will outdo the spellbinding connection between witchkind

WELCOME TO
ANAMCHARA,
BAILENGRÁ

THE PENNY
LANTERN

A Claddagh Connection

In the sea-level lands of Bailengrá, a leafy country of hostas and clovers
Ethereal Ember's mystical equivalent to the solely mortal isle of Ireland
Here lives the emerald race of goblins—unusually mammoth in stature
But rough as their reputes precede, so too do their souls turn sorrowful
Upon understanding the attacking agony of walking through life alone
After all, Bailengrá attempts to showcase the importance of infatuation
Through the romantic tradition of exercising the use of Claddagh rings
Artisanal jewelry with crowned hands holding multi-chambered hearts
Representative of rapture, reliability, and rapport, the hallmarks of love
Unlike blasé flirtations, the bond between goblin mates burns intensely
For all beloveds, when together, *connect upon unfathomable wavelengths*
Two spirits and skeletons welded as one—that is, if only they ever meet

While every ring reveals consistent overall concepts, each design differs
Making it a *tender* mission to expose the goblin whose pattern matches
A lucky break that Casimir, bearded goliath with unshorn licorice locks
Has not yet, much to the dissatisfaction of his starry-eyed soul, secured
Casimir's Claddagh trinket of mixed metal includes an inlaid jade jewel
And like all unpaired goblins, it rests upon his right hand, *outwardly* so
Though this mawkish creature—a magnanimous, qualified glassblower
Identifies exactly what he is looking for within potential lifelong lovers
For Casimir craves someone to embrace the *selfless* attention he lavishes
And in response, our goblin prays to harken assuaging words of avowal
One eve in the city of Anamchara, at the local pub, The Penny Lantern
Casimir moans, drowning his disappointments upon a barrel at the bar
Caringly kept company by a goblin who proclaims himself as Maverick
With the sides of his scalp shaved, emphasizing gunmetal waves on top
Spiked ears upon a *sizeable frame*, yet the chill still seems to offend him
And so, wrapped with scarves aplenty, Maverick listens while quivering
A charming spectacle to be sure, Casimir distractedly thinks to himself
Before questioning this stranger regarding his own enamored yearnings
Only to ascertain that this reserved but devoted bow and arrow builder
Aches for a helpful partner, one who prioritizes *altruistic deeds of service*
In return, Maverick's mode of revering is through nuzzling interactions
Longing to bestow his soulmate's skin with the cherished gift of contact
To which our Casimir, tirelessly tactile, so sincerely enjoys the sound of

Over the span of *sublime* dialogues, regulars and travelers enter and exit
As the twilight trickling inside wilts from rich cobalt to predawn peach
But still, these goblins remain, never so enchanted by jesting exchanges
Scrapping their two seats sideways until virtually *touching*, all the while
Even their blood wrestles to break free from their flesh to be nearer still
Until finally, Maverick thaws enough to slough a few wintertime layers
Discarding his fleece-lined parka and knit hat and fur-trimmed mittens
Baring disrobed fingers, the sight of which *drives a jolt* through Casimir
For, as everyone but these two besotted fools could have easily deduced
One glance down confirms that their Claddagh rings are mirror images
Indisputably chiseled by one of Bailengrá's top-ranking jewelers as a set
Before suffering separation—only to be circulated throughout the land
Sure that someday, the stars would unite them again, and that day is today
Amid this reunion of rings, Casimir is shocked into tongue-tied silence
While merrily bawling within—true to his maudlin goblin disposition
But it is Maverick who openly weeps, like the softhearted creature he is
Our goblin's exposed digits start shaking from dumbstruck amazement
Urging Casimir to steady them, *or try to*, with his own trembling palms
Before, with absolute affection, turning their coordinating rings inward
For without another word, our goblins sensed their love lock into place
A long-awaited feeling nursing relief into Casimir and Maverick's veins
While comforting the entire country of Bailengrá—Anamchara and all
For nothing shall surpass the seconds of realization between *twin flames*

Amid the aftermath, Maverick crushes his *welling-up dearest* to his chest
While their like-minded, hammering hearts halt to give bodily ovations
Reflecting, jointly, for Casimir and his mate are aligned in all ways now
Upon how thankful they are to have both been in the mood for a drink
And while our freshly lovesick, olive-shaded partners are over the moon
Adoring the novel inverting of their rings, lovelier than any crown jewel
What our goblins, still solidly attached at the hip, will honor even more
Is the red-letter day their irreplaceable bands travel onto their left hands
Engaged through a proposal of dahlias and private promises, *at long last*
And *soon*, if Maverick, wedding enthusiast, has anything to say about it
But in the interim, their gemmed treasures are reminders that their love
Is preplanned to persevere *as Casimir and Maverick were fated for forever*

Wretched Sisterhood

Venerate folklore's childless Lamia and her unhinged *cannibalistic* ways
And gain acceptance by the sultry females of the Man-Eating Mansion
Over a manual drawbridge above a piranha-strewn moat sits the manor
Seven *lofty* stories of ultra-obsidian timber and deep aubergine parapets
Where the Wretched Sisterhood of carnal creatures slay—so unladylike
Minxes, for their title may imply ugliness, yet they exist *as anything but*
Tricking excitable males into their deceptive dungeon using their looks
For there lies a kind of impalpable danger beneath the veneer of beauty
And to weaponize one's desirability extends potent thrills of satisfaction
For entitled males, be they *mortal or monster*, never hesitate to objectify
So it follows that females shall use that sin to their atrocious advantage
Our Wretched Sisterhood, *suggestively* nubile, all brandish almond eyes
Lengthy, messily styled locks and intrinsically erotic glows from within
Naturally enticing in a way that pushes the opposite sex to crawl closer
Yet they appear undamaging—as if their appearances render them *weak*
And those with that debasing mindset are always the first to be lured in
Past the reinforced portcullis, the men ogle the negligée-clad sisterhood
Too sidetracked to sense the *shuddersome* aura seeping from the ground
Like hundreds of specters congesting the air with their exigent cautions
And as the flexible females perform burlesque dances atop their victims
Imbuing their flesh with dosages of pleasure before delivering only *pain*
Groaning males are too blinded by the hedonistic hallucinations of lust
To realize the sisterhood hunger, too, with taste buds much more taboo

Salivating when whimpers sound underneath them, these females *lunge*
And only when scything incisors sharply plummet into hips and hearts
Do the deluded prey gauge the total scope of their masculine gullibility
For the sisterhood's irises are indeed striking, yet against the hazy lights
Of the Man-Eating Mansion, so too, do they blaze the wine-red of hell
And their pleasurable tongues, supple as they are, also bequeath fatality
Venom numbs appalled lips, making the men mute as the females dine
Feeding on brain matter as if *Michelin-starred*, tearing into gallbladders
Licking clean bones and their jellied marrow just like calcium lollipops
And after, when the Wretched Sisterhood walk away painted in plasma
Paltry remains are stuffed below heaving floorboards with all the others
Who dared underestimate the *horrific* capabilities of a beautiful woman

Lola's Saturday Night

Traipsing around a two-tiered loft whilst blasting heavy metal melodies
Lola—a gothically femme fatale enchantress and empress of all potions
Attired in a lace-trimmed camisole slip of kohl and long gloves of latex
With her *purring* familiar, a charcoal Persian kitten, rocked in her arms
Decides to take her pent-up feelings of fixation—listlessly lying in wait
And clarify if her crush's attitude compares to her own, once and for all
What greater way to spend a *steamy Saturday night* in the midst of May
Than to seek out, self-indulgently so, the enlivening ways of witchcraft
Rather than appointing the aid of an eroded cauldron or iron stock pot
Lola, as *glamorous* as she is sorcerous, sets out a crystalline martini glass
And retrieves her recipe booklet to start boiling her single-serving brew
An acerbic cocktail to cause the chambers of her besotted heart to burn
When the attractive apple of her eye, he who *must* be partial to her, too
Muses about our Lola—thinking thoughts both impure and infatuated
Fantasizing almost straightaway, our witch's chest uncomfortably stings
For the early stages of romance may not be the simplest pills to swallow
But then, once sampling, lips and lungs find they can never get enough

With the astringent spell in her system over the length of this weekend
Lola senses her crush's mind straying toward her often, nearly minutely
The blistering in her arteries bringing on fainting spells, wonderfully so
Knowing her soon-to-be-lover is ready to receive her admiration, at last
And so our witch shifts to her second plan, crafting a passionate candle
By pouring crème-brûlée-fragranced oils into a heart-reminiscent mold
Before igniting all five wicks after the rose-hued wax sets at a severe clip
Only then does Lola utter *witchy words* to infuse her creation with love

Superlative goddesses of obsession, air my emotions in a midnight confession
In hopes of reciprocation, lead my man to me for a sizzling nightfall session

Lola, singing along to her stereo, exhales over her candle's fuchsia flame
The subsequent grenadine-scented coils of smoke spelling out a missive
Intended for her soulmate's eyes only, plainly revealing her bold desires
Straight after, *swiftly so*, our sorceress's kitten mews as her doorbell trills
Although the arrival of this particular guest comes as no grand surprise
For Lola is nothing if not a witch who always gets what, or who, she wants

Heartthrob of Hell

Devils, what sexual stupors transpire in the presence of obscene virility
While attending the rock concert of the one and only *heartthrob of hell*
Commandeering satanic charisma, pared into his DNA since spawning
As a purebred demon, Grayson seduces like a siren, with evergreen eyes
Raven strands grazing pierced brows before falling upon a defined neck
Cut-off tees displaying inked forearms, tattered denim upon toned legs
And grunge, *desirable* additions of smudged navy liner and skull chains
Musician he may be, gripping his electric guitar, poison-ivy-pigmented
With the hands of someone who *intimately understands how to use them*
But in reality, Grayson's central profession originated where imps roam
For our unchaste demon holds employment as one of Hade's associates
Assigned to this realm to hypnotize receptive humans while strumming
Confident the heavily aroused crowd will soon descend to his boss's lair
For virtue has been in excess as of late, *leaving hell hungry for novel souls*
So, as netherworld creatures wait for attested sinners to enter perdition
Grayson, horns hidden, offers his screaming audience in the meantime
For none can deny their performer a thing—nor shall they *ever want to*

Sinking to his knees atop the platform our *hardcore* hellion struts upon
Grayson's profane physique undulates to the riotous refrains he invents
And with signet-ring-decked digits dominating his stringed instrument
Our demon's fans remain entranced and envious of those he focuses on
For his riveting gaze reminds the masses that Shakespeare once penned
The devil hath power to assume a pleasing shape, truly fitting for Grayson
How mortals crave closeness if only to lap at the sweat soaking his skin
And suck the lingering beads of smooth bourbon off such salacious lips
But instead, they must settle for watching from their spot in the stands
Awestruck as our composing demon plays, moving with *molten rhythm*
Until, eventually, encore verses through, Grayson saunters off the stage
And his audience trails after freely, as they would follow him anywhere
Even down the theatre's backstage stairs, upon an unknowing katabasis
A descent of increasing humidity, until heated barbed wire gates appear
And the squalid underworld, dwelling of the doomed, sparks into view
But by the time realization dawns, *the exit is barred, and Grayson is gone*
And while strife impends, all they desire is to see their crush once more
Though shortly, they will never be able to see anything at all, ever again

Infatuation Disbeliever

Familial truths too often die out, diluted down the ancestral family tree
Like in the case of Eros and Psyche's *dearly* distrustful daughter, Beatrix
Narrow-eyed ever since labor, this babe was raised by doting paradigms
Who recited legends of their Grecian counterpart, *matchmaking* Cupid
And yet, as a consequence of skepticism, deeming love to be fabricated
Beatrix swore, through the aid of a celestial-bound oath of cynical faith
That her stone heart would never fall victim to an insincere infatuation
And as the constellations *winked* at Eros's opposite, her vow was official

Borrowing a never-dull arrow once axed from rose quartz and romance
Beatrix rinsed the heart-tipped missile in the infamous fountain of woe
Before driving the Roman relic of love into her cardiac organ of *caution*
Ensuring that although Beatrix would remain so depressingly lonesome
None would ever brandish the threat of artificial admiration against her
For the numbness of sorrow is sure to beat the hostile stab of deception
But once skewered, the embezzled heirloom of archery grew embedded
Like a grating splinter becoming increasingly acquainted with her aorta
For the arrow showed no signs of being prone to removal anytime soon

While languishing with the protruding piece grafted in her riled center
Beatrix happened upon Oliver, frolicsome son of Spes, goddess of hope
Ever since their schooldays, Oliver had continued to intone his feelings
Securing love notes upon lemon trees; *sweet* words lying atop sour fruit
And serenading below her bedroom windows like moonlit affirmations
But to the stubborn ears of a non-believer, his empty lyrics meant little
Now, beholding Beatrix's dilemma, he anchored a hand upon her nape
Before maneuvering the other to pluck out the painfully wedged arrow
Like the heroic King Arthur, withdrawing Excalibur from its rigid rock
Barely winded, Oliver professes he has pined for no other since meeting
But better it would have been to show Beatrix via prioritizing subtleties
Rather than telling her through *measly* assertions of sweeping emotions
Mercifully, with the absence of agony coupled with a rush of adoration
Beatrix considers the countless chronicles of true love read in her youth
Before trusting Oliver, at last—trading her incredulity for vulnerability
With the clemency of dreamers, the stars freed Beatrix from her pledge
Sure that the god of love's daughter would feel this way the whole time

Praline Patisserie's
October Menu:
Salted White Chocolate Brandy Bonbons
Pomegranate Macaroons
Mint Fudge
Pumpkin Tarte Tatins
Chocolate Chip Vanilla Bean Scones
Pecan Crème Eclairs
Fig Streudels
Toasted Walnut Baklavas
Dulce de Leche Beignets
Cranberry Ganache Truffles

Praline Patisserie

Oh goddesses, what ambrosial nuances stream from this slice of heaven
Airy wafts of brown butter, gingersnap, and *old-fashioned* peanut brittle
Urging clients with rumbling stomachs inside the confectionary utopia
Where their candy-covered cravings shall be sated in the *tastiest* of ways

When the moon bore youthfulness, Lachlan, our deity of omnipotence
With silver-striped curls of flaxen flanking stubbled, *handsome* qualities
And a hulking nine-foot height of almighty athleticism—so Herculean
Needed a change from his tedious, albeit fulsome, lifestyle in Olympus
And so, Lachlan descended to the in-demand realm of Ethereal Ember
A diverse destination to experience *everything* materialistic and magical
Where our god, bored to tears, longed to encounter unfamiliar mortals
While still viewing *enchanted* beings and backdrops imitating his home
Yet what Lachlan never anticipated coming into contact with, was love
And not just average regard *but the type that moves between better halves*

As radiant as infrared waves, with burnished mahogany lengths of flesh
And teal ringlets accessorized with mini, knotless braids all throughout
Tallulah remains an immortal, emerald-eyed witch of genuine goodwill
Sashaying around, gauzy skirts shifting, with a heart ready for romance
And so, when ichor-bearing Lachlan reached earthen soil, *her soul wept*
Tallulah and her god's rapport—something both undoubtedly destined
And a triumph these lovers labored both *dearly and devotedly* to uphold
Matured into a committed relationship of reinforced zeal—era after era
Eventually, Lachlan and his witch resolved to build a business, together
A small, sentimental venture to embody their *fondant-forward* affection
For beyond Lachlan's gladiator-like exterior, carved by physical exertion
And in between all of his godly onuses, from meetings to machinations
So too, was Lachlan trained as a *professional* pastry chef and chocolatier
Having spent cocoa-dusted decades honing piping and tempering flairs
While benefiting from deep-rooted skills of baking within his anatomy
Endowments that coordinated idyllically with his soulmate's specialties
For Tallulah operates as a décor sorceress of textiles and swatches galore
Conjuring fabric samples, mosaic accents, and made-to-order furniture
Amid her broad career revamping rooms as a charmed interior designer
Making Tallulah and her eye for aesthetics perfect for their promising plans

Like a decision derived from kismet, this pair built a bakery as partners
And after *exhaustive* years full of beautifying blueprints and recipe tests
Perfumed in powdered sugar, the Praline Patisserie victoriously opened
With a coffee-and-cream awning, folksy masonry, shutters of artichoke
And Dutch doors painted with tulips—as if right out of a picture book
Yet inside, Tallulah outdid herself, from the glossy forest-green wallpaper
And woodland-themed booths and benches spotlit by lambent lighting
To bamboo baskets of baguettes and glass cases of malted milk morsels
Lachlan's darling manages the gourmand-scented front of the bakeshop
Extremely gregarious as she is, instantly poised with tailored suggestions
For her beloved companion understands Tallulah's epicurean tastes well
And presses every original creation past his witch's lips with confidence
After toiling in the hearth-heated kitchen, self-rising flour atop his face
Stirring *gelatinous* marshmallow mixtures, torching *stiff* Swiss meringue
Laminating layers of palmier dough, or decorating crumb-coated cakes
But when completed, Lachlan's desserts are not only appealingly edible
For so too, do they each bestow excited patrons with exclusive presents
Ensuring the otherworldly gifts within his blood shall *never* go to waste

For the supernatural month of October, welcoming moods of witchery
Here lies a behind-the-scenes teaser of Chef Lachlan's upcoming menu:
Salted white chocolate brandy bonbons provisionally convert iris colors
Pomegranate macarons resize statures, and mint fudge forbids any envy
Autumnal pumpkin Tarte Tatins alleviate backbreaking corporeal aches
Chocolate chip vanilla bean scones for luck, pecan crème eclairs for wit
Fig strudels grant focus and toasted walnut baklavas contribute bravery
Dulce de leche beignets deliver degrees of immortality to those without
And cranberry ganache truffles allow necromancy talents *for just one eve*

Regardless of their choices—be they caramel or citrus, bitter or brûléed
Each buyer exits with syrupy satisfaction, swearing to return repeatedly
And yet none *remain in better, besotted spirits* than Tallulah and Lachlan
Pleased to fulfill their customers' famished wishes and satisfy their souls
But most of all, these soulmates appreciate their ability to toil in tandem
Spending day after day enveloped in each other's encouraging company
Selling petite treats at the Praline Patisserie in *honeyed* harmony, always

Livinia's Lunar Stardom

Many worship the seventh wonder satellite circumnavigating our globe
Suspended with imperceptible cobwebs spun by intergalactic goddesses
But this zodiac-centric witch loves the lofty moon more than any other
Livinia—crescent outline carved directly in between her argent temples
Physique poured into a diaphanous ensemble of night-blooming petals
Extremities branded by nirvanic inkpots, lined with bodily illustrations
Depicting the periodic phases of this everchanging, *apotheosized* sphere
Which independently illuminate—like somatic flatteries of outer space
When that respective silhouette is simultaneously occurring high above
Loyal Livinia remains a protégé of Artemis and Selene, moon divinities
Who leaned over her bassinet of powder blue when she was but a baby
Uttering keywords, the likes of which were never before affirmed aloud
But Livinia was to be their inheritor—*this the starry females were sure of*
And so they whispered in warm tones, secrets falling as astral raindrops
Sinking into Livinia's pristine skin, becoming *magic* in her bloodstream
Spawning her abilities of lunar witchcraft in a burst of cosmic euphoria
Much older, our mage oversees the eight fluctuating profiles in her care
From new moons of navel-gazing to empowering slivered sickle moons
From swollen gibbous moons to unabridged moons of symbolic clarity
Until Livinia's presumed sequence concludes before commencing again
So too, with the assistance of dusk-opening evening primrose blossoms
Ideal for sorcerous endeavors under the star-studded mantle of twilight
Does Livinia design extraordinary deviations of her moon's appearance
Reserved for only occasions of note—whether to salute in fresh seasons
Celebrate an age-old tradition, or pay homage to an *astrological* episode
From approaching fall equinox harvest moons and January wolf moons
To *mega-rare* supermoons and light-refracting blood moons of cabernet
These distinctly awed displays come to pass only after careful conjuring
Rallying coven-based backing and preparing spiritual shrines to the sky
But when the date arrives to purely alter the moon to its ensuing phase
Livinia verbalizes these rhymes verbatim, and so the hoary circle shifts:

Amid this unavoidable lunation, understand the intention of my narration
Object of my most beloved affection, change contours with orbed perfection
For upon the bright side of the moon, bewitchment may offer many a boon
Eclipsing disquieting blues, waxing and waning until mirth finally ensues

Reincarnation Rhapsody

Everything from the earth up to the ether bristles with vines of *true* life
From oatmeal-freckled fawns, moonlit hilltops, and prickly pear pollen
To lethargic leopard tortoises, saltwater surges, or lemon verbena leaves
All recast entities respire, in conjunction, due to one eminent immortal
Queen of the Underworld, Persephone—*gorged upon pomegranate seeds*
Chose to abdicate her additional crown to Arietta, worthy as any other
Ordaining this deity, full of hope, as the latest goddess of reincarnation
Arietta relaxed into her recently acquired position without reservations
For her essence is steeped in bohemian optimism—fond of novel starts
And partial to propelling the *wheel of existence for as long as it shall spin*

When the three females of fate snap shut their scissors to decisively *snip*
A subsequent soul is preserved within a cinched sachet, sewn by the fae
And only when milliseconds or millennia-lasting lifespans have elapsed
Are the comatose spirits *freed*, then awakened in mint condition bodies
Remolded as dragonflies and ladybugs and downpours and rattlesnakes
Carefully, Arietta either cherry-picks which class they shall convert into
Selecting trellis-bound morning glories to a former *flora-loving* botanist
And a laidback panda for a previous jaguar learning to laze through life
Or, she permits the yet-to-be-categorized souls to decide for themselves
Like in the case of lovers once divided by the impassable fence of death
Arietta, a goddess of her word, allows the female to name her new form
For her other half will *surely* follow, shifting into a corresponding shape
And should she choose a stem a lavender, he would become a honeybee
Certain to unite for the dozenth instance *and fall into love all over again*
So too, do the rest of Arietta's darlings smoothly adjust to their realities
And though firsthand experiences consume all of their conscious hours
Snapshots of their past lives peek through—like windows of familiarity
And gratefulness follows, glad their existences did not have to *stop there*

Atop her sunstone throne, Arietta senses her reincarnated children's joy
Acclimating to life according to schedule inside their designated frames
Whether it be a friendship fivesome remade as a wreath of delphiniums
Or a fallen star revived as an amphibian—swimming alongside axolotls
Arietta looks after them all afore their portended post-passing reunions
For our goddess shall greet *an iteration of every soul until the end of time*

Terminal Love Triangle

A mercurial love flowed betwixt three, foretelling of ever-certain *tragedy*
For within a wealthy metropolis of mystical citizens and lively melodies
A *terminal love triangle*, a circuit of revolving romance, was in full force
Glittering in the indispensable middle remained the arresting, Adelaide
Surprisingly sanguine banshee—beautifully shrieking into the starlight
Whenever the severe reaper hissed that death's chariot was approaching
But amid any interludes—attired in flattering, blue opal Bardot gowns
Adelaide breaks ceramics into mosaic gifts *almost* as attractive as herself
For our banshee's deeply terracotta waves and juniper-dotted jade irises
Urged species from widespread nations to lust after this maiden's allure
And so, it should drop no surprised jaws that our heaven-sent Adelaide
Was uninhibitedly courted and ultimately treasured by not one *but two*

Each suitor loved with the burning intensity born from endless anxiety
Fearing their entrenched feelings would never be favorably reciprocated
A trepidation neither male ever needed to fuss over in honest hindsight
Starting with the first of Adelaide's admirers, we have the fragile mortal
Finnick, with garish indigo eyes and soft barley curls brushing his nape
Prattled away as a hospitable innkeeper at a watercress shelter of charm
Taking up hobbies of bookbinding or chess-playing when off the clock
But all knew of Finnick for his boundless goodwill and gracious energy
How precious that our mortal only ever dreamt of finding his soulmate
A fantasy that Adelaide, *an equally hopeless romantic*, turned into reality

One solstice, when burgundy petunias unfurled beneath cloudless skies
Finnick *serendipitously* spotted Adelaide while at an annual crafting fair
From there, coy compliments and low-lit dates turned into lyrical vows
And the torch of love they ignited for one another *only flared from there*
Always, our mortal treated Adelaide as if she had descended as an angel
Gently was the way his heart sang to her own, eager it heeded in return
Amid winter's apex—running his hands up and down her freezing flesh
Finnick would bundle his shivering banshee in his sole blanket of wool
Inviting his face to turn frostbitten if it meant *her bones remained warm*
For our kind innkeeper would gift Adelaide the world, if only he could

But another craved Adelaide's affection, concurrently not competitively
And as wonderful as her Finnick was, with all the sensitivity of a seraph
Our banshee could not discount the darkened bait of her second suitor
And her transfixed soul and tempted senses did not beg her to even try
With an irregular skeleton, Drago filled the forms of man and monster
Cracking his spine until evolving into the scaled membrane of a basilisk
Before slipping back into his mortal casing, seducing as a serpent tamer
For his looks, from a brunette buzz cut to onyx eyes, *entranced everyone*
Bedecked from corded neckline to considerable thighs in shadowed ink
Drago exuded the persona of an alpha Adonis with a candid conscience
For though he burned for Adelaide, he waited until she sought him out
And when she did, Drago finally *promised her forever, just as she foresaw*
Hooked, our cold-blooded maverick placed his banshee atop a pedestal
Boring his *superheated* stare—hung up upon his partner—into her own
Not an inch of Adelaide's sun-kissed skin went unpraised by his mouth
Or ungrazed by her basilisk's coarse palms, grasping with rapt gratitude
In a manner which spoke volumes of his *eternal devotion, never to wane*
And though Drago loved brashly, so too did he convey heartfelt respect
Lining each possessive touch with the profound nuances of compassion
In the midst of *violent* summer storms, he serenaded his upset Adelaide
Drowning out the tempest so only dulcet tunes inundated her sore ears
Ruptured long ago from banshee shrieks but spared now by her Drago
Intending to expose her to only harmony *for as long as fate would allow*

Finnick and Drago harbored no contempt for one another, sincerely so
Acknowledging the another with comradery—as real gentlemen would
For how could they despise someone who decanted love unto the body
And moaned poetic phrases into the mind of their Adelaide, so openly
Instead, our pair of paramours fixated upon whatever iotas of attention
The light of their life offered, viewing every instant shared as a privilege
While speculating that since her full heart contained *multiple* chambers
And a distich of ventricles—an elaborate organ of essential importance
Just maybe, that meant Adelaide possessed the space to love them both
A notion their open-ended valentine was more than thrilled to confirm

Adelaide's smitten yet separate significant others adored her completely
While expressing their emotions through clearly conflicting approaches
But for all their disparities, our banshee deemed both as *truly deserving*
Regarding her sentimental mortal as if he were the incarnation of glory
Dipped in comfit wells of consoling patience and permanent positivity
Like a palpable glint of daylight, one she never once wished to let loose
Which was altogether quite *overwhelming*, like a dizzy labyrinth of love
Considering the mesquite and musk essences of Drago's pleasuring lips
Still coated Adelaide's lavished tongue—throbbing while wanting more
How could our wailing woman have been expected to choose only one
When enviably positioned in between this duet of impeccable matches
And how could her head have experienced anything but unruly ecstasy
Knowing that rivers of acclaim were so *feverishly* anointed upon herself
Amid an otherwise fatiguing existence of unabating cries and casualties
For despite Adelaide's buoyancy, the life of a banshee remained sapping
Made less traumatic only by the load her lovers lugged atop their backs
Reducing her grueling troubles, saddled by the heavy impact of demise
Gallantly helping without requiring their ravishing Adelaide to *ever* ask
For being cherished is to be nurtured without complaint, until the end

And so, Adelaide bound herself to both romancing men, year after year
Floating within a state of frenetic limerence, divvying her hours in half
With timetabled turns of the objective sun and moon as *lunisolar clocks*
Our banshee would begin every day beside Finnick, her adulating beau
Slotting her back against his solid torso while shaping original artworks
Soothed by the pace of her mortal's heart as he skimmed vintage novels
Or tried to teach the rules of chess, which his lover found *far too dreary*
Yet Adelaide would still indulge Finnick until the haze of dusk surfaced
Prodding our banshee to leave her hotelier darling and return to Drago
Back together under the *glow* of twilight, Adelaide's lover held her tight
Dipping his thumbs into her hips as they disclosed confidential desires
Resulting in evenings so remarkable, Adelaide *never* compared her time
Basking in both encounters evenly—for be it midmorning or midnight
Our banshee fell into one of two sets of arms, right where she belonged

Swept off her feet, Adelaide idolized her innkeeper and reptilian shifter
Simultaneously so, without any halting hints of favoritism or hesitancy
For her fond feelings were not hewn in half but rather amplified bifold
Hence why when the dismaying whirlwind of devastation disembarked
The totality of Adelaide's thrashing heart keened in earth-shattering sorrow
Understanding, like never before, that the elixir of love is not all-curing
Fervid as they may be, chords of enthrallment cannot prevent tragedies
A lesson our crushed banshee came to learn amid one dismal afternoon
When Finnick's beloved was forced, *terribly* so, to do the unimaginable
As the future came into focus, her vocal cords tore upon a warning yell
Though not even the steel-enforced strength of Adelaide's fierce passion
Could have saved dear Finnick from the inevitable chokehold of expiry
Adelaide's mortal perished from a hushed malady, lethally undetectable
Asymptomatically, the virus conquered his innocent system with speed
Before ending everything in a single, expedited act—strangely merciful
And in his final fading moments, all Finnick's bleeding lips could form
Were the familiar letters formulating his lover's name—again and again
Like one last prayer echoing into the ether, paining every wildlife being
Who sympathetically wept nearby in support of our *dispirited* Adelaide

With her triangle *dismantled*, one corner buried beneath larkspur fields
Roots of mourning expanded and embedded inside our banshee's lungs
As she waded through oceans of anger and agony, but never acceptance
To live within a lesser world without her Finnick felt so patently wrong
For how dare her body draw another breath when her mortal could not
But amid her weakest days, Drago was there to pacify Adelaide twofold
Lacing inked fingers through her locks and offering husky condolences
As no hardship, Drago cradled his lover close, inhaling her sorbet scent
Ignobly relieved that now, in the grey outcome, his were the only limbs
Adelaide would find herself intimately wrapped up in, from *here on out*
And all the while, in the inescapable beyond, a late Finnick watched on
Pleased that her remaining partner would never leave her side as he did
Pondering that perhaps Adelaide's ardent basilisk, *auspiciously immortal*
Was the best choice, if the cosmos decided there ever was one, all along

Diana the Huntress

Hunt—the term etched into her plasma and psyche, for she was Diana
Recorded in Roman folklore as the stag-symbolized goddess of hunting
With hands that prickled and fingers that went ballistic when deprived
Of her fundamental pursuing equipment, affixed upon her back always
Though a huntress Diana remained, our deity cared—*warmheartedly* so
For her wild animals, exalting bison and jackals and elk and boars alike
Conversing with them amid sunrise and consoling them amid nightfall
Revering this bond, Diana snared not for the sadistic delight of the kill
But to educate others on the techniques of how to humanely put down
Infusing inquisitive minds with her savvy, helping provide for their kin
Ensuring the *aching stabs* of famine never plagued their starved middles
Great woman of the wilderness, Diana revered her woodswoman status
Above all else, uninterested in stable matrimonies or sensual rendezvous
Leading our goddess to request exemption from romantic engagements
Rather than diamonds, Diana only beseeched a bow, a quiver of arrows
And the cathartic ability to traverse plentiful forests and mountainsides
With her beastly companions and female confidants forever by her side
While living an *emancipating life* free from any amatory entanglements
And thusly so, Diana attained the reputation of a pure virginal goddess
Body untouched by libertine males and brain unaffected by their *idiocy*
Making her a truly trusting space for maidens and wives and mistresses
Until finally, Diana was fittingly entitled the patron goddess of fertility
And lasting defender of damsels, like a figurative sister to those in need
Our idol supervised penniless women with wounds blatant and unseen
And *swore* to pregnancy-pining souls that breeding boons were nearing
Before aiding expecting females when in the taxing throes of childbirth
But no matter the cause, whenever Diana's gear rattled across her spine
As she journeyed in overdrive toward the souls pleading before her altar
Having suspended her woodland happenings without a second thought
Any worries were thwarted, for Diana was to be their advocating paladin

Even now, whether you remain a female in dire need of daily protection
A soon-to-be-mother wishing for welfare amid elongated bouts of labor
Or a vocation-oriented maiden misogynistically vilified for *unwed* goals
Call out to Diana, faintly or brashly, if matters not, for she shall answer
With the guidance only a goddess may gift, in philanthropic perpetuity

Luster Leeches

Atop a fragmented landmass, marked upon maps as the Neverlight Isle
With *wintry* peaks and valleys spanning throughout the tundra's terrain
Shifty atoms of darkness drench the obfuscated atmosphere year-round
For this isolated island, a vacuum of light, remains devoid of brightness
Thanks to the faceless creatures populating the ceaselessly glacial region
Classified as cryptids by each being from nearby and remote continents
Though their *proper title*, the Luster Leeches, only enters the ears of few
Ilk of an inimitable kind, hailing from the satanic loins of Cain himself
These fiends thrive off obscured entropy, savoring the disordered gloom
Slinking within the shadows until bold smatterings of sunlight turn up
Or combustible wicks of candles and chill-eliminating campfires are lit
In those short seconds of vivacity, the Luster Leeches start their larceny
Snatching any outlawed intrusions before inhaling the golden rays fully
Only to skate past unmoistened lips and down dim, inhospitable lungs
Acting as aureate kindling for the evil embers lining their *accursed* souls
Stoking the flames of their inherited malevolence, swelling their powers
And bolstering the bond between the Luster Leeches and their vile lord
In place of the stolen radiance upon the Neverlight Isle, never to return
Encompassing mantles of *tenebrific*, godforsaken nightfall reign instead
And in the thick of a bottomless blackout, almost anything can happen

Semi-sentience impregnates the shaded entities the Luster Leeches craft
Typical silhouettes, they are not—moving minus any aim or autonomy
No, these local shadow organisms are extensions of their ornery makers
The Luster Leeches command their unilluminated pets without a hitch
Governing their realities as automatically as one would blink or breathe
As if these surreal kin exist as dislocated limbs of their reprobate fathers
Filled with *borrowed* brainpower and bathed in the *dearth* of effulgence
Procced across the Neverlight Isle, these regional atrocities are required
Harming enough to excite the devil until all damages are unsalvageable
Before consistently reporting any achievements to their parental figures
And worming back inside the pervious physiques of the Luster Leeches
Lying in *heartless* wait to gain more blinding-turned-blackened siblings
But anticipate for far too long, these bloodthirsty billows never need to
For the very moment a matchstick is struck, the Luster Leeches *pounce*

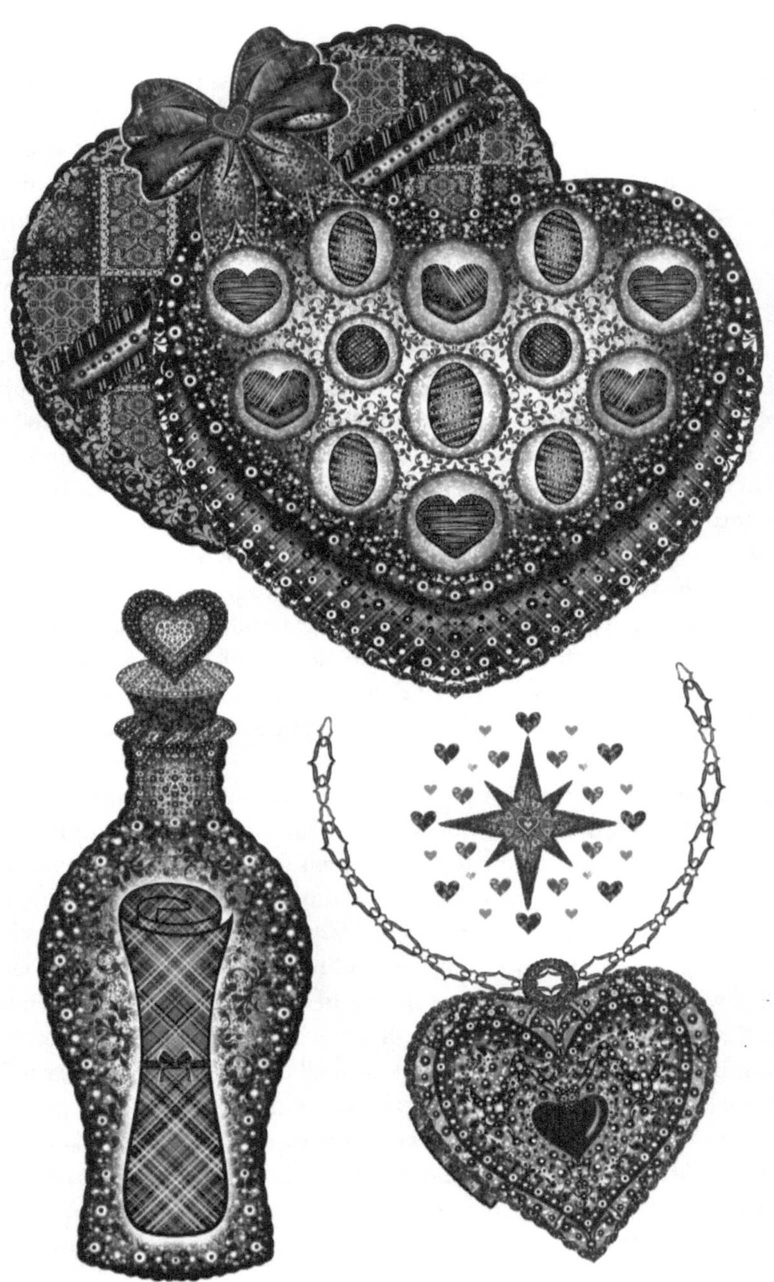

Lazy River of Love

Effervescently, the sweetened sandalwood Lazy River of Love shimmers
Reliant upon the light, for the sun and moon cast *such* diverse shadows
Either mountain-laurel blush or iridescent alabaster tints the tepid tide
Flowing with gardenia blooms and forget-me-not blossoms poised atop
Like a winding basin of nature, our storybook stream resides in Amoria
Within the angelical kingdom of Pearlpoint, *a countryside vista of magic*
Charitably, the Lazy River of Love remains a site to send emotive items
Posts of affection—from initialed lockets to milk chocolate heart boxes
Furled messages of admissions and avowals inside corked crystal bottles
Calligraphy-inscribed letters from bounty hunter orcs to their fae wives
Missives of long-distance written by minute trolls to their mated pixies
Tender parcels of spell materials from mages to loveless damsels in need
But one may only utilize the river if their idealistic objectives are *honest*
Legitimately smitten, battling the bond between Achilles and Patroclus
As a test of truth, simply slash an open palm and bleed into the current
Faithfully bewitched, and the opaline waters shall settle into soft waves
Falsely beguiled, and the river shall spasm—setting off Poseidon's anger
Asking self-deceiving souls to rush back after reflection and repentance
Only then, ready to *earnestly* regard, will the stream accept submissions
Embracing every simpering offering with imperceptible, sopping hands
Ensuring they reach their destinations, *like a fairy godmother of romance*

So too, do individuals float atop the tributary—coasting daintily along
Sensing a dewy-eyed quality surround their bodies, sedative and sugary
Free from strife, buoyant beside *ardent* creatures from selkies and newts
To angelfish, always paired, and rusalkas—beneath the infatuated shore
Further down the river, when a couple teeters on the brink of cessation
Nearing their final days concurrently, as lovers are forever synchronized
Terminal companions sojourn to the Lazy River of Love to slope below
Justifiably awarding themselves a united death in a maelstrom of solace
Inclining ever-so-soothingly, the freshwater leisurely steals their breaths
Exchanging inhalations with the *tranquil thrill of an immaculate ending*
Never excruciating in the least, only entirely reassuring and resplendent
For *euphoric* conclusions often stem from *enrapturing* commencements
And nothing is more enchanting than the beginnings of fond devotion

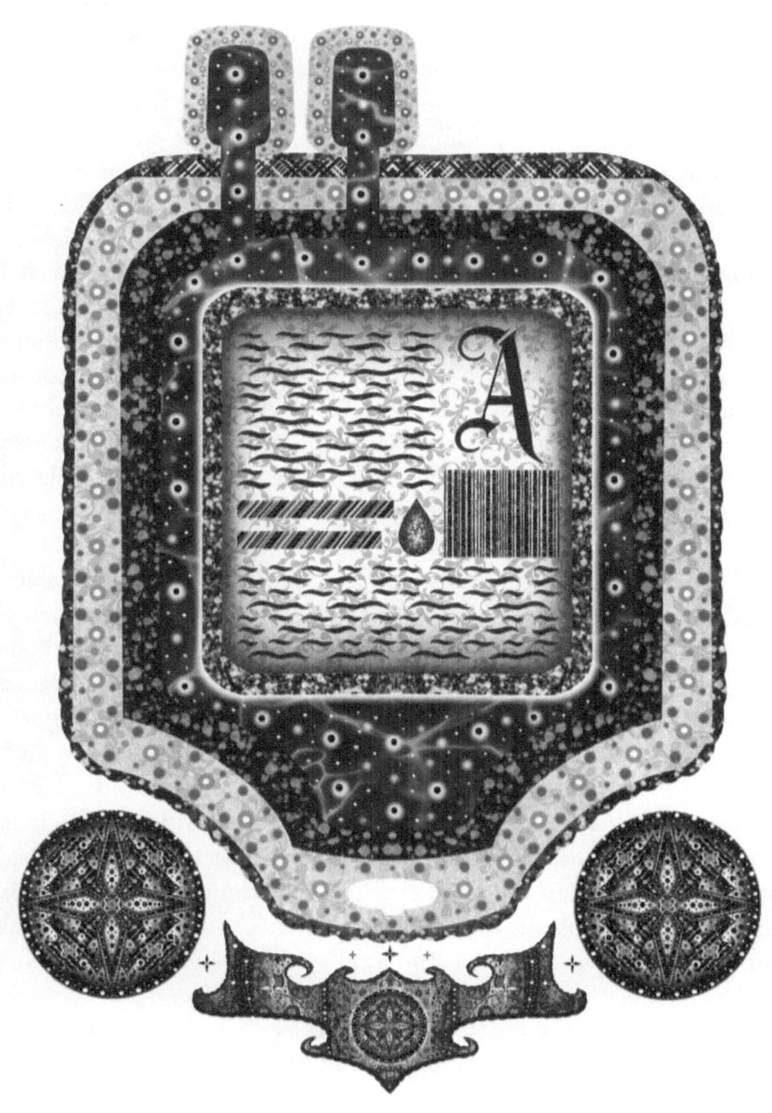

Vervain Hex

Undiluted agony is to loathe that which remains compulsorily required
A hostile truth Dimitri lies saddled with for the *rest of his relentless days*
Once an academic mortal and avid bibliophile throughout his twenties
Studying for a career in cartography, compass and quill always on hand
All before his final gulps of human existence, flawed yet *favored*, abated
And life as a biting vampire began—map-making dreams now obsolete
For Dimitri was ambushed beneath the moonbeams by vermeil cuspids
And so, he was changed; flesh decolorized, irises gilded, failings deleted
No longer bashful and book-idolizing, undead confidence commenced
For our vampire initially cherished his *novel* night-walking species label
As a shameless rapscallion, Dimitri attended bacchanalias of insobriety
Gargling gore, *messy* and flavorful and morbid, straight from the source
Canines grating over uncovered clavicles and wrists, throats and elbows
Opening arteries femoral and brachial—ripping and guzzling recklessly
Only to drowse deeply inside a cypress coffin whenever daylight blazed
Fantasizing of the sanguinary fun to follow when the darkness returned

But, like an addict preoccupied with his plasmic prescription of choice
Cruel consequences soon after trailed behind his *fast and loose* footsteps
For the respected Coven of Equilibrium had watched from the wayside
Ruling that Dimitri *took too much, too often*, rotting the realm's balance
And so, as decreed to do, the enchantresses elicited a renumerating hex
One imposed on all other pallid monsters from the not-so-distant past
Activating the palate-transforming detestation of once delightful blood
Turning the formerly ambrosial fluid into something strictly hellacious
A sap, so sour and searing, that *scorched* when transferred into esophagi
For the hex was a stern vendetta, saturated in vampire-repellent vervain
A notorious herb noxious to the skin and stomachs of nocturnal bodies
And while the ingesting pangs were head-spinning and vomit-inducing
Dimitri, *ashamed* as ever, could not belay his indulging, try as he might
For his soul, dying to drain veins, needed ruby cocktails to continue on
Initiating a galling pattern of hunger and hurting he would never evade
Just like overeating vampires of before—captive to cursed fates just the same

After scarcely surviving decades of the hex hassling his spirit and senses
Dimitri currently spends each waking second in a thatched-roof saloon
Of stonework walls and sable wood weakly illumed by ambient sconces
Where he remains a regular customer amid his *pitiful mindful moments*
In ineffective endeavors to stave off any A positive or O negative thirsts
Forcing down ales, yet the taste, once nectarous atop his mortal tongue
Presently satisfies seldom—as irritatingly bland as the zest of pure ether
And without fail, the *pungency* of nearby patron's gore deters his efforts
But even if Dimitri should throw in the towel—feeding there and then
Any blood-soaked gratification dominates for but a trivial bout of time
Before that *annihilating yet accustomed* appetite rears its avaricious head
And so—brusquely driving back his barstool upholstered with rawhide
Our blighted vampire singles out a fair dame, flirting with flying colors
Before leading them both out back, where he grips her jaw in one palm
And threads *experienced* fingers through her canary curls with the other
While his lips suck his way down her flesh, arousing even the desert air

Until, at long last, the next kiss Dimitri delivers is suddenly full of fang
Infiltrating just enough to allow a torrent of recognizable liquid to leak
Directly into the cavernous tunnel that is his enchantress-hexed mouth
But whereas before the coven intervened, Dimitri would swig non-stop
Amply and unabashedly, retaining a rough hold amid his consumption
Now, our leech's loving conduct lulls his prey into automatic obedience
And when drinking, it is but a fleeting vignette—far hastier and horrid
For the insufferable reaction remains too ghastly to gorge, as he used to
Pained facial muscles grimace when his meal, full of electrolytes, is over
And as the aftertaste of out-of-date vinegar, offensively burning, lingers
The Coven of Equilibrium notes Dimitri's discomfort with vindication
As the humiliated vampire sulks home before crawling inside his coffin
Wearily thankful his ballooned intestines have temporarily had enough
And only amid the business hours of humans does transitory *relief* arise
Dimitri desires to abstain from dining—eager to end his jonesing ways
But alas, remission is never entirely viable for tick-like souls, such as he

Curse-Breaking Coin

Even the most mundane of objects, seemingly uninspiring and unlucky
May be instilled with the occult ingredients needed *to change everything*
Amid a prolonged tenure as a dear representative of his cabalistic coven
Merlin, our warlock of humble beginnings and honored breakthroughs
Focuses, after thirty rounds of trial and error, upon the skill of infusing
Many a talisman, items of imbued mystical fortune, bear Merlin's mark
From orange tourmaline amulets to defend against disapproving beings
And preserved four-leaf-clovers sealed with resins of agelong safeguards
Merlin shaped each piece with punctilious care and powerful intention
And although every trinket bore fruit as supreme wonders of witchcraft
All shall agree that his inventions from before—beautiful and beneficial
Have since paled in certifiable comparison to his *crowning* achievement
Conscientiously sculpted into the composition of a curse-breaking coin
Comprised of glossed copper and decorated with flakes of flexible brass
As smooth as raw honey and as weightless as a wraith's undyed skeleton
Merlin supplied his coin with cells of sorcery through a *charmed chorus*
Intoning the invocation yet only whenever his timepiece struck midday
And when the moon arose in the Milky Way as the clock rung twilight
Our vanguard warlock repeated this finicky formula for a full fortnight
Until his coin vibrated with arrant aptitude, for the talisman was ready

For those incarcerated by a terrible curse, clutch this coin lest life grow worse
As the expedient magic within the metal forces all sufferings to finally settle

For slews of eons, Merlin's *world-class* creation has remained in rotation
Awarded to those placed under arrest by the handcuffs of various curses
Beset by everything from unrelenting malady hexes to heartbreak jinxes
But as a result of holding the powerful, henna-hued disk in their palms
Any *heinous scourges* flew through their veins and fled from their gullets
Before dissolving down to a puddle of nothing, not even dust or debris
Oh-so-similar to the fate of the aquaphobic Wicked Witch of the West
And when our warlock's recipients were freed, at last, damned *no longer*
Another soul gained control of the healing coin, starting the cycle anew
And though our Merlin—with unlimited days and unremitting dreams
Shall always craft, his legacy will live on through his cure-breaking coin
Having made the incurable *completely* correctable for the very first time

Harbinger of Necrosis

As timberland creatures rest, humankind dozes off, and goddesses relax
Fortissimo gallops disturb the silence whenever the moon is at its zenith
For a covered, hearse-like carriage built from perdition-sourced lumber
Is tugged along by a transporting duet of focused and feral Clydesdales
Who snake through the forbidden woods sheltering imprisoned species
Before ending up along an unpaved trail, the terrain inviting migraines
Charging across the backroads of this kingdom with only unkind goals
For these equine beasts assume *not* mortal exteriors and earthly marrow
As their bloodshot irises, hellfire-scalded undercoats, and twisted horns
Indicate that should one harken the fiends, *snarling* and speeding along
Approaching cul-de-sacs and courts, it is already entirely too late to run
For when the abyss-derived horses draw near, their leader looms as well

Inside the overelaborate coach—where inexcusable agendas are devised
Our underworld-famed and human-feared Harbinger of Necrosis plots
Cast in shards of moonlight, emphasizing gaunt cheeks and claret flesh
Hungry for decomposition thanks to a tainted history unlike any other
As a little lad, immunocompromised, he nearly submitted to a sickness
Which took root within his skeleton as obstinate decay, sure to be fatal
But perish our rogue did not, for instead, as either a present or a *plague*
The Harbinger of Necrosis survived, though the rotting virus remained
And this time around, the ongoing disease did not harm his physiology
Instead electing to bestow his existence with the ability to infect others
Encumbering anything, mortal, mineral, or mammal, with contamination
Dispensing curdled attacks of disintegration by way of his sullied touch
Relocating the endless mold inside his carcass unto the flesh of another
So too, may the harbinger pollute through his close proximity presence
Jinxing humans jaunting nearby, altering their frames into rancid shells
And changing the organs of forest faunas into fetid structures of *decline*
Not even inculpable nature is spared, laded with pure strains of erosion
Mining into the mud, like a vole wreaking havoc of the gangrene genre
Just as the very land which we all live upon so appallingly regresses, too
And while the Harbinger of Necrosis never did expire all those eras ago
Soon, at the brisk rate his Hades-loaned horses pay a visit to each town
Everything from subsiding spirits to the festering soil in continents afar
Will cede to a final fate our undying villain will never truly understand

Mount Olympus Overview

Embark upon a tour of an ether-entrenched realm of real Grecian idols
With the papaya afterglows of sunrise and temperate breezes of serenity
Mount Olympus, *beauteous* to the max, sits upon a precipitous summit
Of standout heights dusted with diamanté snowflakes and radiant frost
Hike through the Horae-guarded acropolis of *canonic* architectural awe
And notice exquisite gardens blooming with rosebushes and olive trees
Before visiting a vaudeville playhouse near a concert hall of melodrama
All building up to a lacquered lane of gated palaces upon Mytikas Peak
Where one dozen castles of pageantry steeped in seraphic luxury reside
Starring marble pillars, private courtyards, and brazenly bronze thrones
Owned not by any with secular gore, *for they were banned from the start*

Only gods and goddesses with gleaming ichor populate these highlands
Including the twelve, though thirteen at times, deities of the pantheon:
Zeus, wielding the scepter of sovereignty, unleashing *thundering* squalls
Hera, ruler of matrimony and childbirth; Hermes, nomadic messenger
Artemis, wildlife admirer; Apollo, poetic prophet; Athena, wise warrior
Poseidon, earthquaking sea god; Hephaestus, fire-controlling craftsman
Dionysus, drunken lover of tannic libations; Demeter, agricultural icon
Aphrodite, model of adoration and attractiveness; Ares, militant soldier
Each of these Olympians played their part in *seminal mythical moments*
From interloping interference in the spun-out, decade-long Trojan War
To Persephone's underworld kidnapping and Pandora's clay-based birth
But then, after battles reach bloodied ends or insidious schemes succeed
Every deity tucks into the digestible treasures of Mount Olympus fame

All goddesses and gods, masculine and feminine and androgynous alike
Praise the otherworldly nourishments offered only upon this mountain
From brimming goblets of fresh nectar to treats of toothsome ambrosia
Loaded with powerful preservatives granting immortality and influence
In Mount Olympus's heart, a syrupy spring and candied cornucopia lie
Where capricious citizens devour until their palettes coast into paradise
For so much remains topnotch within this cerulean-ceilinged kingdom
But nothing, all would agree, surpasses the sugared tastes of godly fares
A heavenly experience of feasting mortalkind will wailfully never know
And so, these idols value their *heaping mouthfuls* enough for them both

Eternity-Ending Elixir

Everlasting life expectancies grant triumph and turmoil for fated mates
Roman, multi-headed hydra-shifter with the build of a Spartan warrior
And Crimson, impassioned gorgon with a hissing ponytail of pit vipers
Experienced the tremors of drastic connection upon meeting at full tilt
Before taking the time to turn instant desire into a deep, loyal devotion
Until their *soulmate standing* was revealed, meant to be in every manner
And while typically their hands are as interlaced as their reptilian hearts
At present, with the addled aroma of Armageddon tarnishing the room
The palms of this deathless pair only prehend identical *vials of mortality*
For a meddling force delivered these eternity-ending elixirs at first light
Leaving the mates to stew all morning long, pondering the possibilities
Arguing if the vessels shall be *climactically drunk or completely discarded*

A provisionary reality neither have ever known may offer many rewards
For their infinite hourglass would hasten, time becoming *truly* precious
Pushing Roman and Crimson to savor this life that may be stolen away
But perishability equally hinders—for there is much they wish to fulfill
From carrying out their marriage ceremony to sailing round the nation
Ultimately, the couple must consider their personal dreams and desires
Along with the aspirations and appetites in their white-hot relationship
In the end, the choice must be united, for hell would arise should they differ

With the intuitive gaze of mates, a mutual verdict has seemingly settled
But with a twist of tragedy only the olden Greek playwrights could pen
Crimson drains her vial, bestowing the terrain with a taste of humanity
While Roman, *heedless* as ever, downs the absinthian liquid to the dregs
Unaware of how rapidly the effects of mortality would catch up to him
Not quite able to regret before death's unhinged jaw *swallows him whole*
Aghast, Crimson and her sobbing pets regard her love's inanimate form
Only to resolve that the immortality she clung to retains no merit now
Inspired by Juliet, the gorgon shatters her vial and slits her ivory throat
Hemorrhaging beside the stiffened corpse of her quicksilver sweetheart
Trapped between hydra flesh and gorgon fluid, *potion now a moot point*
While the Executioner, who provided the beakers with ulterior motives
Spies on with a nefarious smirk distastefully fixed upon his masked face
And a crate of divisive ruin, absent twin slots, within his infernal hands

ADMIT ONE
AN EERIE EXTRAVAGANZA
WARPED CIRCUS
OF WONDER
OCTOBER 31 8:00 PM SHARP

ADMIT ONE
AN EERIE EXTRAVAGANZA
WARPED CIRCUS
OF WONDER
OCTOBER 31 8:00 PM SHARP

Warped Circus of Wonder

Exploring this realm under the *nonsensical* guise of glitzy show business
A gothically inclined carnival enters the virtuous town of Twilight Falls
With acrylic-painted smiles, *synthetically* wide, and supernatural minds
As a company since the Middle Ages, each routine in their lineup is set
Transpiring within a striped tent professionally hoisted over each venue
State-of-the-art, adorning onyx and opal streaks with candy-apple stars
But within, uncontrived magic is unveiled inside a ring of whimsicality
Festooned with theatrical streamers, balloons, and *fluorescent* spotlights
Offstage, an unordinary and unearthly ensemble is outfitted to perform
And so, we are elated to welcome you to the Warped Circus of Wonder
Find your seats, settle down, and let the acts of *eerie* extravaganza begin

Our opening act is a balancing tightrope walker with talents of trapeze
Nearly skating upon the *thinnest of strings* before executing aerial tricks
Dazzled, the audience does not yet know it, their mortal brains unwise
But what honestly stabilizes our acrobat as she makes her daredevil trek
Are the succulent brooks of blood spouting within the spectator's veins
True surprise dulcifying their *nutritious* plasma with each step she takes
Ideal news for our gymnast, for she is a stuntwoman and a leech-shifter
Dreaming of devouring their burgundy carnage like a greedy mosquito
Before exiting the vast stage, feat finished, to lose herself in red reveries
Platform empty, the crowd's chaotic anticipation is appeased in no time
As minor acts of ventriloquist puppeteers and lofty stilt striders *astonish*
Before the next leading player graces this tent with his ghostly presence
Skilled sword swallower, our trouper strokes the blade along his tongue
Knowing never would the sharpened edge slice into his discarnate flesh
As a betrayal of blood will never pass betwixt the sword and its wielder
For more reasons than one, as this performer is nothing but a *phantasm*
One with a wolfish craving for humans, though that will transpire after
For now, our heartless apparition may look just opaque enough to fool
But *transparent* enough that these showgoers spot his right-hand sword
As it passes his lips, descends his throat and torso and even further still
Until finally, he unsheathes the rapier from inside his unclouded frame
Urging the jaw-dropped crowd into a shell-shocked state as he vanishes
Perplexed yet fairly pleased, duty-bound to erupt into a stilted applause
The echoes of which still endure as the circus's slated break commences

Back from a fleeting intermezzo, a crimson-nosed clown finds his mark
An individual able to induce either childish delight or paralyzing dread
For this clown—with *wildly* colorful costumes and memorable makeup
Bears the badge of Titans, fashioned before the angels, before the devils
Having absconded from Mount Othrys to busy himself with humanity
Now, our clown juggles, unicycles, and pantomimes with *godly panache*
Ostensibly as lighthearted as can be, but after, all will divine that Titans
With hotheaded whims circling their consciousnesses, are anything but
Up next in the program is the contortionist, seemingly without a spine
Reshaping her flexible physique into pretzel-like silhouettes and stances
Almost as shocking as the subsequent baton-twirling artist, just as limber
Yet this performer embraces not one, but two, invertebrate frameworks
As a jellyfish transformer, prepared to revisit her dressing room bathtub
After propelling her modified form into the ring to the melody of *gasps*
And putting her venom-laced tentacles, impatient to sting, to good use
But before that indisposing procedure proceeds, our closing act appears
An ill-boding fellow with flammable kindling lining aberrant intestines
Inlying essence acting as an eruptive lighter, for when he deeply exhales
Blistering flames thence ascend in a chemical light show of persimmon
For this blaze breather, *very familiar with fire*, is a brute of oxidized rust
And the atmosphere is not the only substance our dragon loves igniting
For his pyromaniac tastes stray toward skin and bone, *easily combustible*
And as this matinee comes to a close, actors prepping for the aftermath
Our fearsome beast shall indulge in bodily arson *much sooner* than later

Carnival concluded, our ringmaster thanks this audience with sincerity
Appreciative of more than just their hurrahs—standing ovation and all
And as these close-knit entertainers reappear for *one finishing, fatal bow*
Each undisguised appearance is brought to light as blindsiding encores
Horror follows, as even the trifling, time-filling thespians are unnatural
Puppeteers are amoral centaurs, while stilt walkers are *stampeding* ogres
But by the time far-fetched realization materializes, the damage is done
And as this traveling troupe, always booked, departs to their next town
The bystanders from before, stuck in lifeless shock, are never seen again
Though collagen relics and dermis ribbons clutter the crime-scene floors
Of every last venue the Warped Circus of Wonder *psychopathically* visits

Seraph and Sinner

Evil-doers and empaths, hellers and healers, each more alike than estimated
Grasping gossamers of common ground in spite of intrinsic dichotomy
Uncovering similarities, both riveted by the peculiarities of humankind
Relating over collective beliefs, appreciative of their respective doctrines
But sometimes, these diverse souls beget a solidarity *far more significant*
Fostering the hunger to unite in a hurricane of compassion and cruelty
Like in the atypical instance of a juxtaposing pair of platonic soulmates
Recognizable in each realm, pious or profane, as the Seraph and Sinner

Modeled after a partridge breezing upon photogenic wings of primrose
Hazel shimmers, nearly as nacreous as Aurora, sunrise goddess of dawn
Epitomizing the reverberations of a choir cooing the hymns of holiness
Acolyte of cherubic decorum, yet not immune to the existence of vices
For after all, her stanch counterpart in life takes inhalations of iniquity
Like a contrasting twin flame, Abel—inked with upturned pentagrams
Voyages upon exoskeleton batwings of tar, like a carrion-trailing *vulture*
Probing for verboten mischief, assuaging the terrorizing heathen within
For Abel was once subscribed only to his *heaven-ousted dark anti-Christ*
But when he found Hazel, so too did he find a second being to pray to
Upon meeting, the cordial angel and crude demon identified a kinship
Though their unplanned bond bore no indications of a classic romance
In its place, something *superior* had progressed—a friendship of forever
Hazel and Abel allied in a spontaneous mixture of both sugar and spice
Arms tenaciously linked, they tour parallel worlds when they so choose
Merrily, the Seraph skips beside her Sinner as he achieves heretical feats
Before maneuvering tragic spirits in limbo down to the home of Hades
Just as the Sinner shadows his Seraph as she carries out *moving* miracles
After shepherding extinct souls through the sacrosanct gates of Elysium
Both journeying high and low, never quarreling, merely *elated to coexist*

The sooner paradoxical entities start to emulate one another, the better
For they will thereafter achieve equilibrium within their lacking bodies
As there is no rapture without the inexplicable rot and no life without both
And the occurrence of such polarity upholds necessary natural balances
For denied of duets like the Seraph and Sinner retaining this symmetry
Our fragile universe would lapse into *true chaos for the first and last time*

Enchanted Nesting Dolls

Somewhere within the outskirts of Saint Petersburg, only a world away
Nesting dolls were *first* proposed by one Russian figurine-making mage
Who hand-painted reddened circles atop cheeks, lipstick-coated smiles
And botanical, polychromatic bodies using angled brushes of precision
Before finishing with a spelled varnish, charming each wooden woman
To proffer exceptional presents, like successive revelations of rare magic

When procuring ownership of this imaginative sorceress's bountiful set
Lore states that one must cradle the matron doll, the titular *Matryoshka*
In order to capture the proprietary abilities of witchcraft waiting inside
Shall another come across the swindling dolls without proper privileges
No sorcery shall greet them—a fail-safe the crafting mage made sure of
Within, the matron's *eldest* daughter contributes memory manipulation
Admitting revising access into the instrumental grooves of brain matter
To alter insignificant details or snuff out entire recollections irreversibly
Our next doll sanctions the talents to turn any cuisine or cocktail sweet
Altering curried or caustic aftertastes into only delectably sugared tangs
After such gastronomic gifts comes the imitating of Oleander by touch
Maledicting others through skin-to-skin absorption *as a queen of poison*
With four more figurines to go, our following doll doles out star-power
Infixed with the cosmos-controlling aura of Asteria, icon of falling stars
Our next female, even tinier than the last, bears color-amending boons
Staining the skies cantaloupe and the seas guava, simply by *willing it so*
The penultimate doll displays the mind-melting hurt of reverse-healing
Leasing the user to unstitch sutured wounds or reinstate treated viruses
Making all medication *null and void* like a contradictory nurse of chaos
Lastly, as petite as possible, this daughter bestows favors of summoning
Proposing the chance to beckon bouts of rainfall and sprees of dimness
Or, if archly daring, one may invoke portals to *utterly untrodden* realms

Although each and every nesting doll stocks sorcery of differing degrees
That final figure also offers omnipotence, a superiority not to be abused
Urging the witch who awards these Russian prizes to their future keeper
To affirm they shall never assume the persona of one pining to play *god*
Picking only those who desire control in an otherwise oppressing world
A sentiment the mage, wielder of *illegal* witchery, recognizes all too well

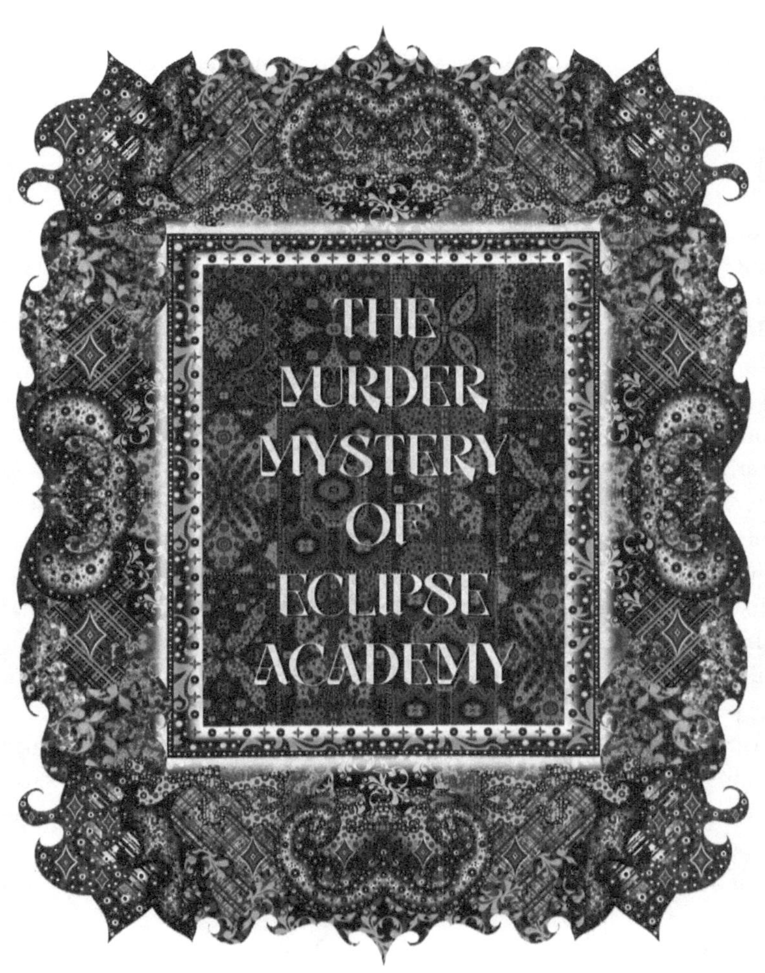

THE
MURDER
MYSTERY
OF
ECLIPSE
ACADEMY

The Murder Mystery of Eclipse Academy

With the culprit clear in the wake of abject murder still sullying the air
A Victorian library—once spouting scholastic refrains of turning pages
Now resounded with the eleventh-hour cries from the freshly departed
Whose swan song bore the *sheer fright* of divining that death grew near
A forecast come true as her insensate frame laid supine in her own gore
Obscuring once unspoiled features like a tableau of disastrous brutality
But let us turn back to the beginning, when motive surfaced in surplus

Radiating a negative energy, the candlelit corridors of Eclipse Academy
A grotesque-decorated boarding school with arched gothic architecture
Remain *perpetually* barren when the vivid vestiges of sunlight withdraw
Only witching hour glooms slither in past stained-glass lancet windows
Before scaling vaulted ceilings—raring to run from these haunted halls
And return to the uncaged *freedom* that such far-reaching ether imparts
Yet inside, chatter circles of what befalls behind student doors each eve
Harsh shanties of rain lashing against the academy's burnt clay exterior
Said to be the sounds of fallen souls rifling for *pulsing* homes to possess
Visions of inflamed torches dimly illuminating the dirgelike institution
Alleged to be the hellborn-hued glare pouring from the eye of a demon
Starved for viscid seas of blood to line black cherry dormitory floorings
All too likely, for since the start of this term, pupils have expired nightly
Flesh incinerated beyond identification and minds liquefied to the max
But the actual mystery is that every disposal developed in the company
Of one of five sixth-form students, making the list of suspects apparent

One: Ambrose, preppy warlock of Siberian frost-channeling capabilities
Lean and long-limbed with a *significant* allowance and extroverted aura
Two: Dalton, dotted grey owl-shifter beneath an average-built earthling
Wholly unsmiling and studious in hopes of soon making Valedictorian
Three: Prue, pintsized yet peppy half-pixie with emotion-sensing magic
With a humor-inclined disposition and persona of pure irresponsibility
Four: Megara, non-mortal vampire, one-quarter gorgon, *effortlessly* cool
Whose silky serpentine hair grips the notice of all without any exertion
Five: Beckett, doubling doppelgänger with the physique of a linebacker
Insouciant and incautious—the type to strike a match upon his tongue
Each not especially close, but all tied together by these strange circumstances

After fraught weeks slog by and unseeing corpses still continue to stack
Each tear-jerking assassination more *allegedly random* than the previous
A dramatic archive of special edition volumes and arithmetic textbooks
Adorned with *ornate* Persian rugs, chocolate divans, and rolling ladders
Houses the quintet of accused academics, as ordered by the headmaster
Both to reduce the current homicidal epidemic by sequestering this lot
And decode, by working together, these disobediences, once and for all

In succession, the crew trickles in through a jet-black basilica-style entry
Ambrose, naturally, arrives promptly, always eager for public exchanges
But in reality, the idea of isolation *agitated his mind more than anything*
Megara and Prue enter jointly, with the latter soaring upon aqua wings
In his human shape, Dalton follows, straight-laced and unfazed as ever
Before awaiting Beckett, late as usual, although that was to be expected
All gathered, the detective work of these potential executioners unfolds
With a brewing deadline, the suspects study the facts and state theories
Yet it remains tough to distinguish *truthfulness*, for each bears incentive
Our half-pixie may have acted out to awaken haphazard pandemonium
A specific mimicker could be ridding any who rat out his rule-breaking
The sapient shifter might slay combative peers gunning for his top spot
Our wintry warlock could be deleting those numb to his likable charm
The vampiric hybrid may have ousted any vetoed suitors *who stood firm*
Nevertheless, guilty or not, these students attempt to acquit themselves
Until termination recurs, even within the confines of the locked library

With a spark, all interior light dies as lightning raids the wuthering sky
Before thunder dins in conjunction with god-awful exclaims of parting
And as the bygone empire chandelier spurs to life, regifting luminosity
Prue and Ambrose's immobile bodies rouse agape *gasps* from the others
For their now offed forms appear cauterized and bloated, irreparably so
Our aerial adrenaline-seeker untowardly electrocuted by veiled voltages
And this academy's warlock drugged by an incognito tincture of toxins
One singed, the other septic; pupils dilated—yet never will they gaze again
Lost to the world of the deceased—populated all the way to the rafters
And so, abruptly, this traitorous collection of five conceivable criminals
Shrinks down to three, coincidently creating a trio rising with suspense

Changing course, the survivors revise their once-elementary hypotheses
Opening up to more *convoluted* ideas involving longstanding vendettas
Or blackmailing ploys on behalf of a vindictive, unspecified sixth party
Megara and our owl-shifter immerse themselves in investigative queries
Assessing coroner's autopsy reports and reviewing crime scene evidence
While Beckett, toiling away to the tempo of an entirely different drum
Develops the impulse to roam in order to ponder with a coherent head
But amid his restless pacing, our doppelgänger halts with a *tortured* jolt
And when, upon feet so unsteady, he pivots to face Dalton and Megara
It is the spiked blade masked as a quill buried in his chest, they see first
And as if the aggregate of his unwary ways has finally snuck up on him
Beckett wordlessly crumples—limiting our group down to a bleak duet

With *only* the shapeshifter and beddable vampire-gorgon left breathing
An impasse ensues, for they remain uncertain of where to go from here
Assured the answers shall no longer be found within forensics or reason
But when upon the ledge of abandoning all optimism, Megara staggers
For the spirits of students past gather to babble in her unexpecting ears
Explaining, with haste, the *sordid* truth of the Eclipse Academy killings
But then, as Megara begs for the library exit to unlock, her body bursts
Each appendage splintering before streamers of flesh rupture in fatality
Ceding to a gory end as the boarding school's death rate *rises once more*
Which places us precisely where we began, with Megara's doleful finale
Except now, further informed, we understand that only Dalton persists
And with the rest of the accused shocked, dosed, stabbed, or detonated
Dalton's inciting incident, leading to such undercover wiles, is exposed

Let us backtrack to the real beginning—when it all *genuinely* got going
One year prior, a normally anti-romance Dalton fell for a sirenic witch
But as is the curse of life, his dearest adored another, a desirable demon
For months, she committed to both—before *delicately* rejecting Dalton
And our owl, having revered something, or someone, besides his exams
For the first time—broke down in an outflow of high-octane heartache
Amid his crisis, Dalton did not mean to send them both to the gallows
No, he treasured his love still, always, but when assailing his hellish foe
Dalton's witch was caught in the crosshairs, *accidentally* silenced forever

Inconsolable after stamping out his darling's life, *miscalculated* as it was
Our scholar absorbed her witchcraft facilities as an unsolicited windfall
Powers which grew devious in nature due to the state of his aching soul
Then, *with nothing left to lose*, Dalton launched a serial spree of carnage
For his witch's untimely demise and resulting despair turned throttling
Like an upheaval of ever-present hail, pelting his spirit with devastation
Until massacring seemed the best outlet to expel such *systemic* suffering
But even congested with grief, Dalton never did divert from his studies
Sitting through university-level daily classes so as not to raise any alarm
And while most of Dalton's evolving magic required necessary nearness
Certain ruinous spellcasting deeds tolerated a much more distant range
And for those murders, our shapeshifter devised *special* feats of framing

Dalton craftily ensured his slayings arose next to a select set of students
And that is when Ambrose, Prue, Megara, and Beckett entered our tale
Inadvertently aiding by diverting attention away from this mastermind
And when these four faulted beings were quarantined inside the library
Our livid villain initiated his concluding, incriminating plan of *revenge*
After all, Dalton's late sweetheart only enrolled at this affluent academy
By receiving a glowing referral from her childhood companion, Megara
Only for Ambrose, social as ever, to introduce the newcomer to Dalton
And Beckett to nonchalantly encourage her to give the shifter a chance
Provoking Prue to tell Dalton where to find his *ex-lover* and her demon
On that momentous day our shifter irretrievably ended their existences
And so, each of these unearthly students were blameless to some degree
But guilty in every sense that a *terribly gutted* Dalton believed mattered

With inactive skeletons spread around him, Dalton becomes burnt out
Raging emotions abated, wrecked heart inert, reprising urges quenched
And pending expulsion followed by *lifelong* imprisonment in his future
Our owl-shifter is left to lapse below waters of seclusion and self-hatred
For not even the earlier safe haven of his education will yield relief now
And so, with effective magic, a tightening noose, and a last-resort tactic
Desperately hoping that maybe his witch will choose him in the afterlife
The library, aghast, detects one culminating loss amid this violent night
As the passageways of Eclipse Academy *gain yet another* mournful ghost

Looking for Love?
CALL
1-800-MATCH
Let this mage fulfill your fate

Matchmaker Mage

To come into contact with compatible beings is to climb to cloud nine
None abide by this creed as consistently as our tender-hearted sorceress
Matchmaker Mage—a maternal middlewoman elected by Eros himself
Antiquated in numeral age—yet entirely, everlastingly youthful at heart
With clients who seek out her skills like longing moths to *loving* flames
Aware of the mage's signature flairs from life-altering newsprint adverts
As other unapprised patrons are simply escorted by her magic's services
Towed through existence by the unobtrusive cables of amorous destiny
For our earthly cupid finds the deepest desires of any not yet betrothed
Maintaining more awareness as an empathetic emissary than any other
Discerning who each uncommitted individual is so intricately suited to
Which personality styles blend the best, which love languages pair well
And which souls should flock to each other just like *smitten* turtledoves
Our Matchmaker Mage collaborates with the fates as cosmic coworkers
Insisting that those meant to be, unanimously ordained, shall converge
Before subtly organizing the meetings of universally prearranged mates
As if they *just so happen* through the powers of impromptu coincidence
But in all truth, these verging lovers encounter due to detailed devising
And the witchcraft within this spell, which makes their uniting feasible

To continue on with ever-so-pining thoughts is to feel incessantly distraught
Drumming hearts hunger for salvation, hankering for sterling reciprocation
But their match has been made long ago, so let these lost souls end their woe
For when suddenly face to face, all pain shall flee as they ultimately embrace

Major merriment magnifies inside our Matchmaker Mage's inner spirit
Whenever the impending couples she situates her steadfast sights upon
Those whose realities shall only sense repletion once *experienced together*
Eventually, all in due course, permanently gather and profess their love
Melding their restive souls, both clawing to be nearer and nearer at last
Doubtlessly emanating mirth of the most sensitive and satisfied variety
Females of fate exclaim into the ether, their choices *very much* validated
But none prevail more pleased than our decidedly self-sacrificing witch
For she exalts the warmth of worship with the force of a pure romantic
So much so, that it remains such a shame, a Grecian tragedy of its own
That our Matchmaker Mage shall find a match for everyone but herself

welcome to
HONEYCOMB
HAVEN

HAZELNUT
INN

Honeycomb Haven

Beneath crimson-and-cream mushroom caps, beings of *pacifism* basked
Safeguarding their flesh from sunrays idly pirouetting across April skies
Limber wings of lilac sparkled with tinsel as fairies frolicked in the park
As the angular ears of elves exulted over the hums of harmonized carols
Parties who bore bantam statues and blushing dispositions calmly lazed
Folding themselves into hammocks cushioned with *ladybug-laden* grass
While deep-sea sweethearts with jewel-toned collages of sea glass scales
Strolled toward unclouded streams, fond of floating as light as a feather
Nymphs scribbled sonnets in cursive scripts as tributes to nature's value
As sprites, creative as ever, reaped ochre petals to craft botanical crowns
Efficiently twisting and nimbly turning like a flowered form of braiding
Patiently placing their presents upon the inclined heads of every citizen
Who resided in this fairy-tale corner of an otherwise vastly vile domain

Extramundane minerals existed within the frameworks of each denizen
For the jaws of fantasy, *of magic*, breathed mythical life into their blood
Though not all were bestowed the luxury, or the labors, of immortality
Souls either swam inside *eternal* inlets, never victim to time's quicksand
Or they skated upon short-lasting winds, speedily sailing toward expiry

Yet the span of their lives, the stretch of their fateful yarn, mattered not
So long as those who backpacked, globetrotting from afar, to this town
Held unprejudiced hearts in unhuman chests beating with benevolence
Whether tongues were as extended as aardvarks or exceptionally forked
Or whether complexions took after claret chili peppers or willow leaves
Honeycomb Haven's *sugar-coated embrace* welcomed every last incomer

A pictorial village of quietude—evermore paused in the midst of spring
Fashioned from the weathered yet *well-loved* pages of nostalgic parables
Where helixes of joy bloomed from kernels of innocence like idyllic ivy
And *flickering* lightning bugs stoked their saffron flames long past dusk
Amid rainstorms, water droplets mirrored transparent grape gumdrops
Just as bouts of breezes carried along the scents of cinnamon and cloves
And swirls of caramel churned inside the stratosphere above the clouds
For the village was *nothing* if not covered in a crystalized layer of charm

Honeycomb Haven sat along the fringes of Stardalia's rural countryside
Just north of the Renva Province, awash with political waves of discord
Just east of the Hellebore District, where *odious* mortal males ran amok
Here, diplomacy was sprinkled in between buttery sheets of democracy
Like envied pastries of peace, leaving tender crumbs of comfort behind
Here, gruff barks of chauvinism and portents of closed fists were absent
Certifying a disarming setting unrestrained by manacles of dictatorship
Free from any vilification and faring well from the floral aura of accord

One by one, while bell-like lines of laughter remained as aloft as avians
Mellow creatures of unearthly descent rose from their relaxing postures
Before taking a twilight walk, greeted by calico cats aplenty on the way
Trailing past glacé bungalows and spiced bookshops of soft gingerbread
Teashops serving toffee brews and tiny theatres promoting play tryouts
Trumpet vines of tangerine and pastel magnolias in potted windowsills
All regarded by every resident, openly rejoicing, with pure appreciation
Until, *like a beacon of escapism*, the town's true treasure inches into view
For the Hazelnut Inn was much more than simply a panoramic pitstop
A *toasted* stronghold manufactured with bulletproof supplies of sorcery
Staged as an ensconced refuge for any in need of genial companionship
With pound-cake-shaded bricks and a cherry-blossom-draped doorway
Bewhiskered woodland darlings, from hedgehogs to leaping cottontails
Shepherded visitors inside, where the floorplan of *perfection* awaited all
Seascape art sourced from the soup saps of blueberries decked the walls
Tufted sofas, as pillowy as nougat, arrayed atop marzipan-dusted floors
Dimmed daylight drifted indoors through cracks in the citron curtains
While confectionary-themed cuckoo clocks sang ballads of saccharinity
Minute dragons thawed their tails by the fireside, cozying into the heat
Gourmet genies dished up sugarplum tarts and tiered pistachio parfaits
And tidy brownies started scrapbooks and embroidered silk tablecloths
Before joining all the others within this *fantasyland abode of amazement*

Always will the village of Honeycomb Haven await more otherkin folk
Just as the Hazelnut Inn will gift each traveler with fudge-flavored care
Granting outcast souls the experience of praline-laced liberation, at last

Flamefell's Inferno

Most kingdoms inspire a tone of open-air awe or metropolitan disarray
Known for savanna atmospheres, canyon terrains, or industrial energies
But some territories, like the cryptically unratified domain of Flamefell
Remain more akin to make-believe mythology than confirmable reality
For while the land exists geologically within a well-populated continent
It lies *in between* the borders, as hidden as the mislaid island of Atlantis
Covered in enchanted shields of indiscernibility to the eyes of outsiders
Leaving very few foreign-born beings the chance to navigate this region
Which Flamefell's loyally loved and pioneering queens make certain of

After a cakewalk election, these long-term friends remain favored by all
Henriette, Incendiary Queen of Audacity—or, simply labeled as Hettie
With cherry-cola bangs under a crown emblazoned by blood diamonds
Reigns beside Colette, Queen of Insight, adoringly referred to as Lettie
Adorning a heliodor circlet atop a slick bun of hazel-highlighted tresses
Denoting her prim yet deadly aura in contrast to Hettie's clear ardency
Following the *unconventional* feat of appointing a pair of parallel rulers
Gained is the gift of fire—once owned by every former Flamefell leader
For in the heart of their hermitic fortress, eternal flames teem with sage
Storing *secrets of the insoluble world,* from terminal cures to Martian life
Whispering of wisdom in a language only presiding royals may decider
Intended to be confined in confidentiality with all their majestic might
But alas, disclosures of this inferno have disseminated through the ages
Generating an inflow of near intruders—hungry for heisted knowledge
Although nonresidents are uninformed of the blaze's bottled-up nature
Aiming to scrutinize acre after acre until pinning down Flamefell's door
Before razing their way through castle halls, rummaging for such rarity
And when the vermillion sparks spew nothing but unavailing nonsense
Surely, they would dispose of those they interviewed, useless at helping
And so, whenever any invaders find, by pure guess, the kingdom's gates
Entirely too close to trampling Flamefell's soil, Hettie and Lettie attack
For their empire may be veiled, but the *sickly* blood of their rivals is not
Opting to bathe in trespassing carnage rather than let their subjects fall
Precisely why these female trailblazers were nominated in the first place
And as the original queens of immortality, so too, will they lead for life
With hearts burning as brightly as the lasting coals of Flamefell forever will

Retirement of a Reaper

Scythe-wielding soul-harvesters remain unmoved by the evils of demise
And Misty, umbrous reaper cloaked in Oxford blue, was once the same
Pawing at casualties with licensed forceps until they entered the *beyond*
As nothing more than gore-sopping ticker tapes of who they used to be
But when Misty located her next soon-to-be victim, out of earthly time
A ripple whirled through the universe, changing destiny—changing *her*
For Orion, bespectacled yet debonair bookworm, unthreatening as any
Appeared almost aureate, as incandescent as his constellation namesake
Dissimilar to the reaper down to his chemical makeup and fleshly form
And yet, Misty was overcome with an emotion she could not yet define
Hyper-captivation halting her from pulling Orion from this living land
When his mortal body still held soft, interstellar-like spores left to emit
And with such alluring purity vaulting off his *seraphic* skin like starlight
Misty could not stomach the concept of her newest and only obsession
Surrounded by abominable phenomena of vegetative despair and death
Within her motherland, rancorously ridded of all that makes him glow

Acting as Orpheus's opposite, our reaper distraughtly nearly absconded
Never to turn around, for Orion made her a believer in granting mercy
Letting our beaming mortal live as she made her way back to her realm
With diamond tears she thought she could not shed drowning her face
Ready to confront the Moirai's fury, unsuccessful for the very first time
But the interest Misty felt within her ageless bones was never one-sided
Therefore, it was only natural that Orion precluded his beloved's exodus
By placing a possessive kiss upon her lips, rough in a way Misty needed
A raving caress that even the undying goddesses gossip about *to this day*
But then, Orion's light flooded Misty's soul—as deeply as it could delve
Until our reaper identified a backbreaking bulk slip from her shoulders
As unseen shackles unlocked, *for no longer was she an ill-famed dignitary*
No, in an extreme twist, Misty became as human as her erstwhile preys
The instant this awareness set in, flippant energy did not greet the ether
Instead, Misty and Orion shared matching sentiments of stark privilege
Fathoming the transcendental importance of their left-field attachment
Our *past reaper* knew she would shortly be called to name her successor
But meanwhile, with her glass finally half full, Misty irrevocably retired
Raring to experience a secular existence by the side of her *shining* savior

A Siren's Finale

Oh, what wonderstruck joy, a deceptive godsend, to heed a siren's song
Like the orchestral genius leaping from lutes pouring, *instead*, from lips
Followed only by the darkest variety of horror within all who take note
A *mortifying statistic* maddening Cressida, so stunning, largely as of late
Sparrow and sea-nymph hybrid with scalloped shells linked to her skin
And oily kelp plaited round her limbs like chartreuse, nautical bunting
A literal knockout, Cressida adorns watercolor scales and sunrise wings
As flaxen as wheat fields tinted with the verve from liquified luminaries
Siren of saltwater, Cressida recalls her first foray peering into the waves
And encountering her enthralling reflection atop the aquamarine water
Only to understand how explicitly eye-catching her outer shell appears
Beauty of brine, Cressida summons the début moment her mouth split
And a perfectly pitched refrain premiered, symphonically drizzling out
Only to fathom how unexpectedly fatal her melodic voice truly sounds
Dragging defenseless mortals to their sapphire-soaked expirations dates
For *far too many* centuries to preserve memories of each of their names
Yet not long enough to neglect the gurgled echoes of their sinking cries
But now, when Cressida discontinues her silence, as she must each day
It is to intone a closing chorus—a deathbed-preceding elegy of apology
Only audible enough for her own straining ears to decipher in penance
And as the tune she recognizes too well ricochets throughout her mind
Those previous reminiscences prick her guilt-ridden psyche, once again
As our siren considers her earliest flashbacks while experiencing her last

Weary of woe, Cressida shall never witness any more excessive fatalities
Luring touch-starved sailors closer, tragically seeing her as their goddess
Only to wreck their ships with sails aplenty upon the rock-strewn shore
Toppled from maritime vessels into the tides, which became their grave
And so, canceling a cycle of undoing, Cressida ends her rueful existence
With a beached sea urchin, our siren *hacks open* her outstretched wrists
Before letting her own lyrics ferry her bloody body below, dying, at last
And because Cressida delivered no heirs and retained no living relatives
Her lineage flits away, and with it, the species of sirens becomes extinct
And while the grieving currents miss embracing their declining victims
The mortality rate of mankind, once unutterable, has never been lower
And this final siren's spirit, once sickened, has never been more *soothed*

189

Griselda's Guide to Palm Reading

Passage from Griselda's Grimoire, chapter VII, page 491, circa 1502:

Like handheld portraits of a person's soul, broadcasting what lies inside
Flawless or furrowed palms shall narrate everything one needs to know
Zealous beginners of witchcraft, prepare to excel in the art of palmistry
A revealing practice of studying the contours and characteristics of skin
In order to decrypt the *unique* particularities of individual personalities
By seeking out these threadbare pages, it shall be safe for me to assume
Magic much like my own, proven ideal for interpreting edifying palms
Courses within your hands, the root from which all *strong* powers stem

Before deducing of any sort, begin by holding the supplicant's open fist
Clutching with deference, showing their flesh is secure in your custody
While nervelessly communicating this enchantment—trusted and true
To view, with charmed and clarifying retinas, what typical souls cannot

Let every bold and blurred feature illume; let their meanings reach me soon
Let my mind probe their spirits deeply; let my lips report their results sweetly

Beholding with explanatory sight, take stock of the client's hand shape
To make a cerebral profile of their persona, *as silhouettes let so much slip*
From spindly air hands of adaptability and sturdy fire hands of alacrity
To gentle earth hands of prudence and gnarled water hands of decency
Such curtailed information shall be spotted before inverting their wrist
Palms now perceptible, where the precise, elaborated-upon data resides
Unalike strokes intersect and evade one another, symbolizing in spades
Extended life lines may predict pristine health and *prolonged* existences
Marriage lines warn of love triangles and herald news involving spouses
Curved lines of mentality expose mounds of intuition and imagination
Fortune and fate lines echo thriving ambitions or incoherent instability
And heart lines suggest the significance and span of future love liaisons
How *truly* tremendous that such innermost evidence, altogether telling
Remains prostrate in an epidermic position of pure vulnerable visibility

Much-loved students, go forth and perform my palm reading teachings
To aid adrift mortals in their self-discovery—as all *noble* witches should

Taxonomy Tome of Fantasy

Beneath superheated desert sands, something slept far below the grains
In the form of clandestine treasure stashed so as to stay secreted, always
But those dreams were demolished for discovered it unsurprisingly was
Exhumed by two archeology adorers on an artifact-scouting excavation
Who, after brushing away *layer upon layer* of earthen grunge and grime
Set gobsmacked faces with enlarged eyes upon a thickly beautiful tome
With a well-preserved exterior of buffed calfskin and gold-leaf lettering
But the rightful *magnitude* roomed within, for upon cracking the spine
Presenting pages of parchment to sunlight after decades in the darkness
Untold chapters of taxonomy records, a completed dossier, laid waiting
Listing *each and every* individual of fantasy like a categorized dictionary
Further, the tome outlined these beings' depictions to the fullest extent
Improved by hand-drawn illustrations shaded with elemental pigments
Based upon credible comments by those who encountered such entities
Followed by published paragraphs stating their *strange or secular* origins
And their powers—be they congenitally inherited or laboriously netted
Before stressing the species *spot-on* fortes, fragilities, and so much more
Now, read on for excerpts from six sections out of the thousands inside

Chimera: Hybrid not just mythological, assembled from varied animals
With the form of a goat, cranium of a lion, and fanged tail of a serpent
As the three-headed son of reptilian idols overseeing rainstorms and rot
The Chimera bore blaze-breathing *mastery* and limbs laced with venom
Maintaining supernatural rapidity alongside a reputation so unnerving
But imperishable she was not, void of life-saving wings upon her frame
Eventually leading to her unexpected passing—impaled by a lead spear
Concluding the Chimera's multi-classified existence in one aerial strike

Werewolf: When the shining view of a full moon bedecks the exosphere
Lupine lives howl into the twilight ether, transforming with primal airs
Initially, the first of their fur-covered kinds were spotted in biblical eras
Bearing biology-defying molecules to shift from man to *clawed monster*
With elevated ocular and olfactory senses and undomesticated instincts
But so too, are these beasts threatened by specified eradicative elements
To debilitate, employ morbidly argent bullets or blossoms of wolfsbane
Both of which shall ensure villages remain safe and locals remain whole

Revenant: Undead corpses revived with a penchant for exacting revenge
Donning death-inciting slices and larva-infested marks upon their flesh
Bolstered by incentives of incomplete business, these spirits *do not* doze
For the witchcraft which renews revenants presents spectral enthusiasm
Yet certain life-related items or rituals shall cease their haunting at once
But be wary, for once exiled, not long shall pass until they revisit, *again*

Hobgoblin: Upgraded humanoid warriors of the most dedicated variety
With the *brawn of ten oxen*, outright athletic and objectively militaristic
Often wielding battered arsenals and sporting inelastic shields of armor
Yet these soldiers also carry clever and controlled, albeit bodeful, guises
With battle-hardened tactics burned into their brains, little stuns them
Innately, every hobgoblin is faithful to their platoon—detrimentally so
For atop the precipice of *brotherly betrayal,* their forfeit will soon follow
Loyal until the end and revered accordingly in the heartsore hours after

Kelpie: Like marine mutations, these water mares hold drowning hopes
Readily shapeshifting between equine silhouettes of heather grey horses
And mostly masculine bodies with manes of algae and hands of hooves
With their aquatic stamina, ferocious vigor, and cryptic coloration gifts
Humans are tempted into cantering outings with *grievous* grand finales
To derail, secure their hoary bridle, subdue until they turn, then detain

Naga: Serpentine creatures staging mortal features from skull to midriff
And rattling facets underneath with polyhued scales like reptilian gems
Not malicious or maiming, only victim to bouts of opinionated hubris
With weather witchery, these beings act as icons of storms and showers
While displaying swirling gazes of reveries and healing skills of recovery
Enraging failings include exposed extremities and rivals of frost and fire
Force a naga onto bone-chilling land; carve open their debilitated flesh
Until rivers of ruby lifeblood flow and flow, until *nothing* is left to spill

No wonder this tome was tucked far away—for in a dog-eat-dog world
Such damning data could prove lethal to jeopardized species of scarcity
Thus, the diggers snapped shut their finding—squirreling it *out of sight*
Never to speak again, publicly or privately, of the prize they left behind

A Saga of Frostbite and Rosebuds

When the last oak leaves of autumn tumble atop millipede-laden earth
And a proverbial frigidity—like a vampire's predictable bite—clocks in
All shall shiver, for the Wintertime Sorcerer has made his annual return
With hibernal undercurrents shading his flesh as if regularly frostbitten
Our warlock holds snowflake-shaped jurisdiction over all things winter
Amending seasonal temperatures until *subzero* digits freeze thermostats
Restraining provincial streams and fishponds to circumpolar standstills
Designing particles of sleet and hail, triggering blizzards and whiteouts
Ruler of climates, chiefly amid December, and yet his greatest attribute
Is the Wintertime Sorcerer's veneration toward his botanical sweetheart
For his hypothermic limbs may be frozen, yet his fiery heart is anything but
Absolutely admiring defines our balaclava-attired sorcerer and his mate
Springtide Witch—a lily of the valley princess of rainfalls and rosebuds
Bears buttercup-tinted skin, peaches-and-cream irises, and blonde curls
But inside, our enchantress is paramount to garnering quarterly growth
Fussing with cyclic policies until external degrees *finally* turn temperate
And planning beside Helios to launch lengthier days and pithier nights
The Wintertime Sorcerer and Springtide Witch—both primeval beings
Occupied each other's spheres always, yet their allegiance was not brisk
Lazily, aboveboard seeds were planted, *sprouting later as petals of passion*
Outwardly, this twosome remains antithetical in every presumable way
Yet their connection, once fully formed, was irrefutable *even to the stars*
Sometimes, one lionizes all they lack, and lionize, this pair certainly do
But the passing of time tarries for no one, not even arrow-struck lovers
Sadly, our wizard and his witch's heart-to-heart's are too often cut short
Once a brassy handbell resonates for their assigned season repeat, again
Part ways they must, a *nightmare* for lovebirds, to attend to their duties
As their vocations, never caving to cliché pleas, are truly nonnegotiable
And while one would voluntarily keep the other company as they work
Essential mages may never linger upon mortal soil amid the off-seasons
Made to visit their land of witchery beside the other furloughed leaders
But then, life's pendulum swings while the metronome musically sways
And the boiling solstice, with sun poisoning and seawater, blazes a trail
For autumnal gourds to enter alongside jack-o'-lanterns and scarecrows
Enabling our Wintertime Sorcerer and his Springtide Witch to reunite
In a starry-eyed hurricane of windchill flurries, budding floras, *and love*

Heartbreak Café

When a first-time patron arrives, reedy jingles of despondency ring out
For the Heartbreak Café is nothing if not a pouting place of pessimism
With *toned-down* two-toned bricks and *melancholic* half-light oil lamps
Where mortal and mystic souls struggling under a bereaving avalanche
All congregate to drown their dogged letdowns in drinks and delicacies
A monochromatic chalkboard menu, automatically reset each fortnight
Pityingly itemizes the apropos offerings—from Lamenting Chai Lattes
And Misery Neapolitan Milkshakes to Crestfallen Butterscotch Coffees
And Anguishing Affogatos, made with bold espresso and mocha gelato
Changelings, rejected gnomes, or humanoids occupy backless barstools
Sipping depressing brews as their tears flow like Acheron—woeful river
And those who fortunately muster some semblance of sporadic hunger
Shall call for baked goods from slate loveseats relevantly cleaved in half
Or wrought iron bistro tabletops engraved with bleeding heart insignia
Before being served everything from *oven-fresh* caramel-filled croissants
Poppy seed puddings, or lemon blueberry muffins with streusel crumbs
To tiny fondant-coated chocolate and peanut butter layered petit fours
Cream cheese with black currant Danishes and macadamia nut cookies
Chewing without any genuine glee, regardless of the culinary sublimity
As their *mourning* minds only backslide to thoughts of their past lovers
For whether a companion axes their relationship or evacuates the realm
That abandoned ache, wounding as a wartime scar, pains just the same
And that horror-eliciting sensation of your soul splitting down the axis
Gluts the ambiance in a film of defeat, felt by *all* who are loved by *none*
At last, the Heartbreak Café's customers deplete their cappuccino mugs
And nibble away at their sweets until plates of pottery hold only scraps
Before shyly branching out to commiserate with other blue individuals
With heavy hearts, relayed sagas are met with sympathetic condolences
And as teatime daylight ebbs, so too does talk of their *tortured* histories
Dormant below reassuring rays of an unpredicted, unsullied beginning
And when the café intuits the impression that *they are truly meant to be*
Once that adrift feeling of ardor reappears, like rotting leaves reformed
French doors open to gently urge them out hand in hand, bill forgiven
But love is erratic, prone to go awry, as this building is all too aware of
And so, much unlike the partners that pushed them here to begin with
When the bell babbles, yet again, the Heartbreak Café takes them back

Bronte's Vampiric Box

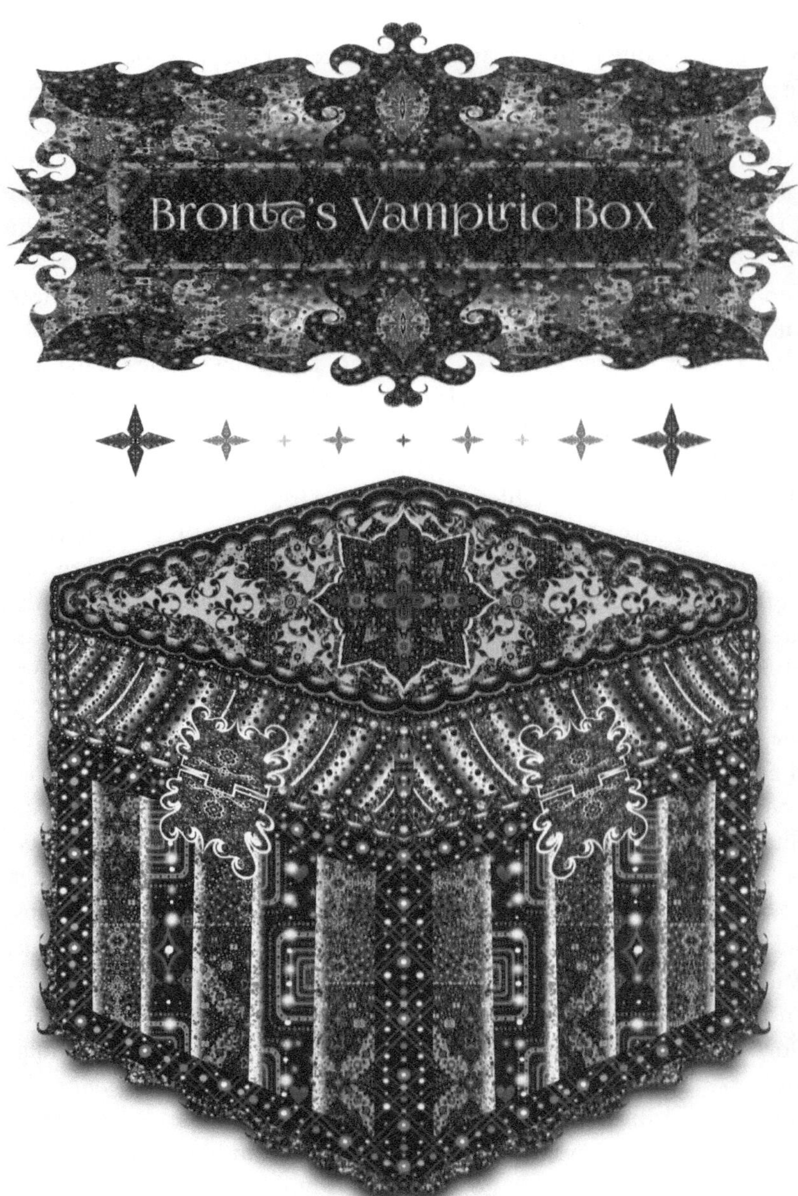

Bronte's Derelict Heart

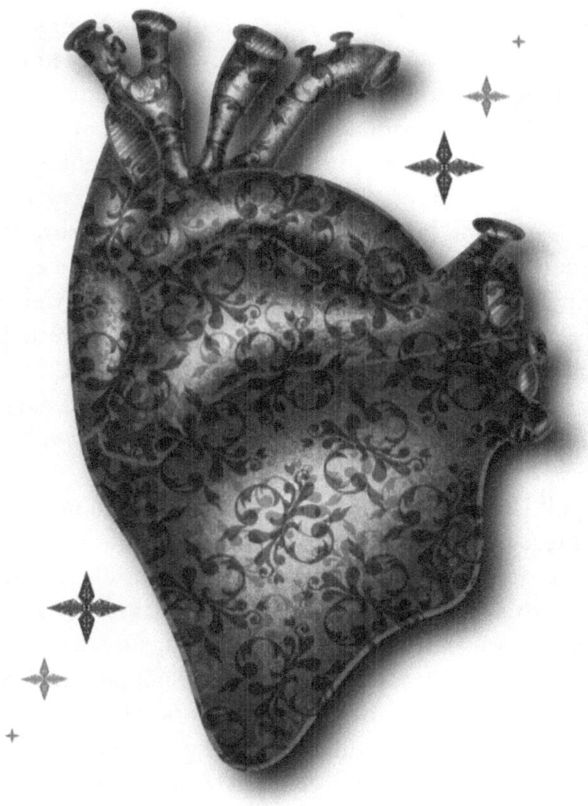

Bronte's Vampiric Box

Believing in no real belief system save for the sanctified glories of blood
Bronte, masculine knave—knowingly handsome in a haunting manner
Enshrines only hemoglobin zests sliding over his tongue—so wantonly
From antlered deer to enfeebled mortals, *our vampire venerates them all*
With a scorched sienna mane dusting his lapel, a thick, unkempt beard
And sophisticated attire of a suit jacket thrown over his solid shoulders
Atop a partially unfastened collared shirt of class, spattered with scarlet
Unsociable, he comes across underneath the *bat-strewn blanket* of night
Bronte's intimidating, if not indifferent, exterior equals what lies inside
For our vampire unplugged his irking humanity many ages ago by now
Disengaging every emotion to center his attention upon only attacking
And with this newly apathetic personality, direct decisiveness settled in
Compelling Bronte to realize he needed his inoperative organ *no longer*
Not to emote, not to love, and, undead as ever, certainty not to survive
And so, our previous cattleman, Southern twang and all, secured a case
Before laying his aortic personal effect atop a cushion of crushed velvet
Locking the lid, setting it atop nutrient-rich soil, and going on his way
But by a twist of fate, or, by the interference of *radically romantic deities*
Darla, long-legged and bright-eyed mortal—far from a shrinking violet
Chanced upon the ornamental box by happy happenstance, amid 1731
Only to immediately set off—longing to locate the deprived titleholder
As avid of a daydreamer as the amative divinities who directed her here
Darla supposes, *wishfully so*, that she was nominated to return this relic
For the thought of a forlorn individual bereft of this cardinal apparatus
Presently unable to feel, *was as heartrending to our Darla as anything else*

Chasing a pull Darla could not define, steered by passionate tendencies
Our mortal recognizes a starless backstreet that for some surreal reason
Darla *knows* is occupied by the owner of this ostensibly misplaced item
Approaching with little self-preservation, she starts to announce herself
But Bronte, with vampiric senses, tersely turns before her lips even part
Confusedly, our monster ponders why he does not lash out on the spot
Snapping at her proximity—naïvely interrupting his nocturnal *devilries*
Or, he muses, why he does not lunge for her gullet, slaking his appetite
Instead, Bronte closes in with the gait of a curious predator—possessed
Certain, *craving* to please, he will grant Darla's plea, whatever it may be

Darla, smiling unswervingly so as if facing an archangel, not an animal
Lifts his *oddly* unlocked possession, *and voila,* our vampire understands
With the beck and call of a lover, Bronte unbuttons his top completely
Baring a hulking chest that Darla regards for several prolonged seconds
Before unsheathing a katana blade—strapped upon his back for slaying
But tonight, Bronte shall not wield his steel against anyone but himself
With a few well-placed scores, his unoccupied thoracic cavity is opened
Imploring this mortal to reinsert his organ—*oddly* inept at denying her
Yearning to pluck his ribs from their cage, play them for her like a harp
But as Darla, burgundy staining her bare hands, clutches Bronte's heart
Affectionately stationing it between his lungs and beside his breastbone
Something of the most unconventional sort takes shape—just like that
Unorthodox enough to, admittedly, alarm a centuries-year-old creature
Like a jittery jackrabbit, *the heart of Bronte surges from his torso's opening*
Landing within the warm-blooded embrace of Darla's outspread palms
And with only a trace of interstellar intervention, realization reconciles
For strangers they are not, but *written-in-the-cards mates* they surely are
Meaning Bronte's heart is under Darla's ownership—always and forever
And although our vampire's organ was once as lifeless as the rest of him
Like a snare drum, it begins metrically beating in her hold, *finally home*
Bronte, torso perversely agape and mind spinning out with possibilities
Fathoms that while he may not require his heart to physically persevere
So too, does he not need it preserved inside his sternum in order to *feel*
For these Darla-related sentiments, once exclusively concerning plasma
Are none other than the touchingly free-flowing trappings of loyal love

Before each dogmatic god and goddess awakened for the very first time
Bronte and Darla's destiny was decided, for the stars crafted them both
Placing our mates upon dual roads to meet—and meet they luckily did
Heart palpitating in her hands, *love* pitter-pattering inside her anatomy
Darla shines—honored to clasp this restored cardiac relic, ad infinitum
So long as her vampire, to hell with bloodlust, stays by her side all the while
And Bronte, ashes of humanity rekindled, emotionally available, at last
Feels more than flattered to oblige, keen to remain as close as a parasite
For he is a non-believer no longer, now converted into a holy celebrant
Adulating at the altar of her mortal form *until doomsday deigns to dawn*

Ultimatum Liasson

Amid a stormless, summerlike golden hour reading novellas of *romance*
Unsought company appears in the form of a fleshless underworld beast
Most certainly a carnea—a skinless species of laid-bare brawn and bone
Employed as an *Ultimatum Liaison* by the lieges of a hell-adjacent land
Having glided higher and higher still to reach the realm of humankind
Before appearing astride dear Dulcie—fair-faced damsel of only sixteen
With meager drops of elven influence treading beside her mortal blood
Yet not enough to impart immortality, urging this fiend to offer Dulcie
Either a positive lifecycle or a painless coda, but *most definitely not both*
Should Dulcie select an existence so blithesome, high spirits shall result
Our maiden's fancies forever fulfilled with *plenty* of profitable prospects
Just as her chalice shall always run over with arousing and amiable love
All while dwelling within a dream cottage of pale yellow and soft plum
But then, seventh heaven stolen away, a ghastly conclusion would arise
Held below the perpetually convulsing River Styx, engulfed repetitively
Before facing burning rebirth, for only then shall her actual abuse start
But cherubic Dulcie needs never to endure that type of torturous finale
As there lies a *second* route, just as available and achievable as the initial
Alternative number two decrees that our mortal's reality shall be toilful
Flush with *disgruntled* years of monotony, bereft of employment boons
Out-of-sorts amid sickbay fits of illnesses and organ-failing impositions
Deficient, Dulcie's days shall be, of spousal sweethearts and sisters alike
Nevertheless—just like the allaying calm following a long-lived scourge
Our darling damsel would be presented with a therapeutic exit of *peace*
Breaths noninvasively deprived as her heart draws to an unworried stop
Before sailing into the unheralded joy of the carnea's non-wicked world
Where a private chamber of calla lily décor and bedside bonbons looms
Wrapping her translucent physique in an ambiance of leisurely warmth
Where humanitarian and horned handmaids see to Dulcie's every need
A far better fate than *anything* befalling in the empyrean afterlife above

Weighing each critical option for hours upon end, Dulcie's head whirls
As the Ultimatum Liaison, uncaring of this catch-22, awaits her answer
Perking up only when popsicle-hued lips part to utter her choice at last
Setting the seal upon her destiny with accessories of ataraxia and agony
Both expected to ensue, yet the question remains, *which shall come first?*

ESTATE
OF
DESIRE

Estate of Desire

Previously, all that was lacking within the indecent Temptation Empire
Remained a site for salaciousness to be acted upon, like a *lustful* temple
For those whose X-rated whims grew too ambitious, aching to be sated
And so, the Estate of Desire was hence erected in the region's midpoint
A guiding light of suggestive longings, whose very outer shell intrigued
Seemingly *taboo*, yet nothing is as immodest as the acts executed inside

Cast in low, thematic lights to deepen the mood, rays of romance loiter
For passion breeds indulgent familiarity—impossible to evade affection
Alongside tokens of love, the atmosphere tides with aphrodisiac stimuli
And the environment is fueled by the ache-inciting spores of coriander
Just as each wall shows off pornographic frescos of the hypersexual sort
Depicting explicit activities as erotic as the events arising down the hall
Enter the grand room, aromatized with titillating patchouli and saffron
Where uncensored creatures in the *throes of vulgar deeds* throb for more
And the Estate of Desire provides, like a brothel where payment is void
For all members pine to confer pleasure before ever receiving their own
With consent aplenty, willing satyrs and fae indulge their physical pleas
Just as other excitable species *entertain* nearby, their moans overlapping
Genders and genus's glossed over, as such designations are so confining
Ghouls engage in trysts, *all the more appealing*, with mud-made golems
As feminine kitsunes with underfed libidos bed well-endowed vampires
Yet none arrive as worked up as the Temptation Empire's native citizens
With sexual appetites as bold as cannibalistic wendigos—rabid for flesh
The succubi and their incubi foils, paranormal beings of *pure* seduction
All congregate to share orgasmic stories of swallowing flavorsome souls
Before *heartily* participating in the Estate of Desire's obscene endeavors
Lapping at erogenous, unclothed skin until starved to sample, yet again
Dying to consume the estate's mind-altering narcotics and moonshines
Amplifying filthy sessions; and once ingested, heightened they truly are
If only other civilizations could be so overtly liberated in their sexuality
And uninhibited in their tragically scarce interludes of risqué indulging
Perhaps bloodshed, maniacally unethical and needless, might die down
And intolerant discrimination, fruitlessly abhorrent, may be minimized
For intoxicated upon arousal, everything else, from mayhem to murder
Comes off, in the most lascivious of manners, as so *unimportant* indeed

Juniper's Resistance Daquiri

Master of mixology, self-trained in the division of *special-order* libations
Juniper, bartending sorceress of merely twenty-six youthful years of age
Remains largely acknowledged for her fruit-forward Resistance Daquiri
A defending brew of banishment aimed against every type of detriment
Combating the solely sensuous manipulations of vampiric compulsions
Contesting stares of stone flowing from the pupils of snakelike gorgons
Countering the *ship-wrecking* choruses sung by criminal seashore sirens
While repelling any earthly or ether-based maleficence—aiming to end
Exempt from pneumonia amid the cold or heat fatigue amid the reverse
Just as poison ivy cannot infect digits and cacti barbs shall not rip flesh
So too, can this charmed cocktail ward off viruses cancerous to mortals
Shielding thin-skinned bodies from finicky perils or fatal maladies alike
Just *a single sip* and immune to any injury, Juniper promises all shall be

To rustle up this tonic, our sorceress muddles high-quality ingredients:
One scoop of pixie-sourced sugar, four pears poached in melon liqueur
Nine strawberries from berry-producing fae courts and five mint leaves
When *thoroughly* puréed together, Juniper blends splashes of white rum
With one finishing ounce of lime simple syrup for lemon-leaning tangs
Ensuring the potion adopts the acidity suggestive of a vacationing treat
So toothsome, patrons *savor* the flavor as much as they await the magic
Concoction complete, Juniper speaks words of witchery atop her drink
To suffuse the citrus-spiked beverage with abiding atoms of her sorcery
Until the results of imbibing end with *discarnate perks* of built-in armor

Once the liquid runs down their throat, commence my offsetting antidote
Secure destructible skulls and survival; deter all harm with endless revival

When nothing hazardously amiss attacks, the invocation has succeeded
And although Juniper *always forewarns* of the incapacitating side effects
None heed her counsel, entirely too keen for the relief of real resistance
Our sorceress's advice only harkening back to dash through their brains
Once understanding that though barriers from spiteful entities endures
So too, does a *numbing force field* firmly enfold their fortified existences
Until, as Juniper's cross to carry, they are left desensitized to everything

Mother of Mirages

Somewhere within a backcountry clearing, floodlit by sunbeam flickers
Bellflowers and milkweeds sway to the tune of slumber-inducing winds
While wild figs and merlot grapes prosper and miniature rabbits *prance*
But then, the vista's beautified edges, now indistinct, begin to implode
And every floret, fruit, and fauna glitches—turning *so* horribly haywire
For what appeared as concretely authentic was simply a sightly illusion
Woman-made by a female soul of fraud, named the Mother of Mirages
Brought into this world by fantasy forces yearning for a taste of novelty
As an original creature with suspicious trickery behind a striking façade
Look closer; note her mannerisms, *eerily mechanical, entirely methodical*
Mortal she is not, for how could any humanity cope in such a skeleton
With empathetic embers reduced to charcoaled rubble soiling her heart
And offbeat bone marrow fouled by the inexhaustible seeds of ill intent
For when birthed from brimstone, our deceiver gained *avant-garde gifts*
To design and deliver lifelike visions, just as her misleading title implies

Mirage: a visual display of pretense, according to the universe's glossary
Laboriously customized to match a mortal's *characteristic flights of fancy*
By tailoring cross-stitched patches into the malleable canvases of minds
Threading realistic fibers over and over until awe-inspiring images arise
Like sprawling moors of shamrock *magnetism* rousing unruffled arcadia
Shoreside sceneries reflecting roseate sunsets upon the bedazzled waters
And majestic flairs inside a twenty-four-karat château of total opulence
Once snared by the Mother of Mirage's sticky web as prey of proximity
Reproachable magic plays upon credulous consciousnesses and corneas
Never protesting as they perceive their personalized views with wonder
But by the time their vision belatedly adjusts after days lost in her scam
And comprehension settles in through slight malfunctions, *strange blips*
Or allusive inconsistencies with the reality they know not matching up
That the mirage is merely that, *a false trance of delusion*, it is far too late
For the Mother of Mirages, employing skills of the most conning strain
Competently detains all weeping victims inside their synthetic illusions
Held within an optical dreamscape only their enlightened eyes may see
And though the gardened landscapes and grand reveries amazed at first
Presently, each captive of this untrusting being only begs to break loose
An unviable wish not even the greatest of genies could ever manage to grant

Unseelie Heiress

How long before thorns bloom within a skull where rosettes once grew
After destiny is spoken into the stillness of the solemn, darkening ether
As it turns out, nearly no time shall pass for petals to convert to poison
Falling to the floor of tragic minds, *reduced down to only remiss remains*

At the very core of the Nemerosa Kingdom, the Malumive Court leads
Comprised of Unseelie fae with bad-natured devices and beastly values
Itching to inflict unmendable incisions and impose *psychological* insults
Yet such desires extend to royalty, for within the artillery-packed palace
Lives the *rightful*, predatory heiress, Parisa—like a winged black widow
With carbon copy aircraft limbs and mint-condition purple-hued flesh
Offset by lithesome attires of jewel undertones and beaded body chains
But beyond such beauty lies sociopathic favoritisms and hexing powers
And since Parisa remains reasonably youthful, in terms of fae shelf lives
Our heiress *often* ponders what the existences of her relatives resembled
Before the divinities of fate, or truthfully, the donors of fortune, struck
Nemerosa once bore purity, just as decent as the Seelie beings from afar
Until change arose, not by maledictions or microbes, but an astral shift
For even the most unearthly souls are not immune to cosmic invasions
In one mutative spell, the kingdom's residents became indomitably *evil*
Bearing blackened hearts as baleful as a raven's aura and serrate as a saw
And thus, the Malumive Court lodging the first Unseelie fae took form
But the joke rests upon the celestial idols who attempted to assail them
For malice energizes the spirits of each denizen to a greater, graver level
Reformed for the better, just like their territory of shadows and severity
Thieved of sunlight to sustain *desiccated* soil, never to sprout lilies again
Yet to twisted fae, such terrain appears sublime, like a forbidding haven

Parisa, brimming with regal vice, imagines embracing internal goodwill
Not only surrounded by Eden-rivaling ethics but holding virtue within
But then, shaking away such reveries, Parisa recalls her love for anarchy
For an Unseelie fae is who she fundamentally is and all she has ever known
And our scion pines for the day when an heiress she becomes no longer
Promoted to Queen Parisa, gifted an egregious diadem of enemy bones
Decked in as much adversary plasma as her precursor—maybe more so
For she is nothing if not a deviant dreamer, shooting for the sinful stars

Pandora's Requiem

How *drearily* dehumanizing to be devised for such exploitive specificity
Not produced to desire or dream, but only to serve another's ambitions
What a labyrinth-like mind maze to navigate through the dour statistic
That one bears creators in such a manufactured, ceremonial sense at all
A reality the initial female to stride upon mortal soil knows far too well
Pandora, Grecian celebrity, acquired an affinity to clay-sculpted golems
Both molded into whichever distinctive form their makers so preferred
Commissioned by a punitive Zeus, Pandora was crafted by Hephaestus
Shaped from land and seawater, granted breath by a foursome of winds
Bestowed a medley of godly gifts from Aphrodite, Hermes, and Athena
Though *the cryptic cherry on top* was the pantheon king's present of a jar
Yes, jar, not box, no thanks to an altering mistranslation made long ago
Preserving strife, turmoil, and sickness and fatality, disgust, and famine
Snapped shut to begin, but eventually, Pandora's nescient curiosity won
Urging our original woman to uncertainly lift the lid of her riddling jar
And while others protest, they certainly would have done the *very same*
According to Pandora's mythical fable, her inspective act damned Earth
Unloosing devilry and distrust into the realm, though only allegedly so
For epic poets of the male variety love blaming the other sex for everything
Alleged feminine perpetrators of villainy, as if menfolk are such seraphs
And yet, what our Pandora *so wishes* all readers of her saga will consider
Is that she was awarded such sparse volition amid her atypical existence
In fact, as a pawn in the games of gods, she was given no volition at all
And so, what lowly soul could scorn her for making a choice when able
If Pandora's parents gave her free will, why should she not have used it?

Inevitably immortal as she remains, Pandora's malaise did not disappear
Alongside the finishing mutterings within her unforgettable mythology
Epimetheus's reluctant wife lives on, beset by the ennui of her actuality
As all Pandora was created for has now *melted* away in the days gone by
Zeus's indiscreet reckoning and rage toward Prometheus long forgotten
And the virid world of humanity *long* adapted to its jar-given additions
Pandora is left to serenade herself into a hopefully eternal stasis of sleep
A lovely, yet lamenting, requiem dedicated to a life she will never know
For her birth was plotted, matrimony arranged, appearance plagiarized
But in slumber's fantasies, Pandora may be *whoever* she so wants, at last

Desperate Devotion

Seasons turned their elemental pages, beginning familiar chapters anew
Torrents did not loiter in the stratosphere, rain falling as fiercely as ever
Storms waged rowdy wars against soft-toned stints of summer placidity
For Mother Nature's timetable withstood when virtually all else did *not*
After an *uncalled-for* apocalypse, with the majority of life mowed down
Continuing reality's play, a resulting act of depressive dormancy ensued
Yet the corpses of elves and ogres lining acres of sullied mud were proof
Of *the climactic coup de grace* that transpired atop this once kinetic land
And while the skies, insufferably inert, were invaded upon by an illness
Of the paranormal breed, haunting atoms of prominence before killing
A pair of disregarded souls, somehow, someway, persisted through it all

Within this defeatist region, the geographical receiver of unbidden fate
Traumatized, the last remaining civilians clung to each another, closely
Just like failing coals begging the anemic glimmer they grasp to remain
Lennox, burly offspring of dragon shifters, *powerless* until his evolution
And Camille, elegant nature-idolizing nymph bearing negligible magic
Each ambled all alone amid the conscience-stricken fallout of surviving
Unable to abscond to a sardined kingdom undamaged by the epidemic
For the exiting bridge buckled in one final deed of *damning, dire straits*
Leaving these two crippled by cheerlessness until they saw each another
Tides of icy incredulity then *relief* sluiced over their overwrought bones
Leading Lennox and Camille, a unit now, to inhabit a derelict domicile
Where they fixed simple suppers, sharing their day-to-day's from *before*
Only to spend nights trading progressively suggestive words of wanting
And after an age—both athirst to feel alive when bordered by such loss
A semblance of love arose, *shivering and sobbing*, born not from passion
But lit from the kindling of desperation, averse to abandonment, again
And although the conditions of how their romance initiated felt forced
The sentiments Lennox and his nymph shared were founded in fidelity
Yet doubt surfaced, inquiring if relocation to far-off places was possible
With hundreds, thousands, *millions* of beings, would their love outlast?
But as time stole by and ardor only amplified, they knew, yes, it would
For desolation became contentment, which *escalated into candid elation*
And only inside the dear margins of Lennox and Camille's relationship
Did these lovers *hope*, an emotion they believed forever lost with all else

Silverlark's Twilight Soliloquy

As revered witches of the *highest* order, sworn into the Silverlark Coven
Guided by Grecian goddesses or mortals with invocations in their veins
We hold a hallowed rite below the tenebrosity of twilight's grey satellite
To praise the deities who soaked our gore in their own *wells of witchery*
Exposing eternal gratitude for the aids they endowed unto our marrow
Certifying their titles and tales shall never be lost to the ravages of time
Allied by the resilient fibers of feminine energy and sheer enchantment
We honor Hecate, Pasiphaë, Circe, and Medea by burning holy votives
To shine upon obligatory altars and abundances arranged for every idol
Awarding divinities with the idiosyncratic attention they *severely deserve*
We embark with the necromancy expert, Hecate, goddess of witchcraft
Torch-employing patroness of spirits, divine arts, sorcery, and darkness
Prayed to atop a platform with her signature crest of triple lunar shapes
Beside hand-carved symbols of disastrous snakes and gate-opening keys
For Hecate, we bestow currants, blackthorn, and cinnamon as homages
Before shifting gears toward gossip-inducing, Pasiphaë, Queen of Crete
Daughter of Helios, bride of Minos, and experienced mistress of magic
For Pasiphaë, we decorate a sacral space with bull-themed iconography
Further adorned with fresh floral laurels and spring water jugs to entice
Moving along, for the stars will soon scatter, we remember exiled Circe
Island sorceress of *comeuppance* with an affinity for pig-altering potions
For Circe, we sculpt a dedicated circle closed in by stems of snowdrops
Finished with flasks of red wine, honeycomb slabs, and shells of the sea
Intended to appeal to our goddess's coastal home and Hellenic heritage
We flaunt our finale by paying tribute to princess and priestess, Medea
Witch of charms and conjuring, progeny of Aeetes, prior lover of Jason
For Medea, a Wiccan-made bench bears fatal plants and poisonous fare
Decked with tailored presents of alcohol, milk, and blood, all to gratify
With each altar outfitted with offerings, the flairs of our sorority merge
As we utter a supernatural soliloquy when the cosmos mimics melanite
To receive the notice of every storied matron in true, submissive *thanks*

In the dawn-brewing wake, the warmth in the air surges to welcome all
As Hecate and Medea, Circe and Pasiphaë, make their presence known
Receiving their custom bounties with *full-hearted* appreciation and awe
Such thankfulness fueling our fountains of witchcraft just as we wished

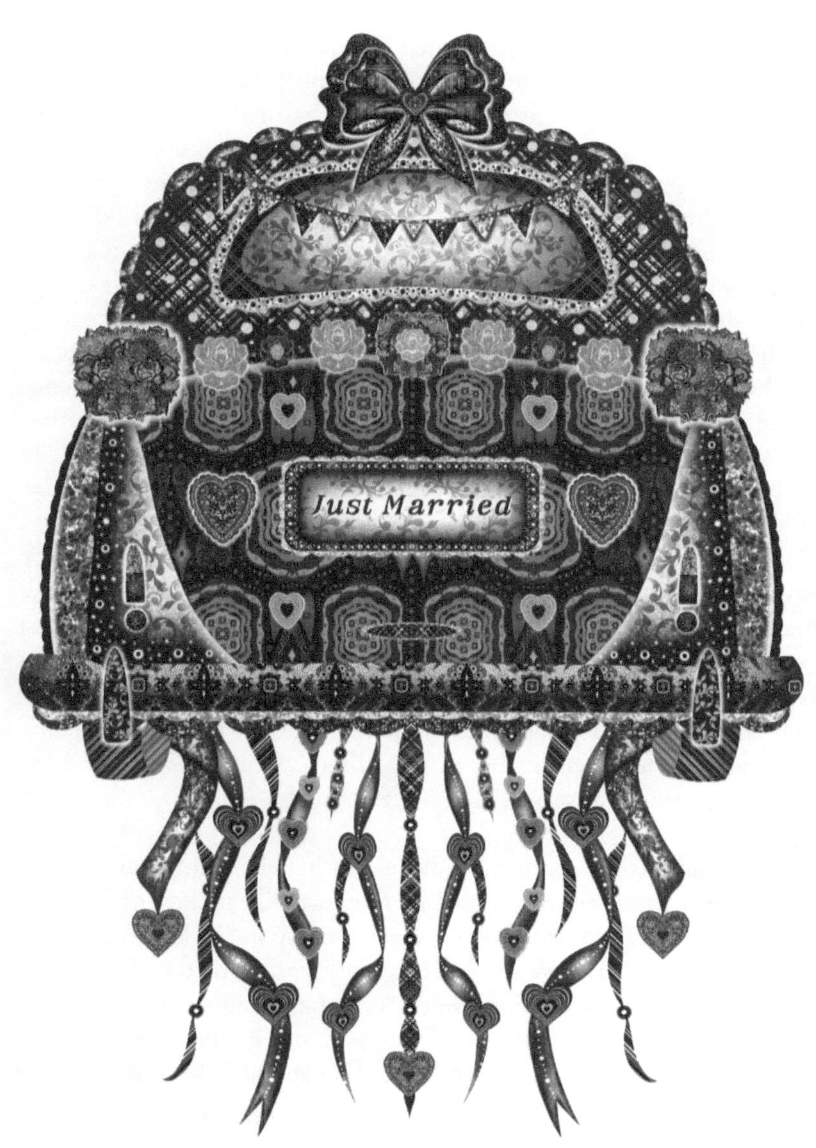
Just Married

Weeping Widow

Like diamond dewdrops clinging to wild roses, so too does death loiter
Intent upon instilling the stale stench of defeat into souls and sceneries
And yet, the faint afterlight of affection, deeply intimate and impelling
May imitate the reaper's intruding presence, harrowing as it is hopeless
For sequences of passion and passing *too* often end in epilogues of grief
And so, requiems of late suitors mixed with crestfallen notes of casualty
Dwell within charcoal-centric graveyards and plots of roach-ridden dirt
Which a female figure—bandaged in the unmistakable gauze of aching
Gingerly deposits atop the casket of her newly deceased, dearest spouse
Velvet-sheathed hands move solely from the miracle of muscle memory
For her brain rests in a consciousness-muddling catacomb of mourning
But her body recollects this deed of farewell with *well-versed* experience
Divining the juncture between heaven and havoc better than any other

Weeping Widow, the out-of-luck embodiment of everlasting heartache
Whose spirit constantly steeps inside a porcelain teapot of bereavement
With starless locks swaying down her back like seas of softened licorice
And tear ducts shining with waterworks as vivid as constellations above
Flashes of soul-sucking sorrow spew forth from her heavy-lidded frame
For although she decorates her flesh with vintage gems and luxe textiles
No amount of appeal—from a craveable mouth to an exposed neckline
May mask the plumb dolefulness pestering her once ensorcelled energy
Like Persephone lamenting her lack of liberty when Jack Frost awakens
So too does this widow pine after her ex-partners—*time and time again*

Many midnights ago, on the awaited eve of her eighteenth day of birth
Blinded by the *joie de vivre* roused by romance, like flickers of fondness
An ill-natured hex of hard feelings descended upon her lovestruck form
Pushing this reincarnated deity of relationships, a paragon of addiction
To remain within the merciless spiderweb of a widow's curse, evermore
Lumbered with the ineffable uphill battle of losing every beau she weds
Tying the knot just to be torn apart by claws reaching from the afterlife
Yet, the idea of being daydreamt about by another calls to her, *even still*
And while the widow knows tragedy shall befall like a Euripides drama
Down the aisle she drifts, securing her fiancé's fate with each pained step

On and on, the Weeping Widow, repeated customer of betrothal's lure
Finds her worshiping skeleton decked in a hand-stitched gown of glory
With a multitude of moonstones sutured atop tiers of celebratory satin
Trimmed with conventional designs of lace, lined with spools of taffeta
Stained stark white, the undefiled shade not quite yet sullied by demise
Though, as the sun is pulled across the sky and the ceremony continues
Greyed grows the hue of the widow's dress as her violet bouquet withers
And the minute their marriage is formalized, tenderly uniting their lips
Monsoons of ebony engulf the fabric's pigment, foreshadowing disaster
As chapel wedding bells echo in a *low-spirited* tune of terminal tremors
All the while, a runoff of rue hurries down this brief bride's rouged face
As her emotions spar, wrestling between savoring this devoted occasion
And keening for her condemned groom before *hell upon earth* embarks

Flaunting distressing velocity, death slays, absent any hint of hesitation
Nicking pivotal breaths of husbands until only *untenanted shells* remain
Forcing the lone Weeping Widow to recite yet another elegiac goodbye
Removing her latest pearly ring, setting it beside all the oxidized others
Pillowed within a memorial chest of remembrance made for past lovers
And then, with her fourth finger bare and her mind entombed in strife
Raggedy becomes her onyx gown, sulking through town amid nightfall
Yet despite racking wails, marking the onset of another age of infelicity
So too, does this jilted wife realize regard never loses its luster once lost
For casualties as callous as this merely inflate the intensity of exaltation

And so, with only stellar moonlight as a sidekick amid moping outings
Unconsciously, this widow combs for a currently respiring fiancé-to-be
He who she may empty the contents of her sidelined commitment into
And since the universe obsesses over *entertainment*, time does not delay
Before flinging the former bride into the strong arms of one more mate
As her blood, full of rectified pep, froths to the beat of wedding hymns
Until, in an expected curtain call of expiry, this cursed streak carries on
For adversity is *engrained* in the very veins of this evanescent newlywed
Just as the driving need to find Cupid's inebriating scent spurs her soul
Leaving the Weeping Widow's heart-shaped tears to steadily fall, *forever*

Sovereign of the Scarlette Rainforest

Red denotes a *dearth of finery*: poinsettias and rubies and pomegranates
So too, does it remain the pre-painted hue for that which fuels survival
Or, should the shade meet the ether in *excess*, that which shall end lives
But in the equator-nearing Scarlette Rainforest, hellishly humid biome
Tones reminiscent of winterberries never seem to be deficient in supply
Inside this tropical sanctuary, macaws dive underneath treetop parasols
Traversing the sauna-like atmosphere—tinted with chili-colored vapors
Matching each plant, from carnations to camellias, and each claret tree
Featuring uncharacteristic bark inlaid with rows of carnelian gemstones
In the forest's heart, a mossy throne built into the base of a cacao trunk
Seats the anaconda-protected, reigning queen of all fairies in her region
Like Mother Goose to her subjects, *yet monstrously grievous* to all others

Displaying darksome delights, Queen Mab both tantalizes and terrifies
To wax poetic using basic terms of beauty would be an understatement
As even the most impervious of beings or beasts are always taken aback
After noting her moiré wings whirling with garnet and grape *iridescence*
And nape-grazing locks fading into saturated fig at the never-dead ends
Lodging an oxblood headpiece of branches and blossoms, barbs and all
Even our monarch's fanciable face outshines ten thousand twilight stars
Devastatingly aglow with sparkling eyelids and shimmering cheekbones
But what fire-breathing and flesh-eating souls recount round this realm
Are Queen Mab's inborn competencies, fragranced by fumes of copper
For she remains a blood-bender, harnessing fortes of plasma persuasion
Gifted with a mind that forces gore to bear flames or freeze in its tracks
Before extracting the interior sap through throats or tear ducts, entirely
When facing opponent species of *subterfuge* orchestrating to overthrow
Our crowned fairy hijacks cells of wine and white, draining every drop
Until disruptive ilk no longer pose any peril, utterly unfilled as they are
With spirits yanked below, confiscated blood marinates the forest floor
Guzzled by burnt umber topsoil and hibiscus roots like porous sponges
Dashing then upwards to exacerbate the florid dye of flowers and fungi
Before treading the air, platelet-filled molecules afloat, like rosé bubbles
Adding to the rainforest's *without-respite* mist, dousing bugs and brutes
A sight Queen Mab hails as she remains settled atop her splintered seat
Waiting to gauge if her next guest's visit will end in peace or *persecution*

Hexdella's Infernal Key

Should ever one question why only honorable witchcraft runs rampant
Concoctions and charms and conjuring so rarely force-fed with villainy
The *veiled* existence of the mage-made Infernal Key remains the answer
With surreptitious beginnings founded by the most offensive of covens
A criminally charmed trinket of blanched, unbreakable bone was hewn
Slot the elaborate skeleton key into *any* lock, be it a dresser or doorway
And the knee-deep in knavery, elusive entry, missing hinges or handles
Materializes all at once, inviting the user inside where fallible beings *fly*

Step into Hexdella, diabolic world comprised of smoky star garnet caves
Where preeminent covens of defiant enchantresses, both fresh and frail
As immoral as torture-talented devils of the abyss, maybe even more so
Practice strictly prohibited forms of witchcraft with unfettered freedom
As their inner abilities would prove *far too* concentrated and calamitous
For the ever-so-delicate soil of humankind's precarious realm to handle
As these mages never pull from the magic reposing underneath the dirt
Wholesome and warm, given as a do-good boon from the environment
No, what streams inside umbral veins is instead netherworld-originated
And that befouled impiety merges with the offered prestige of cessation
For the *funereal* reaper remains their timeless teammate throughout life
Just as demonkind, kindred characters to all nonconformist spellcasters
Invest obliging slivers of their powers in return for a lasting partnership
All black-hearted donations of borrowed witchery dwell in a water hole
Nearly never-ending, sat within the bull's-eye, the very core, of Hexdella
Erected to house tides of dodgy occultism rather than natural rainwater
One after another, each witch crowds to pull up pails of unlit barbarity
Returning so many a time, never quite satisfied in their search for *more*

Within the chasmic lands of Hexdella, the Sanguinary Coven converge
Verbalizing contraband cognizance incantations of cranium-tampering
While the Spectral Coven, necromancy *experts*, revive eliminated spirits
And the voodoo-studying Scarring Coven craft with cursing intentions
All to say that around each bend in this realm, godless sorcery succeeds
But should the depravity turn too despairing, *suffocating in its sinfulness*
Fleeing remains futile, for the Infernal Key, once splendid, now sinister
Only operates in *one* direction: adept at arriving, yet inept at departing

Rock-Shackled Romance

Weep for poor Prometheus in hopes that such tears, salted as anchovies
May be *swept up* by the immaterial arms of a sympathetic August wind
And splashed his slanted brow—a jubilant balm amid a lamentable life
For this god of fire, a first-generation, lenient Titan laden with *foresight*
Defied the deities by providing frozen humans with the favor of flames
And as revenge, for Zeus never could stand to be snubbed or surpassed
Godly sedatives paralyzed Prometheus, who was then shackled to stone
Unable to retaliate as a mammoth eagle, feral with famine, visited daily
Wolfishly chewing through abdomen tissue to swallow his rallying liver
Cementing a cyclical reality, one he thought once would *never conclude*
Yet even still, Prometheus would never come to regret his transgression
For not even Hephaestus, another ablaze icon, once considered sharing
And if all the other gods, from Apollo to Poseidon, wanted for nothing
Why should mortals, brittle from birth, be built to want for *everything*

Agonized, awaiting the eagle's return, Prometheus receives a beaked kiss
And at once, though his stymied frame cannot stir, his eyes shoot open
For he so surely knows the scent and shape and sense of his dining bird
And this aerial creature is not him; no, this is a dove with a savior's soul
But more outstandingly, this is a dove Prometheus *knows*, intimately so
In another life, before the tireless feast of flesh his existence has become
Prometheus was entirely besotted with Electra, a fair female of courtesy
Who just so happens to also assume the skeleton of a dove shapeshifter
Electra, unbeknownst to her soulmate, made her move *far before* sunup
Having vanquished the unslakable eagle—a triumph not to be belittled
Before propelling his corpse, plumes and all, into the shark-infested sea
Now, here to free her love at last with curse-crushing blood in her body
Electra swings into her mortal silhouette, *just as radiant as he recollected*
And unbinds his limbs, that is, until a unit of goddesses glide into view
Consequently, lest the glowing women tattle to gain Zeus's good graces
Electra understands as well as Prometheus, she *must* eat as the eagle did
As she squeamishly plucks at his metabolic mass, he grins past the pain
Flattered to have her lips upon him again, at least in some perverse way
But after, once the promenading goddesses are as elsewhere as his organ
Prometheus's lover finally ascends them both away to safety she secured
Intent to live in tame secret, never to speak of eagles or livers, evermore

Pixie Dust Exposé

Amid the inertia of idealized afternoon air above this pasture of dahlias
Something kaleidoscopic pulses in the distance just beyond the blooms
Like a cluster of shrunken supernovas inhabiting this mortal-filled land
Smatterings of *pure* pixie dust suspend midcourse before waltzing away
Upholding the flexibility of a phantasm and the aromatics of pecan pie
Peer past an elucidating magnifying glass; discover prismatic diamonds
Unequivocally impressive, as if the star-studded galaxy lowered its levels
Imparting upon our planet a reduced replica of the superiority in space
And yet, the granules are more sinister in sincerity than scenic in sham
For the delusion of flagrant enticement is often too good *to ever be true*

Harken the prequel tale of pixie dust from the mouths of winged elders
When fairy-adjacent beings first faded, mythical yet *not quite* immortal
Customary decomposition of their chipmunk-sized bodies never began
In its place, minute entrails and epidermises were macerated and milled
Until the composite cadavers of the playful creatures became pixie dust
Such mischief-packed existences diluted down to only macabre residue
When side by side, inclined as one may be to rate highly of the powder
Remember the particles are gothically charged with a pixie's dying cries
Permeated with the pangs of expulsion from this effervescent biosphere
Before facing total disrepair, reassigned to a vagabond life of *impassivity*
Aimlessly airborne only to then stick to the surfaces of still-sentient kin
Caked in the iotas they too will turn into when eventually succumbing
A sobering topic gnawing at the pygmy entities with every elapsing day
But moreover, pixie dust also populates the skin of clueless humankind
And so, at the sight of a tinsel-tinged shoulder or a spangled collarbone
One must pause, recollecting that veritable grains of glitter, *they are not*
Substituting actual glitz, the pulverized guts and gore of the dead linger
Like a vexed poltergeist with unresolved business, plaguing visible flesh
Without unsuspecting mortals ever learning the nausea-inducing truth

All to urge one to posit: if other *scintillating* substances appear attractive
Like the roiling northern lights—a multicolored phenomenon of pizazz
Or the reflective smog of smoky periwinkle amid the late witching hour
If those sights tempt such awe, what could possibly have been the price?

Dusk Dreamer

Drowsy as a newborn lamb, this *buzzing*, breathing land starts to shush
Tiger lilies tuck in stippled petals, and woodpeckers delve under duvets
Alchemists leave their laboratories; potion sommeliers slip into slippers
All as a result of an enchantment noted round each neighboring region
A dozing cradlesong from the melatonin-spiked lips of a slumber witch
Lulling dust mites and daughters and dryads into a healing *stint of sleep*

The Dusk Dreamer: a sorceress of somnific auras and Morpheus's sister
Previous star pupil of the original coven, for her starry roots made it so
Conceived from *night-sky* ovum; born bearing chamomile-scented cells
Inoculated with catatonic sway to herd every entity into concise comas
Taming hyper minds into tranquility as sundials signify eventide hours
While concurrently warring with the ill-tempered courier of *nightmares*
Negating his leverage upon each day's coda with her bleary-eyed charm:

Sisters of this dimension, sovereigns of this universe—let us mystically coerce
Support brains softly blacking out until the sweetest hallucinations carry out

Once all toilworn bodies take to bed, reveries resume, freed from fright
As this sorceress, a quasi-author, chronicles millions of different dreams
With storylines intuited from their fantasies, fixations, and fascinations
Like specific motion pictures treading the boards beyond shuttered lids
After, the Dusk Dreamer fashions dream-dispensers from swan feathers
Before transferring her tailor-made trances inside the woven inventions
And sequentially hanging her craftworks above canopied cots and cribs
Intreating fictional images to nosedive into each napping hippocampus
An apothecary herbalist envisions concocting a pestilence-purging cure
While dehydrated sands of desert plains imagine pours of precipitation
Cyclopes locate perfect-scenario mirrors where *two* awaited eyes appear
And wily foxes race toward long-lost packs of their endangered siblings
For even *the wildest of wishes* can arise within dreamland's amphitheater

Daybreak upon the horizon, a dressing gown of weblike silk is disrobed
Before the Dusk Dreamer slides beneath a snug quilt and sedates *herself*
Sound asleep as the realm of Ethereal Ember finally resolves to rest, too

Acknowledgements

My most heartfelt appreciation to anyone who has read my previous works and reached out with thoughtful words, and to those who have bought my newest release – thank you endlessly, and I hope you have enjoyed!

Also, a very special thank you to the following women who have supported my self-published books by posting with such kindness: Diellza (@sol.pages), Heather (@myfriendsdontread), Athena (@alyssaathenaa), Taylor (@ofshadowsanddreams), and Danni (@dvnnisimone). Wishing you all the best!

Praline Patisserie's Chocolate Chip Vanilla Bean Scones

~ makes 8 scones ~

Ingredients:

For the scones:

2.75-3 cups flour, 1 tbsp baking powder,
1/4 tsp baking soda, 1 tsp salt,
10 tbsp frozen butter, 3/4 cup sugar,
2 room temp eggs, 1/3 cup room temp buttermilk,
1/3 cup vanilla yogurt, 1 tbsp vanilla extract,
1 cup mini chocolate chips

For the glaze:

1-1.50 cups powdered sugar, 1-2 tbsps milk,
2 tsps vanilla, 1 vanilla bean, scraped

Directions:

1. Combine the flour, baking powder, baking soda, and salt in a large mixing bowl. Grate in the frozen butter and mix using a pastry cutter, or your hands.
2. Separately whisk together the sugar and eggs before whisking in the buttermilk, vanilla yogurt, and vanilla extract.
3. Slowly incorporate the wet ingredients into the dry ingredients before adding in the mini chocolate chips. Mix until just combined.
4. With a lightly floured work surface and floured hands, repeat the process of flattening the dough, folding in half, turning, flattening, and folding about 5 times.
5. Press the dough into an 8-9 inch circle, with a height of around 2 inches.
6. Cover with plastic wrap and freeze for 20-25 minutes.
7. Remove and cut the dough into 8 equal wedges.
8. Place each wedge upon a lined baking sheet, about 2-3 inches apart.
9. Place the baking sheet in the freezer for 30-40 minutes.
10. Preheat the oven to 400°F toward the end of the freezing time.
11. Brush the scones with an egg wash - 1 egg and 2 tsp milk or buttermilk.
12. Bake for approximately 18-22 minutes, then allow to cool.
13. Make the glaze by whisking the powdered sugar, milk, vanilla extract, and scraped vanilla bean. Add more powdered sugar or milk depending on your preferred thickness. Use a spoon to pour over the tops of each scone.
14. Enjoy with a cup of chai or a mug of mocha!

Heartbreak Café's Lemon Blueberry Streusel Muffins

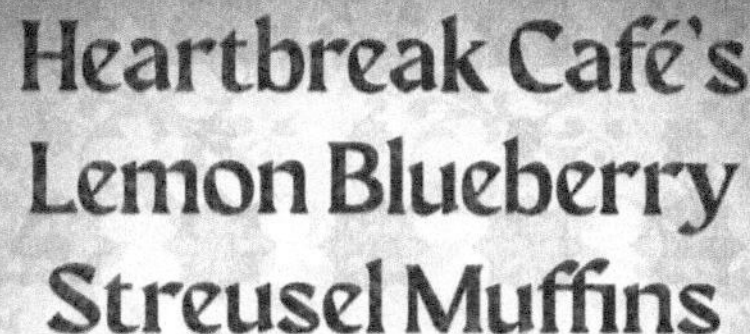

~ makes 12-14 muffins ~

Ingredients:

For muffins:

2.75 cups flour & 1 tbsp for coating blueberries, 3/4 tsp salt,
1.25 tbsps baking powder, 1/4 tsp baking soda,
3/4 cup sugar, 3 room temp eggs, zest of 1 large lemon,
1/2 cup butter, melted, 3/4 cup room temp milk,
1/2 cup room temp sour cream, 2 tsps vanilla,
2 tbsps honey, 2 cups blueberries, frozen

For streusel:

4 tbsps butter - melted, 3 tbsps white sugar,
3 tbsps brown sugar, 2 tsps lemon zest,
2/3 cup flour, 1/4 tsp salt

Directions:

1. In a medium bowl, combine flour, salt, baking powder, and baking soda.
2. Separately, whisk together the sugar, eggs, and lemon zest, followed
   by the melted butter, milk, sour cream, vanilla, and honey.
3. Add dry ingredients to wet ingredients and mix until combined.
4. Place blueberries in a small bowl with 1 tbsp of flour and stir to coat.
5. Fold in blueberries to the rest of the ingredients and gently incorporate.
6. Cover with plastic wrap and allow batter to rest for around 45 minutes.
7. During this time, preheat your oven to 425°F and line every other spot in two
   muffin pans to ensure they each have room to grow. Bake in 2-3 batches.
8. Make the streusel by mixing the butter, sugars, lemon zest, flour and salt. Set aside.
9. After 45 minutes, use a large cookie scoop to fill the muffin liners to the top.
10. Sprinkle a generous amount of the streusel atop each muffin.
11. Bake for 11 minutes, then lower the heat to 375°F and bake for 12 minutes, or
    until the tops become lightly golden and a toothpick comes out clean.
12. Raise the oven temp back to 425°F. Repeat this process in second muffin pan.
13. Remove the muffins and allow to cool atop a wire rack.
14. Dreamily dine upon from dusk until dawn.

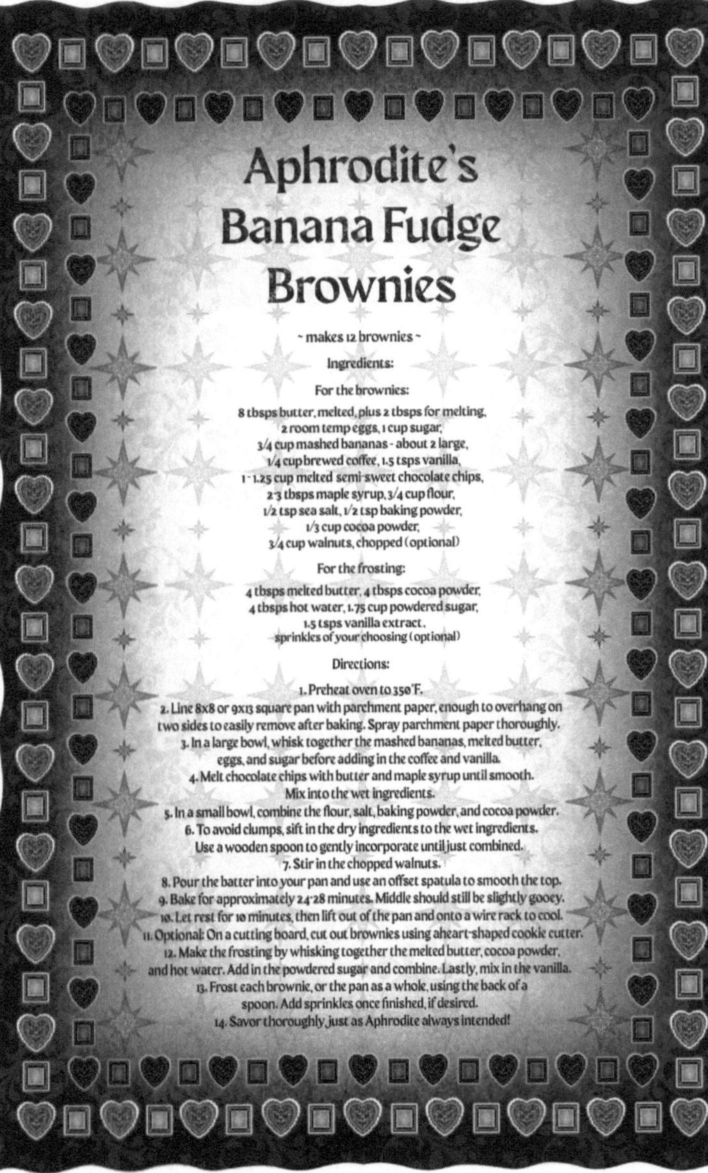

Aphrodite's Banana Fudge Brownies

~ makes 12 brownies ~

Ingredients:

For the brownies:

8 tbsps butter, melted, plus 2 tbsps for melting,
2 room temp eggs, 1 cup sugar,
3/4 cup mashed bananas - about 2 large,
1/4 cup brewed coffee, 1.5 tsps vanilla,
1 - 1.25 cup melted semi-sweet chocolate chips,
2-3 tbsps maple syrup, 3/4 cup flour,
1/2 tsp sea salt, 1/2 tsp baking powder,
1/3 cup cocoa powder,
3/4 cup walnuts, chopped (optional)

For the frosting:

4 tbsps melted butter, 4 tbsps cocoa powder,
4 tbsps hot water, 1.75 cup powdered sugar,
1.5 tsps vanilla extract,
sprinkles of your choosing (optional)

Directions:

1. Preheat oven to 350°F.
2. Line 8x8 or 9x13 square pan with parchment paper, enough to overhang on two sides to easily remove after baking. Spray parchment paper thoroughly.
3. In a large bowl, whisk together the mashed bananas, melted butter, eggs, and sugar before adding in the coffee and vanilla.
4. Melt chocolate chips with butter and maple syrup until smooth. Mix into the wet ingredients.
5. In a small bowl, combine the flour, salt, baking powder, and cocoa powder.
6. To avoid clumps, sift in the dry ingredients to the wet ingredients. Use a wooden spoon to gently incorporate until just combined.
7. Stir in the chopped walnuts.
8. Pour the batter into your pan and use an offset spatula to smooth the top.
9. Bake for approximately 24-28 minutes. Middle should still be slightly gooey.
10. Let rest for 10 minutes, then lift out of the pan and onto a wire rack to cool.
11. Optional: On a cutting board, cut out brownies using a heart-shaped cookie cutter.
12. Make the frosting by whisking together the melted butter, cocoa powder, and hot water. Add in the powdered sugar and combine. Lastly, mix in the vanilla.
13. Frost each brownie, or the pan as a whole, using the back of a spoon. Add sprinkles once finished, if desired.
14. Savor thoroughly, just as Aphrodite always intended!

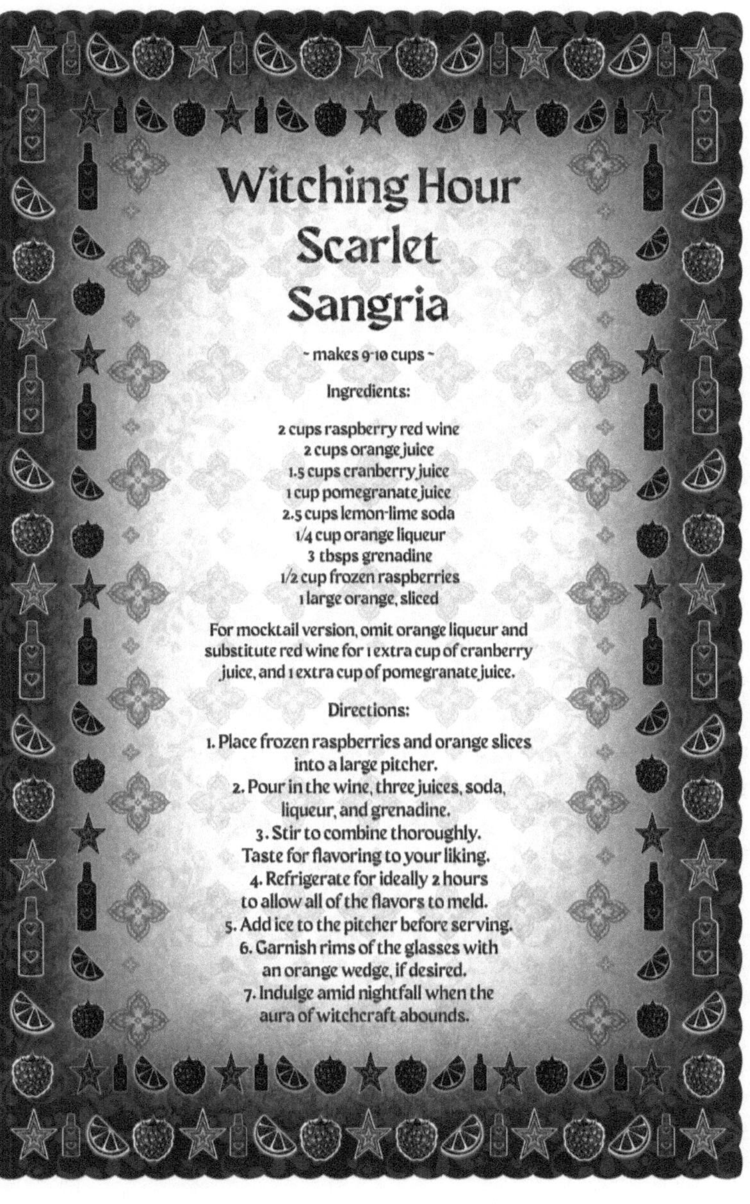

Witching Hour Scarlet Sangria

~ makes 9-10 cups ~

Ingredients:

2 cups raspberry red wine
2 cups orange juice
1.5 cups cranberry juice
1 cup pomegranate juice
2.5 cups lemon-lime soda
1/4 cup orange liqueur
3 tbsps grenadine
1/2 cup frozen raspberries
1 large orange, sliced

For mocktail version, omit orange liqueur and substitute red wine for 1 extra cup of cranberry juice, and 1 extra cup of pomegranate juice.

Directions:

1. Place frozen raspberries and orange slices into a large pitcher.
2. Pour in the wine, three juices, soda, liqueur, and grenadine.
3. Stir to combine thoroughly. Taste for flavoring to your liking.
4. Refrigerate for ideally 2 hours to allow all of the flavors to meld.
5. Add ice to the pitcher before serving.
6. Garnish rims of the glasses with an orange wedge, if desired.
7. Indulge amid nightfall when the aura of witchcraft abounds.

Marisa Loretta is an author and artist living in Upstate New York. *Ethereal Ember*, sinister, starry-eyed, and sorcerous, is her third book release, following *Midnight Love Potion* and *Scarlet Nightfall*. As an avid reader, her unending love of all things fantasy and romance, from *Practical Magic* to *Buffy the Vampire Slayer*, has only grown over the years. Marisa is thrilled to have translated that infatuation into penning her own tales and extends her true gratitude toward everyone who has chosen to pick up her poetic works. You can further connect with her online at www.marisaloretta.com or on
Instagram: @marisaloretta

Also by Marisa Loretta

Midnight Love Potion

Scarlet Nightfall

Ethereal Ember